THE LAST SEAT

A THRILLER

JENIFER RUFF

Greyt Companion Press

THE LAST SEAT

A THRILLER

Print ISBN: 978-1-954447-53-0

Ebook ISBN: 978-1-954447-52-3

Written by Jenifer Ruff

Cover design by Damonza

Visit the author's website for more information. www.Jenruff.com

ALSO BY JENIFER RUFF

The Agent Victoria Heslin Thriller Series

The Numbers Killer

Pretty Little Girls

When They Find Us

Ripple of Doubt

The Groom Went Missing

Vanished on Vacation

The Atonement Murders

The Ones They Buried

The Bad Neighbor

Lies in the Snow

THE FBI & CDC Thriller Series

Only Wrong Once, Only One Cure, Only One Wave

The Brooke Walton Series

Everett, Rothaker, The Intern

Psychological Thrillers

The Last Seat

When She Escaped

Lauren's Secret

CHAPTER 1

The black SUV nearly hits me. I'm so distracted rehearsing the lies I might need to tell that I don't see it until the last second. I throw up an arm and jump aside as it speeds past in the train station parking lot.

Heart still pounding, I climb the stairs to the platform and pull my jacket tighter around me. The bitter Chicago wind cuts right through, making me wish for spring and a reliable car.

Inside the commuter train, heat blasts from the vents, and a discarded coffee cup sits on the floor. Only two seats remain open. I choose the closest, remove my coat, and rest my hands in my lap. Out of habit, I push my thumb into the damaged skin around my fingernails. I'm trying to figure out what my mother wants to tell me. It's something she wants me to hear in person. I'm worried the news won't be good.

I stare out the window and let out a sigh. When I arrive at my mother's house, she's going to ask me about Adam. I'm going to say everything is fine, and the knot in my stomach will grow. We've always been close, my mother and I, especially since my father passed last year. Even as a teen, I never kept secrets from her. That all changed recently. I'm now keeping a lot of important things to myself.

As if on cue, Adam's ringtone chimes from my handbag. I debate letting it go to voicemail, to avoid an argument with him, but I won't. Despite the awful things he said about me, I want to talk to him. Maybe he's finally come to his senses. Or there's an issue with taking care of Moose.

"Adam." I brace myself for the sound of his voice and the emotions it will stir inside me.

"I figured you'd be halfway to your mother's by now. What are you doing at the train station?"

His ingrained habit of checking my location before calling doesn't bother me. We still share a phone plan. I appreciate his ability to pinpoint where I am with a glance. Should I ever end up in a ditch, at least someone will find me. And that's not the only reason I'd like him to keep checking. If he continues, it means he still cares.

"I'm not driving. I'm taking the train," I tell him.

Adam knows I'm no fan of the train. Three months ago, a guy with long, greasy hair had a thing for my blue medical scrubs. He kept asking me if we could "play doctor." It was ridiculous, but also scary. He didn't back off until other passengers told him to leave me alone. Now I prefer driving, even if it means circling block after block in search of an available parking spot. In my car, there's no unwanted attention, and I'm in control. I can play my music and belt out the lyrics when I'm stressed and pull over when I'm ready to stop. But like so many other things in my life right now, like it or not, I'm having to adapt to circumstances I didn't choose.

"Why are you taking the train?" Adam asks. I picture him raising his brows and squinting the way he does when he's skeptical.

"My car stalled yesterday. I'm not driving it on the highway until I can get it looked at. When your engine cuts off without warning, it's terrifying. I'm going to get it fixed. I just couldn't do it today."

"Look, Haley, I could have driven you. I told you I wanted to see her."

Even though Adam is having issues trusting me, he still loves my mother. He doesn't have any family left, not since his grandfather died. My mother is it for both of us.

"I appreciate your wanting to see her, but she asked me to come alone."

"Why doesn't she want me there?" Adam asks.

"I'm not sure, but it's probably for the best. I haven't told her we're separated, and if she sees us together, she'll figure out right away that there's something wrong. I'm not going to put her through that right now. And besides, someone has to feed Moose while I'm gone."

"You'll have to tell her about us at some point."

Adam sounds like he's fed up with explaining this. I am procrastinating, but only to avoid burdening my mother with my problems. She needs to focus on her health.

I pinch the bridge of my nose. "I will but now is not the time."

An argument is not something I need at the moment. It's only going to spiral back to his accusations and turn ugly. I end the call and stow my phone back in my purse. When I finally focus on my surroundings, I wish I hadn't. Across the aisle, a man in a dingy jacket stares at me with unapologetic intensity. He's practically leering.

In front, a college-aged girl with pink and blonde hair extensions frowns into her phone, filming, then pans around the train's interior.

The young man next to me is in his mid-to late twenties. Like so many other people on the train, he has earbuds in his ears. He stares straight ahead as if he's lost in thought. Or maybe not, because he catches my gaze and gives me the slightest nod.

I steal another peek at the man across the aisle, praying he's engrossed in something else. Nope, he's still staring. I can't take it for the entire ride. I grab my bag and move to the empty seat two rows behind me.

The train doors remain open, and a new passenger hurries aboard, wheeling a small suitcase behind her. She's an attractive brunette around my age, smiling in a polite, reserved way. She's dressed in expensive clothing—a white blouse, black slacks, and a camel-colored overcoat. Very classy.

If she wants to sit, she has no choice. The only seat remaining is the one I just left.

Facing me, her brows lift ever so slightly, probably because I'm looking at her. I offer a reassuring smile before she turns around. She removes her coat and settles in. I hope she doesn't become the new subject of the leering man's attention.

The train shudders, resuming its trek, then speeds up into a steady, clacking rhythm. I rifle around in my bag until my fingers close on the smooth surface of my book. Losing myself in a novel might help pass the time.

I open the thriller, prop it against my legs, and reread the same paragraph several times. I can't shake the prickling sense that something isn't quite right tonight.

Dark scenery blurs past outside my window until the screech of brakes announces our arrival at the next station. The leering man gets up, and I'm glad he's leaving. The train slows to a stop with the shriek of metal gears, and the doors open. A blast of cold air rushes in. Before anyone can disembark, a man in a surplus army jacket barges into the car, oblivious to common etiquette. For an instant, our eyes meet, then I look away.

A deafening boom explodes next to me. I jolt upright. Another shocking boom resounds. In the enclosed space, the noise is louder than any clap of thunder. A bolting figure pushes a woman aside and flies through the doors, army jacket flapping behind him. My ears ring with a piercing whine. My heart hammers.

Gunshots! On this train. Right in front of me.

A woman sobs in hitching gasps. Screams echo through the car. The girl with the hair extensions holds up her phone as her mouth hangs open in shock.

I squeeze my eyes shut, willing the nightmare to reset. But it doesn't work. This is really happening. It just happened.

I can't move, can't breathe.

A body falls into the aisle.

It's her, the woman who took my seat. The last one on. She's lying on the floor, looking up with wide eyes. One hand clutches a crimson blossom spreading across her white blouse.

CHAPTER 2

The man beside me elbows my ribs as he yanks something from his backpack. The hair-extension girl is crying and holding up her phone, still filming. Nothing seems real. Not the acrid smell of gunpowder or the primal screams. Definitely not the woman on the floor, her chest rising and falling in stuttering gasps.

The train doors close and the train chugs to life again, as if everything is normal and we can just head on to the next stop and go about our business. As if something mind-blowing and horrifying didn't just happen in our midst with absolutely no warning.

A scream breaks me from my shocked state. I jump into action and drop to the floor beside the wounded woman. The wet warmth of her blood seeps through the knees of my jeans.

The woman's eyes are closed as I search for a pulse in her neck. *Please... please still be alive. Come on, breathe for me.* How many gunshots did I hear? Two? Three?

A bullet hit her shoulder. Another pierced her chest. She's losing so much blood.

"Open your eyes and look at me, please," I say, my voice calm and firm, words I've repeated many times before. "You're not alone, okay? I'm right here. My name is Haley. I'm an ER nurse. What's your name?"

No response, just the gurgling rasp of her shallow inhalations. She's fading fast, losing color, her previously glowing face now ashen.

Passengers crowd in on us. An older couple with silver hair clutch each other's arms and whisper the Lord's Prayer at warp speed.

"Everyone, please give us some space." My hands go to the woman's ruined blouse. I ball up the sodden fabric to stem the bleeding. "You need to take slow, deep breaths. I'm here with you."

I press down against the chest wound to staunch the hemorrhaging. Each weak beat of her heart causes a spurt of blood to leak out from beneath my ungloved hands. There's no equipment here. No medical team masking up to rush her into emergency surgery. I run through a mental checklist of the life-saving interventions I'm lacking. A chest seal, a decompression needle, an entire trauma team. Yet I can't let her slip away. Not like this, where she's so beautiful and alive one moment and gone the next. I can't lose her.

"Did someone call 9-1-1?" I shout, briefly looking up at so many faces staring down at us with stunned gazes. A businessman cringes as he loosens his tie. A young mother shields her child's eyes.

A man's voice comes from behind me. The young man with the earbuds. "I called. They'll meet us at the next station with an ambulance. It's ten minutes away. Is she going to make it?"

I don't answer his question. Instead, I meet his eyes. "I need more clothing to stop the bleeding. Shirts. Scarves. Whatever you can gather."

Materials come at me. I grab a navy sweatshirt that looks clean.

Someone says, "Pull the emergency lever so the train stays at the next stop."

An incessant alarm starts ringing inside the train.

I can't say how many minutes pass as I try to staunch the bleeding, but it seems like forever. Blood soaks her lovely silk shirt, then the sweatshirt. I replace it with someone's sweater. Her breathing is shallow and erratic. The bluish pall of her skin deepens. I should be prepping her for an emergency thoracotomy in the ER trauma bay, pushing blood products and clotting factors, not pressing random garments into her wounds.

"Her name is Lauren," the earbud man says. "I found an ID in her purse." He holds up something that looks like a press badge.

"Lauren." I lean closer to her face. "Lauren, the EMTs are coming. Stay with me. Your family needs you to fight." I don't know if she has a family, but I'll say anything to help keep her here with me until an ambulance arrives.

When the train finally slows, only the faintest of pulses tells me she's still alive.

Lauren's eyes flutter open. She's struggling to focus. She stares up at me. Her mouth moves. I can't tell if she's trying to say something or if she's simply exhaling what could be her final breaths.

"Gray Gloe," she gasps.

Whatever she tried to say matters. Those words might be her last. But I don't know what she means. I'm not even sure I heard correctly. Is it the name of a loved one? Or just garbled nonsense?

"Gray Gloe? Is that what you said?"

She doesn't answer. Her eyes close again, her long lashes settling against her pallid skin.

I look around to see if anyone else heard her. We're slowing down for the next station. They're all focused on the doors, willing them to open and lead us back to safety. I'm sure they want to fly out of here as soon as they can.

When the train finally stops, my attention is fully on Lauren. I hear the doors open and sirens wailing in the distance. I whip my head up as armed figures charge in wearing bulletproof vests.

“Don’t move!” one shouts, aiming his gun barrel at me.

I must look deranged. Hands and clothes drenched in blood. Kneeling over a battered, unresponsive body as if I’m the one trying to kill her.

CHAPTER 3

"Hands! Let me see your hands!" The bark comes from a burly cop, his weapon leveled at my chest.

"I'm an ER nurse. She was shot. We have to keep pressure on her wounds." I'm screaming inside because he's aiming a gun at me, but my years in the ER ensure my voice sounds calm and reasonable.

After a few beats of studying me, the cop shouts, "Everyone else, keep your hands up while we clear the car."

The police march everyone off the train, leaving only Lauren and me inside.

As soon as the other passengers exit, I hear familiar voices coming closer. Two EMTs enter with jump bags in hand. I'm relieved to see Holly, who brought homemade cupcakes into the ER for my birthday, and Matt, who lent me his umbrella last week when I forgot one in a freezing rainstorm. We've worked countless emergencies together at Chicago Main. Until now, they've always prepped patients for me, not the other way around.

Holly's eyes widen when she spots me on the floor, applying pressure to Lauren's wounds with blood-soaked hands.

"Haley?" Matt sounds surprised, but quickly gets down to business. "What've we got?"

"Two gunshot wounds. One to the upper right shoulder, another in the left chest cavity. She's lost an excessive amount of blood."

"Do you know her?" Holly asks.

"I don't. I was just...she was... her name is Lauren."

Matt interrupts my stammering. "Let's get two large-bore IVs in."

I move away to give them space.

Holly cuts Lauren's blouse and takes her vitals.

Matt inserts an IV line, then packs the wounds.

"BP is 76/40 and dropping," Holly warns. "We need to go."

Matt positions a bag-valve mask over Lauren's mouth and nose. He begins rhythmic squeezes, pushing air into Lauren's failing lungs.

In a flurry of coordinated movements, they transfer Lauren onto a backboard and whisk her away. They're in and out so fast, it's as if they were never there.

I let my shoulders drop and say a prayer.

Lauren is headed to the hospital in an ambulance, but will she make it on time?

The sirens fade into the night until I can no longer hear them. My hands are shaking. I wrap my arms around my body and clutch my sides. I can't stop reliving terrible scenes. The man rushing in. The gun blasts. A dark pool of Lauren's blood spreading across the floor of the train.

An officer beckons me to join the other passengers.

The young woman with the pink hair sobs. "It wasn't any of us," she says with tears streaming down her cheeks. "The guy who did it got on and left at the last stop."

Voices merge with hers, speaking all at once until the police shush everyone. "Please don't talk to each other. We need you to be quiet until we interview everyone individually. We have to keep your recollections unbiased."

Everyone stops talking at once. A small shudder runs through me as reality sinks in. I witnessed a crime. Attempted murder. There's blood congealing on my clothes. My hands are still stained with it despite the wipes someone handed me. As my adrenaline ebbs, I'm lightheaded and weak in the knees.

A small crowd stares at us from behind police tape. They're the people who planned to get on at this station, and those from the other cars who also had to get off. By now, they're all aware of what happened, but they weren't there. They didn't see the mind-blowing, sudden, and unexpected violence.

A man in a charcoal suit and blue tie strides toward us. He's well over six feet tall. I have to look up to meet his eyes.

"I'm Detective Millard with the Violent Crimes Division, and this is Detective Desai."

The woman beside him is almost a foot shorter than her partner, but her presence and sharp gaze commands attention. They don't seem real. Nothing does. It's like I'm watching a movie, and this is the detective duo who will handle things from here.

Detective Millard clears his throat. "We need basic information from each of you. Names. Identification. Contact information. Then we'll take your statements."

His voice becomes a meaningless buzz as the event flashes through my brain again in violent snippets.

"Ma'am?"

Detective Desai stands in front of me, forehead furrowed above her brown eyes. "What's your name?"

"Haley. Haley James."

"You're looking a little rough. Let's get you checked out by a medic."

"I'm fine." My reply is automatic. What I mean is I have no physical injuries, but I'm not okay right now. The shooting wrecked me. I'm not a stranger to treating gunshot wounds. I see the aftermath of gun violence in the ER on a weekly basis. Yet I've never witnessed the cause. It happened so fast. So random and senseless. Lauren did nothing to provoke him. It could have been any of us who got shot and bled out on the floor. It could have been me. A pang of guilt hits me. Survivor's guilt, I suppose. I say another silent prayer for Lauren. I could be the one in the back of the ambulance right now, clinging to the most primitive of functions like her. Unless God forbid, she died. Please, no. Please, no.

As I choke out a sob, a hand on my shoulder brings me back to the present. Detective Desai stares at me with a compassionate look I recognize. I see that expression every day on my colleagues' faces when we interact with traumatized patients and their families.

"We'll get through this as fast as we can so you can get home," she says.

My throat clenches, swallowing back my tears. Later, I can succumb to my shock. For now, I need to pull it together. I have to do whatever I can to help the detectives find the gunman. I don't want whoever shot Lauren to get away with it.

CHAPTER 4

Detective Millard speaks to his colleague, gesturing to the train cars. "We'll use these front two for statements. I've got this half of the group. You take the others."

Someone protests about missing their night shift.

"Call in," Millard says. "Tell them you're here until we're done."

My mother. She's expecting me. I should be there by now. I send her a quick message. *I'm so sorry, but I'm not coming. Something happened on the train. Not to me. I'm okay. Call you in the morning. I love you!*

It's going to be a long night. But not as long as for Lauren and her loved ones.

Detective Desai leads me to the front of the train. There's a makeshift collection center set up already. She takes several photos of me. Someone scrapes beneath my nails, then pricks my finger to get a sample of my blood. She notes my name, contact information, occupation, and my reason for being on the train. I can barely remember the basics and wonder if what I told them is correct. Afterward, I get to wash my hands in the tiny train bathroom. I scrub them hard and long, as if I'm the lead surgeon about to operate.

When I've cleaned up as best I can, Detective Desai says, "Tell me what happened. Everything you remember."

"It was totally unprovoked." I grit my teeth. My face is stretched tight. "He just... "

The detective waits in silence with her notebook, allowing me to push past a welling tide of emotion.

I force myself to keep going. "Her name is Lauren. Another passenger found her license or some identification in her bag. She boarded the train at the last station. She was sitting a few rows in front of me. At the next stop, the shooter rushed in, and then... I don't know. I wasn't watching. I didn't see it. He shot her right away, then left. One second she was sitting in her seat..."

"Easy, Ms. James, take a breath."

"Okay. I will. I am." I do what she says and it seems to help me from hyperventilating.

She gives me a few more seconds before asking, "Can you describe the shooter? Any details about his appearance or behavior?"

I close my eyes and picture the series of events again. The train rumbled to a stop. The leering man got up. My relief. Little did I know a cold-blooded killer was getting on. My unease was totally misplaced.

I try to clear my head and start over. A memory returns. The instant when I made eye contact with the shooter.

"He was Caucasian, late twenties or early thirties." I fight to recall every detail I can grasp. I'm shivering. "Average height, dark hair under a baseball cap. Black hoodie. And a loose jacket over it. Like a faded green military surplus piece."

"Good. Excellent recall. Eye color?"

"I have no idea."

"Any facial hair?"

"I don't think so."

"Muscular?"

"Not especially, from what I could tell."

"We might need you to work with a sketch artist later. It's possible you'll remember more then."

I gnaw at my lower lip. "He didn't wait for anyone to get off before he got on. He shoved his way through the doors. I remember thinking he was rude. Then I looked away."

"Did you see his weapon?"

I shake my head.

"Did it appear he knew the woman who got shot?"

"I don't know." I wonder if he was a boyfriend. A husband? A jilted lover? From the little I saw, they weren't a match.

"Did he say anything?"

"Not that I heard. Like I said, he got on quickly and left just as fast." I'm wringing my hands. "He might have said something, and I just didn't hear it."

"Did he take anything from the victim?"

"I'm not sure."

"Is there anything else you remember?"

I shake my head again. I'm having trouble thinking clearly. There are too many emotions and questions racing inside me. Who is Lauren? Why her? How could this happen?

CHAPTER 5

The emptiness in my two-bedroom apartment hits me as soon as I trudge through the door. There's an eerie quiet, and it's not just because it's now two in the morning. It's been this way since Adam forced me to move out of our house three months ago. It was his house before we married, so I had little recourse. With few pieces of furniture, my small living room seems cavernous. I used to complain about Adam's ugly leather recliner and how much space it took up. I hated it, but now I miss it, too.

After the violent episode on the train, my loneliness is stronger than ever. I can't bear being here by myself. In times like these, we need a person we can count on and cry with. Someone who has our back and understands exactly what helps us calm down. For several years, Adam was my person. Now I'm alone.

I switch on the television. I'll take any sound over the silence.

A thumping noise coming from my bedroom reminds me I'm not as alone as I feel. There's Moose, my beautiful gray and gold cat. I love him, but he rarely displays affection. He's as aloof as they come. I think the woman who owned him before me was unkind. He seems to prefer men to women.

I grab a treat before finding him lounging on a platform of his cat tower. While he's sniffing the food in my hand, I gather him into my arms and hug him against my chest. He doesn't love this, and I'm usually respectful of his unspoken wishes, but I'm hoping he'll understand that I need him. He squirms, and his claws scratch my skin as he leaps to freedom. As he runs off, I notice dark splotches on his fur. With a sickening jolt, I realize I've transferred Lauren's blood onto my cat.

From under my bed, he peers back at me as if I'm a stranger.

"Fine. Be that way. I have to shower," I tell him, but there's no snark in my voice. I only sound sad.

I inspect myself first, standing before the long mirror on the back of my bathroom door. Dark crimson streaks my brown hair and clumps the strands together. I can't explain how Lauren's blood reached my hair, but somehow, it did. My jeans are dark and have stiffened.

I can't get my clothes off fast enough. The jeans are a staple in my wardrobe and have been for years, but they go right into the trash. I think of Lauren. Her beautiful, expensive-looking clothes. The softness of her silk shirt before it got soaked through. Again, I wonder what she was doing on the train. Where was she coming from? Where was she going?

Under scalding water in the shower, I scrub until my skin burns, trying to wash away more than just physical evidence from tonight. I need to feel better. Less shocked and afraid.

When I'm clean, and I've finished removing blood from my cat's fur, an act that required several more treats to complete, I crumple over my bed. I'm exhausted, beyond exhausted, but too wired to sleep. My wet hair drips onto my shoulders. The television is still playing, filling the apartment with a weatherman's forecast and windchill warnings, but I need to talk to someone. There are only so many people I can call at this hour. My nursing friends are at work or have to wake up in a few hours to start long shifts.

Others have small children. With my mom needing rest to battle cancer, Adam is the only person I can call.

"Haley? What happened?" He sounds alarmed when he answers. No hint of grogginess though at this hour he must have been sleeping.

Tears pool in my eyes. "You don't have to feed Moose in the morning. I'm not at my mother's."

"What's going on? Is it your mother?"

A hitching gasp escapes my lips as tears spill down my cheeks. I wipe them away. "No. She's okay. I never made it to her place. There was an incident tonight. On the train."

"An incident? Did somebody try to mug you?"

Swallowing hard, I try to tell him what happened. "No, it was worse. There was a shooting. Right next to me. A woman got shot."

"Really? On the train? But you're alright?"

"Just shaken. It was awful. So sad and senseless. She lost a lot of blood. I'm not sure she'll make it."

"Where are you right now?"

"In my apartment."

"Is someone with you? I hear something."

I startle and jerk my head around before realizing he's only hearing a commercial about a mattress sale in the background. "No one else is here. I don't want to be alone. I can't... not after seeing... it was awful, Adam." A shiver rocks my body. My free hand clenches my bedsheet, fingernails digging into the cotton.

Several seconds pass as I wait for his answer.

"Haley, I can't."

He can. What he means is that he won't. He doesn't want to. Yes, it would be a pain to get out of bed and come over here a few hours before work, but a few months ago, he would have done it without hesitation. No, a few months ago, he wouldn't have to get up and drive across the city to console me because we would already have been together in bed. A few months ago, I wouldn't have taken the train because I would have driven *our* good car to visit my mother, rather than the car I have. The one that's old and unreliable but paid off.

"Get into bed and try to get some sleep," he says. "You're probably exhausted. You'll be out like a light soon. Things will seem better in the morning."

"Okay." I feel foolish for asking when I knew there was little chance he would come. "I just wanted to tell you I'm here. And about the cat." I realize then that if I hadn't called, he would have come in the morning to feed Moose. At least I could have seen him then. If I'd waited, he would have been here when I woke.

Adam hangs up in a hurry, leaving me no opportunity to extend the conversation. Instead of trying to sleep, I head to the kitchen. Across the room, a flashing red graphic on the television catches my attention.

BREAKING NEWS: MASS TRANSIT SHOOTING.

I strain to hear the reporter.

"—a truly shocking act of senseless violence occurred aboard an outbound train. Witnesses describe a lone male suspect opening fire and gunning down a female passenger before fleeing the scene..."

One female passenger. The rest of us were the lucky ones. We won't forget that train ride for as long as we live, but right now, we're okay. When the sun comes up, we'll feed our pets, eat breakfast, go to the gym, do our jobs, and hug our loved ones.

Lauren won't be doing any of those things soon. Maybe never again.

Another shudder rocks my body.

CHAPTER 6

Memories from yesterday hit me as soon as I wake. Holy crap. A cold chill sweeps through my body.

My shades are still down, and the room is dark as I turn to one side under the covers and reach for my phone on the bedside table. It's after ten in the morning. I can't believe I slept so late, though I didn't really get much sleep at all. What am I supposed to do now? I can't visit my mother. There's no way I'm getting on that train. Yesterday, I couldn't wait to see her, though I was nervous about her news. But right now, I can barely focus. I'm not ready to face the world. It's safer to stay right here in bed and pull the covers up to my chin.

My mother must be wondering what happened. I call and deliver a watered-down version of the events, focusing on the fact that I'm okay. I try to downplay the incident and the effect it had on me so she won't worry too much. I promise to see her soon and end the call, making sure she knows how much I love her. Watching someone almost lose their life in such an unexpected way has made me super appreciative. Thank God it wasn't me who got shot. That would have destroyed my mother. She's barely over the loss of my father. I can't imagine what it would do to her.

Last night's events replay in a tortuous loop. The man bursting onto the train and shattering any illusion of relative safety. Lauren bleeding out on the grimy floor. Everything about it was so wrong.

I grab my phone again and open my news app. My finger hovers over the newest link about the shooting. I was there. The details are ingrained in my mind. The only thing I'll get from reading these posts is sensationalized retellings of the events I already witnessed. If I refrain from clicking, Lauren remains alive in my mind, along with my hope for her.

Don't look. I shouldn't, but I do. I have to know. Maybe there's good news, and the authorities identified and apprehended the killer overnight.

I click. The anchor's voice comes across matter-of-fact. "Police have identified the victim as Lauren Christensen, a 32-year-old investigative journalist. She's in critical condition at Chicago Main after undergoing emergency surgery for multiple gunshot wounds."

Critical condition. That's good news. Lauren is still alive.

The reporter continues, "Authorities have notified Lauren's family. Her husband, investment banker Kyle Sheffield, was seen arriving at the hospital last night. So far, the police have not disclosed information regarding potential suspects or a motive in this brutal public attack."

Why her? Why did fate or bad luck hand her such a terrible card? I suppose I could ask the same question about nearly every emergency patient who comes into the ER, and sometimes I do. But this is different. I was there for the split second that changed everything.

I'm compelled to learn more. This isn't entirely new for me. I get a little obsessed with my patients sometimes. Not in a stalker way, but because I care. I felt Lauren's life draining away and her heartbeat weakening. I saw her skin turn gray. I heard what might have been her final words. Huge moments like those aren't easily forgotten. They form bonds I can't explain to anyone who hasn't experienced them. I'm invested in Lauren's story now. In her life and her future. I'm rooting for her recovery. I keep digging because I have to.

Turns out I'm not the only one curious. Results appear on my phone before I can type the second letter of her last name. She's chic and self-assured in photos, just like she was when she boarded the train. Almost perfect. How could something so terrible happen to her?

Her investigative journalism record impresses me. She's supported whistleblowers and exposed corrupt corporations. One article has a bold headline calling her a modern-day crusader for justice.

Two theories about the shooting dominate the coverage. First: a premeditated attack. Maybe she was close to uncovering something dangerous with her journalism. Someone was driven to stop her before she revealed all? If that's true, Lauren is a hero. We need more people like her fighting for good.

The second theory makes my stomach churn. A gang initiation.

Some gangs require new members to kill to prove their loyalty. Young, troubled kids get coerced into violence in order to belong. Selecting a random and innocent victim increases the act's brutality, proving the new gang member capable of violence without remorse.

My heart aches at the thought of a kid being manipulated into a terrible and irreversible act. Then I remember the coldness in the shooter's eyes. He wasn't a teen. He was older. And I'm not sure I can feel sorry for him.

If the attack was random, none of us is ever safe. I escaped last night, but what about next week or next month?

I set my phone down. The lack of solid information has only worsened my fear. With a blanket wrapped around my shoulders, I trudge to the front door in my pajamas to double-check the lock. Then, I just stand there in my living room, staring at the wall, hearing but not processing the noise coming from the TV.

Everything is spiraling from bad to worse, and I can't stop it. There's my mother's cancer, and the news she doesn't want to share over the phone. It can't possibly be good. There's my separation from Adam, and the terrible thing he's accused me of, the reason I'm in this apartment and not our home. And now, a violent assault that could very well have happened to me. I shiver, rocking forward on my heels. My entire life seems scary and random, as if terrible surprises are waiting around every corner.

CHAPTER 7

I'm not scheduled to work today, since I'd planned to spend the day with my mother. There's no way I can stay home alone. My mind is on Lauren. I need to check on her in person.

According to my weather app, it's going to be windy with rain on and off all day. The temperatures hover above freezing, too warm for snow in the upper stratosphere, but cold enough to feel the chill deep in my bones. As I slide into my car, I silently bargain with it to cooperate and not stall. The last thing I need is to get stranded in this miserable weather.

Rain hammers the windshield as I drive, forming the background sound to a slew of *what-ifs* rattling around in my brain. If my car weren't so old and unreliable, I'd have driven to my mother's last night instead of taking the train. I'd be with her now, and I'd know what it is she wants to tell me, rather than incessantly wondering and conjuring dark possibilities. Memories from last night wouldn't haunt me. The jolting blast of the gun, the shock on Lauren's face as she straddled life and death. But if I'd driven, would Lauren be alive today? I want to believe someone else on the train could have helped her, but there's no way to be sure.

At the hospital, there's a crowd outside the front entrance. They have cameras and microphones. Reporters. I hurry by with my head down.

My colleagues are gathered around the nurse's station, staring at someone's phone. Cara spots me and waves, more enthusiastic than usual. "Haley! Over here!"

I don't know what's going on, but I have a strange feeling it involves me.

"This is you, isn't it? Tell me this isn't you," Cara exclaims, her cheeks flushed beneath her red hair.

Tamira, the nursing supervisor, snatches the phone and thrusts it toward me. A video plays on the screen. The footage is shaky, and the scene is foreign at first, but soon there's no mistaking what's going on. It's the interior of the train car. Last night's train car.

The angle is different, and I'm seeing some of the chaos in the background in a new way. The shocked faces and muffled sobs. In the center of the video is a figure I barely recognize as myself. I'm on my knees, bathed in blood, focused on saving Lauren. My expression is intense, almost feral. I jerk my head up, stare directly into the camera, and shout, "Did someone call 9-1-1?"

"Oh my God," I mutter.

"It's you, isn't it?" Cara asks with a gleeful look on her face.

I'm still caught up in the video. It goes on and on. Someone—the girl with the hair extensions or someone else—filmed the entire ordeal. All of it is on display. A chill courses through me as I continue to watch.

Tamira claps me on the back. "It's excellent work. You took control and stayed so calm. Way to make us all look good."

"The video is going viral," Cara says, wide-eyed. "You're almost at a million views!"

It doesn't surprise me that the disturbing scene has garnered so much attention. It's got everything people can't look away from. My blood-streaked face. A beautiful woman fighting for her life on the floor of a commuter train while shocked passengers watch. Most people devour that type of life-and-death drama with morbid fascination. I might, too.

Cara taps her phone. "I just sent you the link, Haley. No one knows it's you. Should I put your name in the comments?"

"No, do *not* do that." Tamira's voice is firm, almost a shout. She gives Cara a deep look of disapproval. "Do not put her name on there."

Perhaps it's my first warning of what's coming.

With the scene fresh in my memory, as seen through the eyes of whoever was filming, I answer a barrage of questions from my colleagues. Did I see who did it—yes. Do I know why he did it—no. Did the police catch him? Most unfortunately—no.

"Lauren is in our ICU," Tamira says. "Dr. Condo repaired a damaged lung. She's in an induced coma now. It's a miracle she arrived with enough blood volume to get stabilized."

"I'm going to see her." I get Lauren's room number, then make my way down the hall, pulling a mask over my face as I go.

Inside her private room, Lauren is unconscious, as Tamira said. Tubes and wires stretch from her body and bed to the walls. She's not alone. There's a man with her. I recognize her husband from the articles and online images I saw this morning.

Kyle looks up at me when I enter. I'm not wearing scrubs, but I have my name badge around my neck. From his perspective, I'm an ICU nurse on duty.

He's not as handsome as in the online pictures I saw. His eyes are red-rimmed, and he seems to have aged years in the span of a morning. But he looks much better than Lauren with her sickly pallor. Still, her appearance is a major improvement from when Matt and Holly rolled her out of the train car.

I scan the machines beside her and do a quick analysis of the stream of data her body generates. Her respiration is shallow, but even. Her blood pressure is low, yet relatively stable.

Moving to Lauren's bedside, I speak in a soft voice, although she can't respond. "Hi, Lauren. It's Haley. From last night. Remember me?"

Lauren's eyes remain closed, but Kyle stares, his forehead creased with lines. "Should she? Were you here when she came in last night?"

"I was there when it happened."

It's clear from his expression when he realizes who I am. "The nurse. That was you?"

"Yes. That was me."

"Thank you. Whatever you did for Lauren, thank you."

"Glad I could help. She's stable now, which is the most important thing." I give Kyle a reassuring nod. Lauren may be out of immediate danger, but her road to recovery, both physical and mental, will be difficult.

Kyle probably feels more helpless with her now than I did last night. He can't do much except hold her hand and wait. "Have you had anything to eat yet today?" I ask him. "I can stay with her while you take a break."

"I'm okay. Can she hear us?" he asks, almost in a whisper.

"I'm not sure, but I always speak to my patients as if they can hear me. That's what I'd want someone to do if it were my loved one."

"I'll do that, too."

We stand there in silence, watching Lauren. I pray the confident woman from the train will come back soon.

"I'll check in on her later," I finally say.

"Thank you," he repeats, his eyes welling with tears. "I can't believe I almost lost her." He shakes his head. "If you hadn't been there... I can't even think about it."

"Then don't. Make sure you get some rest so you'll be strong when she wakes up."

I slip out of the room before his tears fall.

CHAPTER 8

My ringer is off, but my phone vibrates in my purse as I'm heading out of Lauren's hospital room. The hospital corridor is busy with health care personnel, so I step into a quiet alcove to answer.

"Ms. James? This is Detective Millard with Violent Crimes." I recognized his gruff voice before he said his name. "We need you to visit the police station to answer some follow-up questions."

"Of course, Detective. Whatever you need." Talking to him sets off a jittery sensation inside me. I don't know what questions he has, but I hope they have a lineup of suspects ready. If they have a photo of the shooter, I'll identify him. I picture his black, beady eyes and dark hair as he pushed his way onto the train car. Except... I told the detectives I didn't recall his eye color, didn't I? Is my mind making up details now?

The police station isn't far from the hospital, but travel is slow in the rain. I arrive with water dripping from my hair after making a mad dash through puddles. At the front desk, I ask for Detective Millard. The woman working there has multiple phone lines, and they're all ringing non-stop. She takes my name, makes a call, and tells me to have a seat.

The chairs in the waiting area are plastic. I'm grateful they're not upholstered. A solid surface is less likely to harbor germs and who knows what else. As a nurse, I worry about those sorts of things.

My phone beeps again and again in short succession, telling me I have new messages. I'm about to check them when a door opens on the side of the waiting area. Detective Millard is ready for me. He's wearing the same charcoal suit. Same blue tie.

I follow him down a narrow hallway, and the soles of my shoes squelch against the linoleum. We pass a room with a partly open door. Inside, a woman sobs with her head in her hands.

The office we enter is small and not particularly welcoming, but it's clean and orderly. Neat stacks of folders cover the tops of the file cabinets against the back wall. The desk's surface is free of clutter, aside from a generic paper coffee cup. The organization on display strikes me as a good sign that whoever works in this room has their life together. It bodes well for the investigation.

Detective Desai sits at a small round table with four chairs around it. There's another paper coffee cup in front of her.

Millard points to one of the empty seats. "You remember my partner, Detective Desai?"

My phone vibrates. This time I worry it might be my mother. I haven't called her yet today, and I'm sure she's worried about me. I glance at the screen long enough to see it's not her. It's a number I don't recognize. Without answering, I drop my phone into my purse and settle onto another hard plastic chair.

"Thanks for coming in, Ms. James." Millard leans back and studies me over steepled fingers.

"Yes, of course," I say. "I want to help."

"How are you?" Desai's question isn't a casual greeting. There's some compassion there. She seems to understand I might be traumatized.

"I just saw Lauren at the hospital where I work. She's in an induced coma for now, but stable, for the most part."

"That's excellent news, but you didn't answer my question," she says, not unkindly.

"I'm doing okay. Just having trouble processing it all. I guess I'm anxious to hear you found the shooter."

She studies me for a few seconds, as if he's trying to decide if I'm telling the truth.

I twist my wedding rings as I wait for them to get to the reason I'm here.

Detective Millard takes a gulp of coffee, then gets to the point. "After reviewing statements from some of the other witnesses, a few discrepancies have come up regarding your account of the incident."

My heart pounds so loudly I'm sure they can hear it. Desai shifts in her chair. Her body dips to the right, but her eyes never leave my face.

Millard continues. "Multiple witnesses claim Ms. Christensen spoke to you while you were helping her. After she got shot. Is that accurate?"

I stare blankly. "I didn't tell you?"

"No, you didn't."

"Sorry. She did try to speak. I'm not sure it makes any sense, but I heard her say Gray Gloe. Or something similar."

Millard scribbles on his notepad. "You're certain that's what she said?"

"She was barely conscious. It might not have meant anything. I've heard many last words. Like 'tell my husband I love him,' and 'tell my children I'm sorry.' But also nonsensical things. I don't know if she was trying to say a person's name, or if she even knew what she was saying." After talking nonstop, I take a deep breath. "Now that I've learned she's an investigative reporter, and her death may not have been random... maybe it was significant."

If only I'd understood her. How much time and energy will the detectives put into figuring out what her last words meant? Except those weren't her last words. Lauren is alive. At that moment, I decide I have to be in her hospital room when she wakes up. I can ask what she was trying to say. I need to make sense of what happened. Understanding will help me move on and stop reliving every awful second on the train.

Millard jots thoughts or observations on his notepad. His pen makes faint scratchy sounds as it moves across the yellow-lined paper. Done writing, he looks up at me. "Why didn't you report this before? The part about what she said."

"I guess I was in shock after the attack."

"We understand the situation was traumatic, but you work in a hospital that treats serious trauma patients. I assume you've handled gunshot wounds before." There's nothing accusatory in Detective Millard's words, yet they make me defensive.

"Yes, that's right. I have. A lot of gunshot victims come in through the ER. But I've never actually seen anyone get shot."

"I see." Millard keeps staring at me as if he doesn't "see."

Detective Desai speaks next. She's all business now. "Ms. James, we need you to tell us everything you remember. Please don't leave anything out, no matter how small or unimportant it might seem to you. We're looking at the shooting from every angle."

We go through the entire incident again from beginning to end, everything I can remember in painstaking detail.

"Have you been reading about the attack or watching it on the news?" Millard asks.

"Yes," I answer in an apologetic tone, though I have every reason to want to stay informed and no reason to apologize for it.

Millard frowns. "That may have affected your recollection."

"Oh, sorry." I don't know what else to say.

Balancing Millard's directness, Desai gives me a tired half-smile. "No need to apologize. Everyone from that night is trying to block out the incident or learn everything they can. People cope differently. You have to get through this, too, in your way."

"Does my story match what the others told you?" I ask.

Millard closes his notebook. "As I said, we don't want to share anyone else's recollections with you because then you'll have trouble separating what you saw and what you learned after the fact. I will share that the descriptions of the shooter vary wildly. Not uncommon."

Detective Desai clasps her hands. "You seem to be the only one who got a good look at him when he entered the train. We'd like you to meet with our sketch artist."

"Okay, anything to help. I saw him."

Detective Desai's eyes narrow. "About that... there's one more thing we need to discuss concerning your safety."

Sensing the shift in her demeanor, I brace myself.

"We've established that you got a pretty decent look at the shooter, which is good." Desai folds her arms on top of the table. "The issue is, regarding your safety... from what you described, he also got a good look at you."

"That's true. He saw me. We looked at each other, but the chances of him recognizing me and finding me are slim, aren't they? Over two million people live in Chicago. He couldn't... " I never finish the sentence. Reality hits me like a bucket of ice water. My mouth goes dry. "Oh, no. There's a video of me from the train."

"We've watched the footage many times." Desai's voice is low and serious. "You haven't been identified on it yet. That could change any minute."

The full weight of their words sinks in. The situation has changed, and it's much worse now. I think they're implying that I'm no longer just a witness. I'm a potential target.

"What should I do?"

Desai's eyes lock on mine. "Be vigilant. Stay aware of your surroundings. Report anything suspicious to us, no matter how small it might seem."

"I understand," I say, even though I don't. Not really.

When I stand to leave, my legs are shaky.

"Just be careful, Mrs. James. That's all we're saying," Millard adds, his final words following me out of his office as I head to meet the sketch artist.

Later, when I leave the police station, Millard's warnings stay with me. How can I be careful when the killer could be anyone, anywhere? How can I go about my life knowing imminent danger could lurk around every corner?

CHAPTER 9

The rain has stopped. I pull into a corner café, grab a large latte, and get back into my car. Heat seeps from the paper cup into my palms, but it can't touch the icy dread mounting inside me.

I scan my surroundings, trying to be vigilant. Every passerby is now a potential threat. There's a man in a hoodie with his head down and his phone to his ear. What if he's the assailant? A tall and broad-shouldered man strides past my car. Could he be the shooter? My eyes dart from one man to the next, and there are of course thousands of men walking around Chicago. I sip my latte and try not to freak out. If Adam or anyone else were with me, I might not feel this way. Alone, I've always been more wary and paid more attention to my surroundings. But never like this.

The only way I'll feel safe is if I lock myself inside my apartment. And even then, I'm not so sure.

My phone is still vibrating. I set my coffee cup in the console and check the first voicemail. It's from yesterday. The morning of the assault. It's rare that I get voicemails. I must have missed it.

"This message is for Haley James. This is Lance Hutchinson from Hartley, Hutchinson, and Associates. I have an important and confidential matter to discuss with you. Please call me at your earliest convenience."

I press the home button on my phone and ask, "What is Hartley, Hutchinson, and Associates in Chicago?"

My phone answers, "Hartley, Hutchinson and Associates is a premier law firm with—"

I ignore the rest. Why is a lawyer calling me? Is Adam filing for divorce? Or worse, is he going to press charges against me? After everything that's just happened, would he do that now? I play the next message.

"Haley James? This is Bridget Quinton from WCTB News. We'd love to have you on our evening broadcast to talk about your heroic actions."

I skip to the next voicemail, then the next. They're all the same. Reporters, news stations, talk shows. I've also got texts. Each is from a media source that wants to speak with me. Obviously, word got out about my identity, and they got my phone number.

My fingers twitch as I find Cara's name and the video link she sent earlier. The video now has three million views. Three million people have seen me. One could be the shooter, watching and committing my face to memory.

When the last of my coffee is cold, I drive home on autopilot. As I turn onto my street, my mouth falls open. I hit the brakes.

News vans with satellite dishes line one side of the street. Thick wire cables snake across the sidewalk, attaching to light stands and other media equipment. A small crowd of reporters had gathered in front of my apartment building. How did they know I live here and not with Adam?

A car honks behind me because I've stopped driving and I'm blocking the lane.

"There she is! Haley James!"

The reporters surge forward, shouting, their cameras flashing. I shrink back against my seat and wish I could disappear. They come right up to my car, right beside my window, staring me down.

I give my car a bit of gas and inch forward. Thankfully, they part, allowing me to pull into my garage. There must be a rule about boundaries they can't cross, because they don't follow me in. I breathe a sigh of relief. I've escaped, but not entirely. My apartment entrance is outdoors. I don't want to go out there, so I sit in my car until I'm shivering.

The side door creaks as I push it open. Their heads snap toward me.

"Ms. James! How does it feel to be a hero?"

"Are you afraid the shooter might come after you?"

"No comment. Excuse me, please." I stride through them, jacket hood pulled over my head, holding my purse in front of my face. I can barely see where I'm going.

Four words repeat inside my head: Please leave me alone.

I don't want this attention.

At the entryway, I fumble with my key, hands shaking. Finally, I fall inside and yank the door shut.

If these reporters could find me so easily, how long before the killer does too?

CHAPTER 10

I hurry from window to window, yanking the blinds closed and removing all the natural light from my apartment. What do I do now? I could use a sedative to calm my rattled nerves, but I don't keep any medicine here. Besides, I need to keep my wits about me.

My phone keeps buzzing with messages from reporters I've never heard of.

I peek at the figures outside the windows. Their presence is a curse and a comfort. I hate being trapped, but if the shooter wants to eliminate me so I can't identify him, surely he won't try anything with so many witnesses.

A heavy weight presses on my neck and shoulders as I sink into the couch. If Adam were here, we could sit side by side and marvel at the fuss outside. Instead, it's me against the world.

I stare at his name in my contacts, resisting the urge to call him. With a sigh, I open my internet browser.

The Internet is still ablaze with theories about the train assault. The first one is something I need to read.

L Train Shooter: Targeted Hit or Random Act of Violence?

The article is packed with speculation. No one except the person responsible knows the real story. The rest are making up whatever sounds interesting. One source suggests Lauren was about to expose a major corporation, which is what I'd been thinking last night. There aren't any solid facts yet. Only conjecture. But Lauren's life is now an open book, whether or not she likes it.

What if they dig into my past? What if they talk to Adam and he shares the reason he insisted I move out of our house? My stomach churns. He wouldn't tell them. It could end my career. He wouldn't do that to me, would he?

I close my internet browser, but the worry lingers, making me uncomfortable all over, as if I'm coming down with a nasty bug.

I pace, rechecking the locks. A sudden thud from my bedroom makes me freeze. What was that? Did it come from inside my apartment? One of those reporters? Or worse, has the killer found me? I grab the nearest object, a glass vase from the hospital's gift shop, and creep towards the sound, every nerve on high alert.

As I approach the partially open closet door, my heart thumps wildly. I'm afraid, but I have no choice. I can't flee my apartment just because I heard a noise. Summoning courage, I fling the closet door open, then jump back, ready to strike with the vase. I catch a peek of gray fur and nearly collapse with relief. It's just Moose. What was I thinking? Am I losing my mind to nerves?

"You scared me half to death," I mutter, setting down the vase and scooping him up. He lets me hold him against my chest and stroke his fur for longer than usual before he leaps away.

My heartrate is back to normal, and a better defense plan is in order. I head to the coat closet, where I've abandoned my golf clubs in the back corner. I can't believe I brought them to the apartment with me, but now I'm glad I did.

The clubs were a gift from Adam, back when he still wanted to share his life with me. Unfortunately, I was terrible at golf. I held everyone up, tested their patience and my own, and never came close to par. But now I wish I could go back to those days and have his arm around me as he corrects my swing.-If I ever play with him again, I'll make the most of it and try harder.

Shaking off the memories, I grab a few iron clubs and distribute them around the apartment. One beside the front door, another within reach beneath my bed, a third near the back entrance.

Night falls. I peer through the blinds at the reporters still camped outside and chatting with each other. Is the killer out there too, hiding in plain sight among them?

It's dinnertime, and I've accomplished nothing today. My fridge is basically empty. Luckily, I don't have much of an appetite. I feed Moose his salmon mix and force myself to eat some plain pasta. I can't shake the feeling of being watched. Makes sense, since that's what's happening.

Sleep seems impossible, but hours later, exhaustion wins out. As I drift off, my last coherent thought is to wonder how long all this will last——the reporters, my fear, and especially my loneliness.

CHAPTER 11

When I call my mother the next day to check on her, she's seen the video. Her best friend Maria showed it to her.

"It will all die down soon, Haley. The reporters will move on to something else. At least it's positive. You should be proud."

"I just want them to go away. I don't want to answer any questions."

"Then keep quiet or say no comment. You don't owe them anything."

"Okay. I'll be there to see you as soon as I can. I'm sorry."

"Don't you apologize to me. Just take care of yourself."

"Wait, what about your news? Do you want to tell me now? I'm alone, and you have my complete attention."

"No, I'll tell you when I see you. It can wait until you get here, Haley. I promise. But come alone, okay?"

"Yes, I will." Her request isn't a problem.

After our call, I hold Moose, petting him for as long as he lets me, then check my phone.

Almost a full day has passed since the video went viral. It's up to six million views now. It's possible everyone in Chicago has watched it. The comments are across the board.

The face of heroism. #haleyjames #nursepower

This is what nurses do. #haleyjames #nursessavelives

Woman gets eaten alive on the train during the zombie apocalypse. #haleyjames #zombieapocalypse

The last one disgusts me and keeps me from reading more.

After changing into scrubs, I put on makeup. Normally, I don't wear makeup to work, just lip balm with a little color, but if I'm going to have cameras taking my picture, I should try to offset my look on the viral video by showing up with my best face.

I'm eager to get to the hospital to be with others and check on Lauren.

Grabbing my bag, I steal a glance out the window from behind the blinds. The memes about me might be multiplying, but the reporters have thinned out. Only a few stragglers remain.

They spot me when I pull out of the garage. I stare straight ahead through my windshield and drive past as they aim their cameras in my direction. I'm like a celebrity escaping the paparazzi as they climb into their vehicles and follow me. It's no high-speed chase, though. The traffic in Chicago ensures we're not even driving close to the speed limit.

At the hospital, they thrust microphones and cameras toward me. I keep walking with my head bowed. Don't they realize they're putting me in danger?

"Mrs. James, can you tell us what happened on the train?"

"Are you here for Lauren Christensen? Did you know each other?"

"Are you and your husband estranged?"

The last question unsettles me the most. How do they know about Adam? I guess it's easy to learn I'm married, and I lived in a house with Adam until recently. Then they camped outside my apartment all night. They saw I was alone. My separation has nothing to do with the shooting or anything that happened on the train, but it appears all aspects of my life are fair game now, same as Lauren's.

I shield my face with one hand and keep moving. A hospital security guard finally spots me. He intervenes and escorts me through the entrance.

The normal hospital bustle is comforting after being trapped in my quiet apartment. Still, every person I pass makes me self-conscious. I wonder if they've seen the video and recognize me. Does that make me paranoid?

"Haley, you're here." Tamira gives a sympathetic frown as I approach the nurse's station. "We've been dealing with the media nonstop. First, about Lauren's condition, then your newfound celebrity. It's been chaos."

"Sorry," I say, though neither Lauren nor I asked for any of this.

Tamira pulls me aside. "Listen, Haley, why don't you take a few days off? Things will quiet down soon, and you could probably use a break."

I hesitate, then remember walking through the reporters and needing help from the security guard. "You're sure?"

"We'll be fine," Tamira assures me. "Besides, you should spend the time with your mom. And while you're with her, make sure she knows how much we miss her."

"I will. I was on my way to see her when the thing happened on the train."

Tamira gives my arm a squeeze. "So go visit your mother and help her. I'm sure she's worried about *you* right now."

"Haley!" Cara's voice comes from somewhere down the hallway. She hurries toward me and then gives me a hug. "Are you okay?"

I force a smile. "I'm fine. Just overwhelmed."

Cara's expression shows the empathy that makes her such a good nurse. "Oh, before I forget... a lawyer was looking for you yesterday. Left his card." She hands me a crisp business card.

I get a chill as I read the name on the card. Lance Hutchinson. The same attorney who left me a voicemail yesterday.

"Thanks," I mumble, slipping the card into my coat pocket. "Did he say what he wanted?"

Cara shrugs. "He only said it was important. He seemed pretty intent on finding you."

Did Adam hire him to serve divorce papers? I can't believe he would subject me to this insult now, when I'm overwhelmed by things beyond my control. Unless the timing is intentional, and his goal is to catch me off-guard. Or is someone suing me for negligence for helping Lauren on the train? Plenty of doctors are afraid to help outside the hospital because the world is a crazy place and good deeds can get punished. I've seen it happen before. Lauren's family is the most likely culprit.

It's also possible Lance Hutchinson is just another reporter trying to trick me into talking. Whoever he is and whatever he wants, it's one more reason to leave town while I can. I'm glad for the opportunity to spend time with my mother. But before I go, I want to check on Lauren.

"Any change with Lauren Christensen?" I ask the ICU nurse on duty.

She shakes her head. "Minimal."

I say another silent prayer. Please let her make it.

There's a security guard stationed outside Lauren's private room. He wasn't there before. Is it a precautionary measure in case there's another attempt on her life? I'm glad the guard is in place. He checks my ID badge and allows me in. When I open the door, Kyle is talking to an attractive older couple.

Their conversation ceases, and he waves me in. "Haley, hi. Meet Lauren's parents."

I step inside.

Lauren is still in an induced coma with the vent pushing air into her repaired lung.

Kyle extends his arm in my direction. "This is Haley, the nurse who saved Lauren's life."

I offer a slight but solemn smile. "Hi. I came by to check on her."

Lauren's mother is a petite woman with Lauren's brown hair and porcelain skin. She comes right up to me and grasps my hand. "Thank you. We can't ever repay you for jumping right in to save our daughter. She is my world, and the thought of losing her is unbearable."

I don't have a child of my own, but I imagine my mother saying the same thing if she'd almost lost me.

"We're aware of the video, but we haven't watched it," her father adds. "We couldn't. But we heard what you did. Thank you. Really, thank you."

I picked my profession because I love helping people, often when they need it the most. My work is rewarding, and most of the time, I get back more than I give. Still, it's always nice to hear when someone appreciates my efforts.

I'm about to excuse myself and allow the family their privacy when her father clears his throat. "We heard you provided the police with a sketch of the shooter. Did they tell you if they have any leads yet?"

"They haven't said anything to me." I glance at Kyle. "Have they given you an update?"

"No, nothing new."

"Is it possible the shooting had something to do with her journalism?" I ask.

"We don't know. The police are looking into it." There's frustration written across Kyle's face. He wants answers and someone to blame. He wants to see justice served on Lauren's behalf. I understand exactly how he feels.

When I leave Lauren's room after speaking with her family, it's nearly impossible to believe they've sent a lawyer after me. Their gratitude seems sincere, which brings me back to Adam as the only other explanation for the attorney trying to contact me. The realization makes my heart ache.

The lawyer's card in my pocket is just one more thing to worry about.

One step at a time, I tell myself. For now, it's all I can do.

I leave the hospital through a side exit, avoiding the reporters.

It's time to see my mother and find out what she needs to tell me.

CHAPTER 12

The drive home from the hospital passes in a blur of lights and signs. I'm on autopilot again, my thoughts racing. Two vans are parked across the street from my building. I keep my eyes straight ahead and drive past them.

Inside my apartment, I drop my keys on the kitchen table. Then I just stand there, leaning on the counter, feeling like I can't move as the weight of everything presses down on me. Think positive, I tell myself. I'm grateful for a few uninterrupted days with my mother. I'm used to seeing her most days at the hospital, and since she hasn't been working, I've missed our regular interactions. She won't admit it, but the chemo has zapped her energy, and she could use my help around her house. But right now, I need her more than she needs me.

I pack without putting too much thought into it, tossing a few outfits into an overnight bag. Soft hoodies and joggers. One nice sweater. I can always do laundry at my mother's house. Then I grab Moose's carrier. It's not going to be easy. The last time I got him in there for a vet appointment left me looking as if I'd wrestled with a tiny werewolf. I can't go through that again. It will be easier if someone comes here to take care of him.

With a sigh, I call Adam.

"Haley, hey... I saw the video. Reporters came looking for you."

"Did you give them my apartment address?"

"Um, sort of."

"I wish you hadn't. Please don't say anything about me."

"Why don't you just talk to them?"

"Because I don't want my face all over the news."

"There's nothing wrong with your face, Haley, but okay, whatever."

"I'm going to stay with my mom for a few days to help her out."

"Good. Did you get your car fixed?"

The answer seems obvious, with all that's going on in my life. "I didn't get to it."

"Look, you can take my car. I'm not going anywhere this week. Drop Moose off here on your way out of the city and we'll swap."

His offer surprises me. It's generous. "Are you sure?"

"It's for your mom. After what happened the last time you tried to see her, the last thing she needs is for you to break down on the way."

I'm glad he's concerned for my mother, but he doesn't sound that concerned about me.

After hanging up, I focus on Moose. With the carrier door open, I move toward him. He stares down with suspicion from atop the bookshelf.

"Come on, buddy. We're going on a little trip. You'll get to see Adam."

Moose understands my intention and darts under the bed.

I drop to my knees, peering into the darkness. His eyes glow as he stares back with defiance.

"Moose, please," I plead and stretch my arm toward him.

He retreats further, backing away until I can no longer see him.

I grab the bag of dried chicken treats and shake it. Moose creeps out, but just as my fingers brush his fur, he bolts. The frustrating chase continues around my apartment. Moose is always faster. When I finally corner him,

I'm panting. I scoop him up, ignoring his yowls of protest, and make a beeline for the carrier.

He twists in my arms, his claws extended. A sharp sting pierces my skin. With a frantic push, I get him into the carrier, pressing the door shut as he heaves himself against it. When it's finally over, we stare at each other from opposite sides of the grate.

"Why do you have to make it so hard?" I ask, adrenaline pumping. "You'll be happy when you get there."

Twenty minutes later, I'm turning into the driveway that used to be mine. Adam is waiting outside, wearing a black quilted jacket I bought him, as if he's excited to see me. He must have tracked my location on his phone and known I was almost here.

When I'm close, I recognize his guarded expression and the rushed look in his eyes. I understand now. He's waiting for me outside because he doesn't want me to come in.

"Thanks for this," I say as I hand over Moose in the carrier.

Adam is looking at the angry red scratches on my wrist. "What happened?"

When I pull up my sleeve, the scratches are visible all the way to my elbow. "He acted demonic about leaving my apartment. You know how he is." I try to make light of the ordeal, but I hate thinking we'll have to do it again when I return.

Adam doesn't ask me inside for a drink or for any reason at all. As we exchange car keys, my gaze drops to his hand. He's not wearing his wedding band. I'm a little shocked, and I wonder when he took it off.

I hand him a bag. "His food, treats, and the coconut oil I put in his dinner."

Adam takes it and says hello to Moose.

I'm about to leave rather than stretch out the discomfort when I remember. "Adam, did you send an attorney to find me?"

His brow furrows. "No. Why?"

"Never mind." I don't tell him I suspected divorce papers. No need to give him ideas or let him think I'm ready to call our marriage quits. We could go back to the way things were if he would just believe me. And apologize, of course.

As I drive away in his Mercedes, I catch him in the rearview mirror. He's standing in the driveway, watching me leave. I wish I could read his mind. Maybe it's better I can't.

I blow out a puff of breath, trying to clear my head. Right now, all that matters is getting to my mother. For a few days while I'm with her, I can pretend my world hasn't turned upside down.

CHAPTER 13

Driving from the city to the suburbs, I vow to shelve my problems and make my mother my sole focus. I've been driving myself crazy trying to guess what she's going to say. My biggest fear is that she's had enough chemotherapy, and she's stopping. If that's what's going on, I'll do whatever it takes to convince her otherwise.

My childhood home, the place where I grew up, is the last modest house on a quiet road. Long, jagged lines stretch across the pavement of the driveway. I've never noticed those cracks before.

From the road, I see the toll my mother's cancer has taken on her gardens. A withered plant dangles from a planter box. Brown leaves litter the flower beds where she usually spreads fresh mulch in late fall. I'm not much of a gardener, but I understand the basics. Remove the dead and dying vegetation to make room for new life. I'll do my best while I'm here.

I kill the Mercede's engine in the driveway and sit there as the air chills around me. I have to stay strong for my mother. After another minute, I climb the front steps and stop beside the faded porch swing. She loves to sit there regardless of the temperature.

I raise my hand at the door, then stop myself. I'll never need to knock as long as my mother lives here. It's my house, too, and always will be. The door is unlocked and opens when I push it. I step inside and inhale the familiar smell of my home.

"Hello? It's me," I call, dropping my purse on the console table and my bags on the floor. Deep dents line the wooden floor from the time I rollerbladed through the house as a girl. My parents weren't happy with me then, but seeing those lines now gives me a wave of nostalgia. So many good memories live in this house. It's just hard to believe my father is no longer with us.

Maria appears in the living room doorway. I glimpse the flower tattoo on her wrist. It's identical to my mother's. They've been close friends since college. Maria lives nearby and visits often, especially these days. Unlike my mother, she waited several years after college before getting married and several more before getting pregnant. By then, I was just the right age to assume babysitting duties for her two children.

Her eyes crinkle with a warm smile, but I don't miss the apprehension there. "Haley, it's good to see you." She pulls me into a firm hug. "I've been following every bit of news about the shooting. Just terrible, but we're all very proud of you."

I step back, not wanting to discuss the train incident here. "How is she today?"

"The same. Just frustrated about not living her life exactly the way she wants to, but she's managing."

"Everyone okay?" I ask. "You and your family?"

"We're all doing well. It's *you* I'm concerned about. The incident was only two days ago. How are you holding up?"

"I guess I'm fine. It's just been a lot. Meeting with the police. The reporters."

"I can imagine. And Adam? How's he handling everything?"

I twist my rings around my finger. "It's a lot for both of us. But things should quiet down for him with me here." I omit the fact that we're no longer living together and pray she doesn't ask me anything else about Adam or my marriage.

Maria seems to weigh her next words. "Haley, I need to give you a heads up. Your mother has something important to tell you. It's going to come as quite a shock. It might be a lot to take in."

"Is it about her cancer? Is she not tolerating the treatments? Because when I ask her, she always says she's doing okay."

Maria shakes her head. "It's not that, and it's not my place to say. Just prepare yourself, and remember, no matter what, she loves you. She has loved you fiercely with all her heart since the day you were conceived. She always has, and she always will."

A chill runs through me. Is she implying I might question my mother's love after hearing this news?

"Maria, what—" I start, but she's already shaking her head.

"She needs to be the one to tell you."

"Okay," I say, apprehensive. "Well, thank you for taking care of her."

Maria's face softens. "You don't need to thank me, sweet Haley. There's no one I'd rather spend time with than your mother. Oh, she hasn't taken her meds yet. They make her sleepy, and she wanted to be clear-headed for you. Make sure she doesn't doze off for the night and forget."

"I won't let that happen. Thank you, Maria. Mom's lucky to have you."

"We're lucky we have each other. Your mother is tougher than she looks. She'll be back to work at the hospital with you soon."

I hold on to those words as I watch Maria gather her things and leave. When she's gone, I summon courage for what's ahead and walk to my mother's bedroom.

CHAPTER 14

With my hand resting on the doorframe, I pause at the threshold of my mother's room. There's no scent of sickness here. Her room smells delicious, like pumpkin and vanilla. It's coming from a fall candle I brought on my last visit.

She's dressed in pajamas atop the covers, with a cream-colored blanket draped over her legs. During her chemo sessions, she opted for a silicone cooling cap to prevent hair loss. It's working. Her blonde hair is as healthy as ever. She blows it out and puts on makeup before each treatment. "The better you look, the better care you'll receive," she always says. As health-care providers, we strive to treat everyone with the same consideration. Yet she still insists it's important to look her best when she's the patient.

She's only fifty-two. For someone who has always been a whirlwind of activity—nursing, gardening, volunteering—slowing down has been a challenge. She didn't want to take a leave from work, but hospital shifts are risky for chemo patients with suppressed immune systems.

I swallow hard around a lump of nervousness. Now that I'm here, I can't handle another disappointment on top of everything else. My father passed a year ago. My mother's cancer diagnosis followed. Then Adam left me shortly after his grandfather died, making this officially the worst twelve months of my life. I want no more bad news.

My mother's face lights up when she sees me. "My Haley." She beckons me over with the same smile that's greeted me my entire life. A smile that tells me I'm loved.

In four strides, I cross the room and clasp her outstretched hand in both of mine. "Hi, Mom. I missed you."

"I've missed you too, sweetheart." We hug, and she holds on longer than usual. "I was so worried. Now, let me look at you." She scans me from top to bottom in a way no one else could do without it being strange. The fresh scratches make her frown.

"Moose didn't want to get—" I stop myself from saying he didn't want to get in his carrier. "Moose did that."

"You look tired. It's been difficult, hasn't it? The train incident and all the attention."

I shrug, trying not to burden her with my troubles and make this visit all about me. "It's been a little rough, but I'm managing."

"Good. I hope Adam doesn't mind my asking you to come alone. How is he?"

This is the question I've been dreading.

"He's fine." I force a small smile. "Taking care of Moose and the house while I'm here."

"Oh, good." Her expression turns serious. "I love Adam, but what I'm going to tell you, I thought it should be just the two of us. You can explain everything to him when you're ready."

Guilt gnaws at me as I continue the charade. "Okay. I will. You look flushed. Are you okay?"

"Yes, I suppose I'm nervous."

"Let me check your blood pressure." I reach for the cuff in the top drawer of her nightstand. I'm putting my skills to good use while I'm here.

I'm also delaying her news. If it's making her nervous, I'd prefer not to hear it. Not yet.

She holds up a hand, then takes my wrist in a firm grip. "No, no. That's unnecessary. I just want to talk to you. This is important. It's something I should have told you long before now, but I couldn't."

My pulse pounds in a whoosh of blood at my temples. The moment I've been dreading has finally arrived. "What is it, Mom?" I lean closer, bracing myself for bad news.

Her fingers slide from my wrist to my hand. For a moment, she looks past me. Then her eyes meet mine again. "It's about your father."

That's not what I expected to hear. I'm relieved but also confused. When my father died last year, his funeral packed the church. Everyone cried. He was a wonderful, kind man. Not a single enemy. His students, colleagues, and the kids he coached all loved him. What could she have to tell me about him now?

It's obvious how difficult this is for her. I can tell that whatever she says next will change everything between us forever.

CHAPTER 15

"What about my father?" I ask.

My mother's eyes glisten. "The man who raised you wasn't your biological father, Haley."

I pull my hand away. "I don't understand. How could he not be my father? You and Dad were together since you met in college. Freshman year, right?"

"We were." Her gaze falls on the blanket across her lap. After a moment, she looks up again and continues in a small voice. "Senior year, your father and I broke up over something silly. I can't even remember what. I had a short fling with someone else. When I realized I had gotten pregnant... this sounds terrible, not information you ever want to hear from a parent... but I barely knew him."

Her words are sinking in.

"Your dad and I were meant to be together. I always knew he was a good person. The best. Even then, I was sure I could count on him to do the right thing for us. For you and me."

My mind is a jumble of thoughts. "So he knew I wasn't his biological child?"

My mother shakes her head and whispers, "No. I never told him. I couldn't."

"What?" My voice comes out sharper than I intended. "He didn't know?"

"There was too much to lose, Haley. I couldn't risk it. I knew I loved him, and he loved me. We were so young, and I was terrified. But we always wanted children, and even though I was pregnant earlier than planned, we knew we wanted you. Once you were born, both your father and I were beyond thrilled. We loved you so much. I didn't see the point in complicating that for anyone. Months went by, then years, and it became too late to tell him."

I'm stunned as I slump into the chair beside the bed. I've just learned important things weren't what they seemed for the last three decades of my life.

"So, who was he?" I ask at last. "The other man. My biological father."

"His name is Elliot Rhodes. He still lives in the area. Near the city. He's a successful businessman." She waits for my response, but I still don't know what to say. We're both silent until she continues. "I reached out to him recently. Just last week. I told him about you."

My jaw goes slack. "You told him? Before you told me? I don't understand. Why now?"

"To eliminate regrets. And I wanted you to meet him, if that's what you want."

I hold up my hand like a crossing guard. "Okay, first of all, the thing about regrets... you have cancer... but you're going to beat it."

"I expect to, but just in case... I'm not leaving unfinished business. And with your father gone, now that the truth can't hurt him, it's the right thing to do."

"Okay." I stand there with my mouth open for a good ten seconds or more. "Why would you tell Elliot before you told me?"

"I debated how to go about this. I decided to first make sure he was receptive to the news."

"Wait. Are you saying that if he weren't, you never would have told me?"

My mother sighs again. "I needed his reaction before I shared the information with you. I couldn't take the chance of his not taking the news well. You know how I am. I never want you to get hurt. I couldn't put you in that position."

I close my eyes for a few breaths. "Okay. You were protecting me. Making sure I didn't get rejected. I get it. What did he say when you told him?"

"He was shocked but also pleased. He doesn't have any biological children of his own."

"I can relate to his shock. I'm experiencing it right now." My skin is tingling, and my thoughts are fuzzy. "Does anyone else know about this?"

"Only Maria. And for thirty-one years, the secret has been safe with her. I trust Maria with my life."

"So, now what?" I ask, pushing hard against my cuticles with my thumb.

Mom lies back against the pillows, her face drawn. "It's your choice now. You can find out more about him. You can decide if you want to meet."

I have so many questions, but my mother's voice is growing faint. I kick back into nurse mode. "You've given me a lot to think about. Let's just take it easy now. Enough talking for the night. I need some time to register everything."

"Sorry, honey," she whispers. "I'm sorry I kept this from you. But I had to."

"I understand why you did what you did. I'm glad you finally told me. Just rest for a while, okay?"

Her eyelids droop as she gives a tiny nod. I lean in, pressing my lips to her forehead.

She relaxes and lets me fuss over her. I refill her water and make sure she takes her meds. The routine of caring for someone helps me calm down.

When my mother dozes off, I move my bags to my childhood bedroom and search for my charger. My phone's battery icon blinks red. I have to replace the battery soon, or the entire phone. With everything that's happened, the task hasn't topped my priority list this past month.

Minutes later, phone charging, I return to my mother's room. She's still sleeping, a peaceful expression on her beautiful face.

I can't imagine keeping an enormous secret for so long, or what it would be like to give it up.

My own secrets feel heavier than ever.

CHAPTER 16

I attack my mother's cooktop with a scouring pad, scrubbing at a stain that's been there forever and won't come off. The counters are next, then the oven interior. I'm on my hands and knees reaching into the back when I realize I've been replaying her words for the past twenty minutes.

She dropped a real bombshell on me yesterday.

What does Elliot Rhodes look like? What sort of life does he lead? Elliot is an old-fashioned sort of name. Is it a family name? Does he have a family? Is he married?

All my memories of my father, the man who raised me, are cast in a strange new light. It doesn't make our relationship less meaningful, just different. I'm a hundred percent certain that if he knew the truth, he wouldn't have loved me any less. It just seems wrong that he never knew, and he never will.

My parents' marriage was solid. They loved each other and didn't hesitate to say it frequently. They showed it by kissing hello and goodbye and holding hands. Their happiness made me believe Adam and I could also last until death do us part. But the marriage I always appreciated was built on a lie. A rather big one. Would the truth have destroyed them?

I want to be angry with my mother for my dad's sake. But she's sick. She's bound to get better, yet there's always a small chance she won't. Cancer doesn't play by rules, and it doesn't care how loved or needed a person is.

Aside from this one enormous incident, my mother has always had my back, no matter the situation. For as long as I can remember, I've looked up to her and believed she could do no wrong. I didn't always show my love and respect during my teenage years because I was a normal teen, but it was always there. She's the reason I became a nurse. I really don't have it in me to hold something against her.

With nothing left to clean, I wring my hands. They're dry and cracked from constant handwashing, the cold weather, and my stress. The skin around my nail beds is more inflamed than ever.

In my mother's bathroom, I grab the small jar of coconut oil she keeps behind the mirror of her medicine cabinet. As I work the emollient into my ravaged skin, I hope Adam remembers Moose's daily dose.

My mother stores family photo albums in the cabinets beneath the built-in bookshelves in the study. I select an album and sit down with it. The photos depict a family I thought I understood. My parents looked carefree and young in college. My mother's blonde hair falls past her shoulders, and my father didn't seem concerned with getting haircuts. His hair is also longer than I've ever seen it in real life. They were Carol and Ethan then. Not Mom and Dad yet.

The oil on my fingertips leaves a touch of grease on the plastic. I grab a tissue and wipe it away.

Next come the wedding photos. My father wore a tuxedo. He told me that was his first and only time in a bow tie. The roundness of my mother's belly is only visible in profile. Her long white dress flows over a slight bump. Despite the rushed ceremony, everyone around them was smiling.

I'm in nearly every photo in the albums that follow. My parents doted on me. In one faded picture, my father cradles me in his arms on the plaid couch that still exists in the basement. In another, we're assembling a Lego starship together. We both have brown hair and brown eyes. Did he ever suspect I wasn't his?

After his death, I studied these same photo albums through tears of grief, consoling myself with evidence he lived a wonderful life even though it got cut short. I admired the enormous responsibility he embraced at such a young age. I couldn't imagine doing what my parents had done. They're not the first couple to have children early in life, but it seems so selfless. I'm not sure I could have cared for my cat properly at that age.

When I finally put the albums back, I have to clear my head and stop feeling so melancholy. I should get out of the house for a bit. Buy groceries before it gets too late.

After leaving my mother a message, I grab my purse and the keys to Adam's car. As I head for the front door, the framed photo in the entryway catches my eye. It's been there forever because it's a family favorite and one of our only professional photos. The three of us sit on a park bench surrounded by spring flowers. I'm about six years old, grinning with a missing tooth and cute pigtails. We all look happy and carefree, especially my mother. Her smile is huge.

Had she stopped worrying about her secret by then? Or was she always afraid the truth might escape?

Until last night, I didn't realize there were any long-hidden secrets in my family. Now I know about Elliot Rhodes.

I wonder how he's dealing with the news.

CHAPTER 17

One Week Ago

I'm reviewing the quarterly reports and eating tortilla chips for lunch when my office phone rings. Expecting another business call, I answer, "Elliot Rhodes speaking."

"Mr. Rhodes? Hello. You might not remember me. My name is Carol Baldwin. It used to be Carol Wizienski."

The name doesn't register. "How can I help you?"

She goes silent for a bit. If this is a sales pitch, it's not a good one, and it's wasting my time. I'm about to end the call with a firm "no, thank you" when she says, "I have important news to share. It's about something that happened when we were in college."

College was thirty years ago. Then it clicks. Carol. A petite blonde with a stunning figure and an infectious laugh. We spent a few nights together at my off-campus apartment. The memory makes me smile.

"Carol. Yes. I remember you. Of course I do. Wow, it's been a long time."

Another pause, longer this time. Is she looking for a job?

"Elliot, there's no easy way to say this, so I'm just going to come right out with it. That weekend we spent together, I got pregnant."

Pregnant? Whatever she's trying to say, I'm not following.

"I have a daughter. She's thirty. Her name is Haley. And you're her father."

I grip the phone tighter. "A daughter?"

"Yes, she's an amazing woman."

My mind is still stuck on daughter. "Why now?" I ask, skepticism breaking through my surprise. "Why tell me after all this time?"

"I couldn't tell you before. I'm sorry, but we barely knew each other." Her voice wavers. "I married someone else. He recently passed away. Now I'm battling cancer, and... you deserve the truth."

I lean back in my chair, winded, as if someone punched me in the gut. I'm not sure how to respond. Who would? "I'm sorry about your cancer," I finally say. "Does your daughter know about me?"

"No. Not yet. I love Haley. We're very close. She is everything to me, and I won't have her getting hurt. I called you before I told her. I had to see how you would react."

"I need some time to process this. I'll have to get back to you."

"Of course. I understand. And Elliot, when you come to terms with this, I hope you can forgive me."

I hang up the phone. My hands are trembling. If this is true... how dare she keep the news from me? But better late than never, right? I'm trying to think this through from a logical standpoint, and it's impossible. I've survived hostile takeovers, the untimely deaths of close friends, and my ex-wife walking out. I thought nothing could shake me anymore. How wrong I was.

"Mr. Rhodes?"

My assistant's voice on the intercom pulls me out of my trance. "I didn't hear you, Jenny. Please repeat that."

"About the board members. That's four now who insist on getting time with you before the larger group meets. I told them your calendar's full."

"Send me their names. Tell them I'll call them back tonight." My voice sounds odd. I can't focus on the reports now, so I get up from my chair and pace. Should I trust Carol? I need advice, and there's only one person I'll go to with this news.

"Lance, I need to see you," I say when my friend answers. "Something wild just happened. I'm coming to your office."

There's a jumpiness in my step as I head out to meet Lance. I jab the elevator button repeatedly—something I hate when others do it—but I can't help myself today.

Dare I believe I have a daughter? My own flesh and blood.

CHAPTER 18

One Week Ago

How many times have I walked into this law office? Hundreds? Lance spends more time here than at home.

Friends since college, we've been through a lot together. Too much, I sometimes think. Personal and professional triumphs, but also devastations. The darkest hours came when his wife Becca died after a car accident. I was with him at the hospital, praying for positive news, only to receive the worst. The loss was so traumatizing that Lance never talks about it. My divorce from Jules, though unexpected and gut-wrenching for me, pales in comparison. There have been career milestones in between, a few failures but mostly successes. Yet we've never discussed anything like this.

Neither of us has a child. I'm always busy, but when I'm not working or playing tennis, loneliness can creep in, along with regrets. Especially after my parents died, and I realized there was no one carrying on their genes. Lance might have similar feelings, but that's not the sort of thing we talk about. Not since Becca died.

Sitting across from each other, with a yellow legal pad between us, Lance narrows his eyes. "So, Carol calls your office out of the blue and says you have a daughter?"

"Yes. I met her senior year at one of Everett's parties. She was a nursing student. We hooked up over a weekend. Several times. It's definitely possible."

"Walk me through what she told you."

As I tell him about the unexpected phone call, memories of Carol surface. Her long blonde hair. A song we danced to, a song that came to represent my senior year in college and all the fun I had. The skin-tingling exhilaration of being with her. The story becomes more real with each remembered detail.

Lance studies me when I finish. "You seem excited, Elliot, but you don't know what this is really about yet. First things first. You need to verify paternity."

"Right. That's what I should do. Before anything else." If Carol is telling the truth, everything changes. If she's not, my life goes back to what it was. That thought brings a pang of disappointment. More than I would have expected.

"I'll run background checks on Carol and Haley. Given your wealth, it's the smart thing to do."

Lance is right. I have to be cautious.

"Would you like to discuss the legal implications while you're here?" He flips a page of his notepad, then walks me through inheritance claims, paternity rights, and their effect on my estate. I want to speculate about how this situation might change my life for the better, but not from a legal standpoint. When I die, most of my estate goes to charities, with a substantial amount going to my ex-wife and her son. If Haley is my daughter, I should change that allocation. But I can't get ahead of things here.

"I want to meet her."

Lance tilts his head. "We need to control how you approach this. Hold off until we get more information. I'll look into it myself."

"You will?"

"Sure. I'm just as curious as you, but more wary."

Despite Lance's warnings, I'm still energized, almost giddy, when I leave his office. I want to like Haley, but what if we don't hit it off? It's not improbable. Some people are difficult and inherently unlikable. God, I hope she's nothing like that.

I type a message to Jenny: *Cancel my appointments for the next few days.*

She responds: *All of them? Even with the board?*

Family emergency, I type back.

Family. It's a new concept. I like it. I'm also aware of the lost opportunities, and that's annoying, but I can't dwell on those. In the business world, they're what we call sunk costs. I need to focus on the future. That's what I can control.

As I drive, question after question fills my head. Does Haley look like her mother, me, or a little of both? What does she do for a living? Is she married? Do I have grandchildren?

At home, I head straight for my study to analyze my life before I share it with my daughter. Correction, the woman who *might* be my daughter. I haven't confirmed paternity yet, but I'm already behaving as if she is.

I grab a piece of paper from the top drawer of my desk. Writing my thoughts down is the best way to approach this situation. It will help me decide what I should share, and what I should hide.

CHAPTER 19

Present

The chemo clinic waiting room overlooks the parking lot. I scan the area, nerves on edge, picking at my cuticles. I have to clasp my hands behind my back to stop. Ever since the shooting, I'm searching everywhere for reporters and the gunman. My thoughts race between potential danger, my situation with Adam, and Elliot Rhodes. My life is chaos.

Then I remember Lauren, who is still in the hospital. Guilt strikes. I'm physically healthy. I have the luxury of worrying about lesser problems while she's still fighting for her life. But I have reasons to worry. The detective's warning echoes in my mind again: "Be hyper-vigilant... stay alert."

There's a man standing outside. He's partly hidden behind a giant blue dumpster, but looking my way, toward the clinic. It's freezing outside. Why is he out there? He's wearing a black cap, his head lowered.

I strain my eyes, trying to make out any details.

He moves, walking toward the building.

I go for my phone. I have to call Detective Millard.

When the man is close enough to get a clear look at his face, my shoulders release their tension. It's not the shooter. He drops a cigarette, mashes it with his foot, and walks into the building through a side door. He was only outside to smoke. How did I not notice his cigarette before?

I might be delusional, seeing threats where there are none. Perhaps I'll only realize genuine danger when it's already too late, like what happened on the train. If only the detectives could identify the suspect, I wouldn't have to be wary of every person around me.

I call the detectives anyway to find out if they've made any progress.

"Millard," his gruff voice answers.

"Detective, it's Haley James."

"Hello, Ms. James. What can I do for you? Have you remembered something else?"

"No, I'm just a little nervous after our last conversation. Any developments?"

"We're following leads. We're using the sketch you provided."

"But you don't have a suspect?" I ask, my heart sinking.

"Not yet, but we're working overtime on this."

"Okay. Thank you. I hope you get a break soon. Good luck."

I wish I'd spoken with Detective Desai instead. She might have given me some comfort. I'll take any reassurance I can get, even if it's fabricated.

Taking a seat away from the window, I check my email and see a name I recognize. Lance Hutchinson. The attorney who left his card at the hospital. He hasn't given up. He's requesting to meet with me about a "personal matter." Maybe it's nothing to worry about. I consider my response, how to phrase my question. *With what is this in regard to?* Is that how I should say it? I'm just procrastinating.

Before I can reply, my mother's session ends, and I help her to the car.

On the drive home, she's a little listless. Her head lolls against the passenger seat headrest, and her eyes close. Her fatigue will increase as the day progresses. Not everyone reacts this way to the drugs, but she does.

She turns toward me. "Have you talked to Adam today?"

"Not yet."

"Is he still grieving over Frank? Though things must be easier for you and Adam now that Frank is gone."

They aren't easier. It's like Frank is still trying to ruin my marriage from his grave, but my mother doesn't know that.

It's been over three months since Adam's grandfather Frank passed away. He died the same day as my mother's visit with the oncologist. We were all upset about her cancer, focused on saving one family member, only to lose another.

I glance at my mother, and I'm grateful she can't read my thoughts. She has no idea how strained things were with Adam around the time of Frank's funeral. That's when our troubles began. Adam's silence. Then, the cold shoulder. At first, I thought it was just his grief. His way of coping with loss. I was wrong.

"Do you want to meet Elliot?" my mother asks, pulling me from my thoughts.

My answer doesn't come right away. "I'd love to meet Elliot, but I have more than enough stuff to deal with for now. I'm not ready yet. Once things settle down."

"Did you search for him on the internet?"

"I thought about it but decided to see him for the first time with an open mind."

Her eyes are closed, but she smiles. "I understand. No preconceived notions."

"What about you?" I ask at a stoplight. "Have you always known where Elliot lived? What he was doing?"

"For years I wondered but never let myself search for him. Not until your father passed."

"Why didn't you look? You must have been curious."

"Oh, I was, but I loved your dad. Pretending Elliot didn't exist was easier."

The light turns green, and we move forward.

I get how it was easier to pretend Elliot never existed than to snatch glimpses of his life. She was smart not to Google him or check out his social media accounts. Smart and apparently gifted with extraordinary willpower. Or maybe she didn't keep tabs on Elliot out of respect for my dad. Still, she must have thought about him. I was her constant reminder.

When we get back, there's a newish BMW in front of my mother's house. A well-dressed man I don't recognize stands near it. Maria walks toward him with her hands on her hips.

I pull up behind the sedan. "Wait here, Mom, I'll see what's going on," I say, getting out of the car.

Maria is already handling the situation. "If you're a reporter, you need to leave," she tells him.

"I'm not a reporter." The man stares at me as I approach. "Haley James?"

Who is he, and how did he find me here? Did Adam tell him where I am?

"I'm Haley." I say with no warmth, crossing my arms. "Who are you?"

For a second, I think he won't answer. He's just staring. I narrow my eyes, and I'm about to tell him to leave, but his next words stop me.

"I work for Hartley & Hutchinson."

The law firm. This is Lance Hutchinson, the guy who has been trying to track me down.

"Why are you here? What do you want from me?"

"I'm here on behalf of Elliot Rhodes."

I wasn't expecting that answer. Why has my biological father sent a lawyer?

CHAPTER 20

The Mercedes door squeaks open behind me, and I give my mother a frustrated look. Of course, she doesn't stay put. Her need to safeguard me is too ingrained. I understand, since I'm the same way with her. When she's standing beside me on the sidewalk, her sharp gaze sweeps over the visitor. "What's going on here?"

I clench my hands. "This is Lance Hutchinson."

Lance gives me an odd look, as if he's impressed I remembered his name. Why wouldn't I? He's left me messages and visited the hospital. I don't have a slew of other attorneys trying to speak with me.

He gives my mother a disarming smile. "Carol, Haley's mother, I presume?"

"Yes." She looks Lance up and down. She's suspicious, though the most remarkable thing about him is that he's handsome, fit, and well-dressed.

He holds out his hand to shake hers. In a flash, I intercept by stepping between them. I don't want her shaking hands with a stranger from the city. She has to watch out for germs.

My mother makes a face. "Excuse my daughter. She worries about me. I'm undergoing chemotherapy."

"I'm sorry to hear that." Lance pulls back his hand. "I also apologize for the unexpected visit. I'd like to speak with your daughter, as long as I'm not interrupting anything."

She turns to me, and I shrug.

"Well, you can't very well have this conversation out here on the street," she says. "Please come inside."

I'm about to protest, but I definitely want to find out why he's here.

Lance accepts her offer, and we all file into the house.

Maria waits until I mouth, "Thank you, we're fine."

"I'll be back later," she says, giving my mother a look only two close friends could understand.

Once inside, my mother gestures towards the kitchen. "Haley, why don't you and Elliot's attorney talk in there? I'll be in the living room if you need me. I'm afraid I need to rest."

Lance waits while I get her a fresh glass of water. I return a minute later and sit down with him at the kitchen table. He has nice eyes and a distinctive dark mole or birthmark to the side of one. A faint trace of his cologne reaches me. It's cedar and pine. I bought a similar scent for Adam on his last birthday because I liked it so much.

"I apologize for not returning your calls," I say. "I had a lot going on in the past few days. Probably happens to you a lot, right? People avoid you and hope you'll leave them alone."

"I'm not used to being ignored. But I'm aware of what you went through. I saw the video. Impressive. You were so calm when no one else knew what to do."

"I'm sure someone else would have realized it was important to keep Lauren's blood inside her body."

"You were in the right place at the right time. Lauren Christensen owes you her life."

The urge to make another sarcastic comment hits me, my default reaction in awkward situations, but I hold back. "So, what is this about? Why have you been trying to speak with me?"

Lance's expression becomes more serious. "After Mr. Rhodes learned about you, he wanted to get a sense of who you are as a person."

I allow my surprise to show with a wide-eyed stare. "He sent *you* for that? Couldn't he just... I don't know. Look around online?"

Lance clasps his hands together above the table. A silver watch clinks against the edge. "Mr. Rhodes prefers to handle sensitive matters through the proper channels."

"And you're the proper channel?" I huff. How interesting. I chose not to find out about Elliot before meeting him, and it appears he's doing the opposite and using a paid surrogate for it.

"Excuse me, this is all a lot," I say, trying to apologize a bit for my sharp tone. "The name Elliot Rhodes meant nothing to me twenty-four hours ago. I've spent my whole life not knowing he existed, and now he's sending lawyers to my house to vet me."

"You just found out yesterday?" Now it's Lance who looks surprised.

"My mother told Elliot first to gauge his reaction. Then I was on that train... and telling me got delayed. If you'd reached me any sooner than today, I'd have said you were crazy and had the wrong person. I'm certain I wouldn't have believed you."

"I see. Well, Mr. Rhodes was equally surprised to learn about you."

I study Lance's face, trying to assess his sincerity. It still strikes me as odd that Elliot sent someone to get to know me rather than doing it himself.

"He's cautious," Lance continues, as if reading my thoughts. "We wanted to ensure this situation was legitimate before anything progressed."

I note his use of the term "we." Elliot has people who protect him. Apparently, he has a lot more to lose than I, but the implication still stings. "If he's worried my mother and I are con artists trying to trick him, I assure you, we're not. Although I guess that's also what a con artist would tell you, isn't it?" I laugh, but Lance doesn't. "And in case you're wondering, my mother truly has cancer. She also has excellent health insurance. This isn't a play for anything Elliot may or may not have."

"Please don't be offended," he says.

"So, what exactly are you here to do? Interview me? Run a background check?" At my questions, Lance shifts in his seat and averts his gaze for a few seconds. Maybe he isn't all that comfortable with the task Elliot has given him.

"I'd like to talk to you. That's all."

This isn't how I imagined my first steps with my biological father would go. Part of me is disappointed, another, suspicious. But if this is the way Elliot wants to start out, I can be reasonable and play along. There's no harm in it. None that I can see. Not yet.

I uncross my arms and set my hands on the table. "Okay. I'd like to get a sense of things, too. Where do we start?"

CHAPTER 21

Although it's strange Elliot sent his attorney, I start talking about myself.

"In a nutshell, I'm a thirty-year-old ER nurse. Almost ten years in nursing." I soften my tone, realizing I sound defensive. "My mother's a nurse, too. We work at the same hospital. My father was a math teacher. He passed away last year. I'm an only child. No siblings. No kids, but I have a cat who behaves like a sullen teenager," I add, wondering what else to share and wishing I'd organized my thoughts better. "I live in a two-bedroom apartment in the city. I'm married to a man I met four years ago at a bar."

As I utter that last sentence, my gaze drops to Lance's hands. No wedding band there. I guess I'm a little curious about the man I'm divulging all this information to.

"Occasionally, I post about my life on social media. Vacations mostly," I continue. "But until three days ago, my life had never been shared outside of my smallish friend group. That viral video was a shock."

"A lot of people have seen it."

I squeeze my hands together, still unable to believe all that has happened. "It's overwhelming. I keep telling myself it'll blow over soon. The attention. I thought you were with the media when I first saw you outside."

"I'm not."

A wave of doubt hits. What if he's a reporter, and he's tricking me? But no—he left a voicemail *before* the train incident. Also, how would a reporter have learned about Elliot when I've only just found out myself?

"What drew you to emergency room nursing?" he asks.

I smile. Nursing is my passion. Asking me about it is akin to opening the floodgates. For the next twenty minutes, prompted by Lance's questions, I try to share the adrenaline rush of working in a busy downtown ER and the satisfaction of helping people in their most vulnerable moments. From children to the elderly coming in from advanced nursing facilities, we see it all. Some shifts bring happy moments, some heartbreak. Making animated gestures, I talk until my throat gets dry and I need a bottle of water.

"Your turn," I say before I catch myself. This isn't about Lance and me becoming acquainted. He's here on Elliot's behalf. "Tell me about Elliot," I add.

While I was talking, Lance only interrupted me to ask follow-up questions. It's sort of embarrassing, but I forgot he's here listening because his client is paying him.

"What do you already know about Elliot?" he asks. "What has your mother told you?"

I lower my voice. It doesn't feel right talking about my mother's huge secret with a stranger, but I'm assuming Elliot filled him in on the important parts. "Elliot and my mother had a short fling during their senior year of college. That's about the extent of my knowledge."

Lance scrunches his forehead as if he doesn't believe me. "Nothing else about him?"

"That's correct."

Declining my offer of a water bottle, he shifts position on the kitchen chair. He does that a lot. Maybe he has back issues.

"Elliot is a respected businessman," he says. "He's also involved in education and healthcare philanthropy."

Elliot sounds like a good person, and wealthy. I mean, obviously, he's wealthy. Who else sends an attorney to handle their personal matters? I wonder how much this conversation is costing him. It's an interesting way for Lance to make a living, though I'm sure this isn't all he does. In fact, I expect he's never done something like this before, at least not for Elliot. Hope not.

"I've never needed an attorney for anything," I say. "Except for when I bought my house."

"You said you live in an apartment."

"Yeah. I do now." I chug from my water bottle. Apparently, Lance doesn't miss much, but I don't need to explain myself. There's no way I'm going to tell him I'm separated when my mother doesn't know yet.

Lance scoots his chair back a few inches and crosses an ankle over his thigh. "Now that you've learned about Elliot, what do you hope to get out of the relationship?"

"What do I hope to get?" I repeat.

"Yes. What are your expectations?"

There's something a little offensive in his question. "I don't believe I have any expectations at this point. Not without meeting him."

"Given the circumstances, we'll need to do a paternity test."

I cross my arms. "Good. I'd like to have the proof myself."

It occurs to me that my mother could be wrong, and she slept with more than one person during her breakup. It's a disturbing thought. I have to trust she isn't mistaken about something so important.

Just when I get uncomfortable because of the questions about "my expectations," Lance lightens the mood. "Tell me about this difficult cat of yours. He or she sounds like a character."

"Moose? You think Elliot wants to hear about Moose?"

Lance smiles. "He might."

As I launch into one of my favorite stories about my grouchy cat, how he learned to open the kitchen cabinets holding his food, I remind myself I don't have to tell Lance everything, and I won't. But have I shared too much already?

Only after he leaves my mother's house do I notice the water bottle that I drank from is nowhere to be found. Not in the trash nor the recycling bin, and it didn't fall to the floor. It's simply gone.

CHAPTER 22

Over the next two days, I do laundry, make meals my mother can reheat, and rake leaves. She's always cared for me and can't handle the role reversal. Despite my insistence she rest, she's offering me food and advice on my diet and lack of exercise.

Staying busy helps keep my mind occupied. It's when I stop one task and before I begin the next that I hear the blast of gunfire or see the face of the shooter. I don't want to revisit any of it. There's nothing I can do beyond waiting for the detectives to do their jobs. As I move from mopping to folding laundry, I focus on Elliot and his attorney. Elliot's wealth is foreign to me. The only other wealthy person in my life was Adam's grandfather Frank, and memories of him make me cringe. His domineering presence hung over my marriage.

Frank mostly ignored me, as if I didn't even exist, while treating Adam more like a servant than a family member. He handed out tasks and expected immediate compliance. I did my best not to complain, though I don't have a perfect track record on that count. When I needed to vent, I went to my mother. She's a good listener, and though my happiness is paramount to her, her advice was to grin and bear it for the sake of my marriage. "Poor Adam, imagine how he must feel," she'd say. "Take heart, Haley. Frank is elderly. He won't live forever."

And she was right.

I pray Elliot is nothing like Frank. But what *is* he like? I still haven't Googled him. Besides my mother, my only connection to Elliot is Lance. He was so attentive during our conversation the other day. It's been forever since a man listened to me like that.

I've been thinking more about Lance than my biological father. That's natural, though. Lance is a real flesh-and-blood person I spoke with in my mother's kitchen. Elliot remains a mysterious concept. An enigma. At least for now.

Later in the afternoon, after digging up weeds—harder work than I remembered—I sit on the porch swing and watch the sunset create streaks of orange and pink across the sky. My mother is napping, or she'd be here, too. It's quiet at the end of the street, and a wave of sadness washes over me. I believe she'll beat cancer, but I'm still anxious about her recovery and my marriage. I need something else to look forward to in my life. Could Elliot be that thing?

I imagine meeting each other face to face. If nothing else, it will be interesting seeing what he looks like. I hope he's nice. And kind. Maybe he and my mother will strike up a friendship, too. I'm daydreaming now, but none of it is far-fetched. I'm excited. And the thing is, I don't have to wait for Elliot to call the shots. I can be proactive. Planting my feet on the porch to stop the swing, I pull out my phone and dial Lance's number.

"Haley," he answers, sounding surprised. "Hi."

I grip the edge of the seat. "I'm ready. To meet Elliot, I mean. Should I call him? I don't have his number. Oh, my mother must have it." I blurt out one word after another before I lose my nerve.

Lance is silent for so long; I wonder if we got cut off. When he speaks again, he sounds a little flustered. "I'll talk to Elliot, check his schedule, and get back to you."

After thanking him and hanging up, my nerves are a little haywire with anticipation. I rush into the living room where my mother lies stretched on the couch.

"Mom, I just called the attorney. He's going to set up a meeting with Elliot."

"What did the attorney say his name was?" she asked.

"Lance Hutchinson."

She tilts her head, clearly considering something, but the moment passes. She takes my hand, and I'm reminded of all the times she's been there for me. Before Adam, I had a terrible flu. She stayed, cleaning my apartment while I was feverish, offering electrolyte drinks and bone broth to get my strength back up. When I was in college and had pneumonia, she drove eight hours to be with me. Even in high school when I drank too much at a party, she didn't lecture. I'd already learned my lesson on the bathroom floor with my head hanging over the toilet. She hooked me up with IV fluids until I felt human again. My lowest points. She was at my side for all of them.

"I can't begin to understand how you're feeling, Haley. I hope you're not too upset, but you have every right to be."

I squeeze her hand back. As much as she shocked me with her news, I can't bring myself to be angry with the woman who's always put me first and shielded me from pain whenever she could.

"I'm not angry. I understand what you did and why you did it."

Her smile reveals her relief. "Good. I love you, Haley."

I grin. "It's impossible not to know that. I love you, too."

"I'm glad you're meeting Elliot. After all this time, he deserves the chance. You both do."

My phone buzzes with an alert from a news app. Keywords grab my attention. I open the link and play the video.

"—possible break in the case surrounding the assault of investigative journalist Lauren Christensen. Police believe they have identified suspects related to her latest exposé of a Fortune 500 company."

I turn up the volume to catch every word.

"Sources close to the investigation reveal Christensen was working on a story involving Granite Global Industries."

Granite Global.

Gray Glow.

Was that what Lauren tried to say on the train? It could be.

Was her investigation into Granite Global the reason someone shot her? Were corporate executives with massive fortunes desperate to silence the journalist? I imagine the arrests and a trial revealing the truth. Lauren fully recovered. Her story published. It's a nice ending to what was almost a fatal tragedy.

I play the news clip again. Please let this be it. Let this tip with Granite Global be the breakthrough.

CHAPTER 23

An hour later, when my mother and I are watching a new Netflix series, Granite Global still haunts my thoughts. What had Lauren uncovered? Did Granite Global hire a hitman? Are they frantic to cover their tracks now?

"Can you hit pause for a minute?" I ask. "I want to call the detectives. Make sure they made the connection."

"Sure," My mother reaches for the remote.

Detective Millard answers my call on the third ring, his voice clipped but professional.

"Hi, it's Haley James. I've remembered something. The words Lauren said on the train. I believe she said Granite Global. That's the name of the company she was investigating. Her words make sense now. Granite Global."

"Thank you for calling, Ms. James. We're aware she spent time at Granite Global, and we're following up on it."

I wait, hoping for more, but the silence stretches. "Do you think this will help the case? Lead back to a motive?"

"It's too early to say. I promise we'll update you when we have something. In the meantime, call if you remember anything else, and continue to stay aware of your surroundings."

It sounds as if he still has nothing. I'm about to ask for more information about their investigation when I get a phone call. I'm surprised at how quickly my focus changes when I see it's Lance.

"I have to go, Detective. Please update me if something happens. I'd appreciate it."

"Yes, Ms. James."

I switch calls. "Lance?"

"Hi, Haley. I hope I'm not interrupting anything."

"No, I'm about to watch television with my mother."

"Sounds nice. Are you free in the evening for dinner the day after tomorrow?"

My stomach does a little flip. Is he asking me out? He knows I'm not single. But the way he phrased it… "I had a nice time with you, but I can't. Did you forget I'm married?"

Silence on the other end.

Oh God. Oh no.

"I mean—" Heat floods my face. "You were asking about Elliot, weren't you? Meeting Elliot for dinner?"

"Yes." His voice is neutral. "If you're available."

Thank goodness he can't see me cringing. I want to disappear into the floor, just melt away. "Right. Yes. Of course. The day after tomorrow works."

"Haley." His tone is kind, almost gentle. "Don't worry about it. I should have been clearer. I'll text you the restaurant details."

"Thank you," I manage, mortified.

When I hang up, I press my hands against my burning cheeks. Did that just happen? Did I really turn down a date he never offered?

His follow-up message arrives a few seconds later with the name of a restaurant in the city. It's perfect timing, as I need to return to my apartment and job soon.

I look up at my mother. She's grinning.

"I guess you heard that." I laugh and shake my head. "How embarrassing. But... in two days, I'm meeting Elliot for dinner."

As I say it aloud, this new reality hits me. Amidst everything else going on, in 48 hours, I'll come face-to-face with a stranger who is my biological father. How do I prepare for this?

CHAPTER 24

On my way back to the city, I glance at my reflection in the rearview mirror. I look okay, better than usual. My hair falls in smooth, styled waves. I borrowed a skirt, sweater and a necklace from my mother, who has an excellent sense of style and updates her wardrobe more than I do. The extra effort I put into my appearance isn't just because of my meeting with Elliot later. It's also for Adam.

While I'm returning his Mercedes, it would be nice if he invited me inside so I can share my mother's earth-shattering revelation. News like mine doesn't come around often. I can't wait to see his reaction.

When I arrive at the house, there's a white car I don't recognize in the driveway.

Curious, I take my suitcase out of his trunk and walk to the front door. I'm about to walk right in, but something stops me. Letting out a deep sigh, I knock instead, out of respect for Adam and his wishes, as much as they pain me. When he answers, his expression is unreadable. It's like that with him. He keeps his emotions well hidden. It's hard to tell what he's thinking. That's why it took me so long to understand he was shutting me out, and his behavior wasn't only the grief of losing his grandfather.

"Hey, Haley. I'll get your car keys."

I step inside and realize I miss my house. Moose is already crouched inside his carrier, ready to go back to my apartment. He'd probably rather stay here. This was his home, too. But Adam had to leave me with something. He couldn't take everything from me.

"How did you get Moose in the carrier?" I ask, trying to keep my voice light.

"It wasn't too bad," he replies, then surprises me with, "I got your car fixed so it won't stall. But it's an old car. It's not going to last forever. The next problem will be something else."

"Thank you." I'm genuinely grateful. Car maintenance is the sort of thing Adam handled for us before we separated. If he's still doing it, not everything has changed. He still cares.

"How's your mom?" he asks with his back to me.

"She's hanging in there. It's strange to see her so subdued, not her usual energetic self, but she'll get through it."

He turns and faces me with my keys in his hand. "Did you tell her about us? That we don't live together anymore?"

I shake my head. "No, not yet. I told you it's not a good time. I don't want her worrying about me. About us. But... she shared some pretty incredible news. That's the reason she wanted me to come alone. Wait until I tell you. It's—"

My gaze shifts past Adam, and the words die on my lips.

A woman has just emerged from the bedroom. The one Adam and I shared. She's striking. Long honey-colored hair, a shimmery coral hue on full lips.

My jaw clenches as I struggle to process what I'm seeing. I'm going to be sick right here on the hardwood floor I used to vacuum every Wednesday and Sunday.

"Hi. I'm just leaving." The woman sounds apologetic. She tilts her head, and her gaze flickers between Adam and me. "I know you need to get that car out, and I'm blocking the garage."

That car, she says, and I read so much into it. The old car. The damaged car. The one that needs to be replaced. The one that's in the way... just like me.

Adam clears his throat. "Right, um, Haley, this is my friend Jessica. Jessica, Haley."

I'm too stunned to manage even a pretend smile. Who is she? Is Adam seeing her? He must be. She's obviously not here to fix the plumbing or the electricity. Not in the dress she's wearing or those heels. She carries an attractive bag, and it's large enough to accommodate an overnight stay.

An awkward silence falls over the room. I turn and stare at the refrigerator as if there's something important on it, but the stainless-steel is bare and streak-free because Adam is obsessive about keeping it clean. I bite down on my lower lip. I won't cry in front of them.

Jessica leaves quickly. She and Adam don't kiss or hug each other goodbye or even touch, and for that, I'm grateful. I think it would destroy me.

Adam hands over my car keys.

"Thanks for letting me borrow the Mercedes." I try not to sound shell-shocked as I search his face for an explanation. I want him to say it's not what it looks like, but what else could it be? A new colleague? And they were working in the bedroom? Not likely.

"It wasn't a problem." Adam's expression is as guarded as ever. "You said your mother told you something?"

After seeing Jessica, I'm in no frame of mind to tell him. Maybe I should stomp around and yell, remind him we're still legally married, and we never discussed seeing other people. But it's all too much. I'm embarrassed, confused, and overwhelmed by his betrayal. I simply can't right now. I turn away and scoop up the cat carrier.

Outside, Jessica is already backing out of the driveway.

I put my suitcase in the trunk, place Moose in the back seat, and then climb into my old car. A cold sweat has spread over my body. I'd like to collapse over my ripped steering wheel and sob, but I've got to get out of here while I still have some dignity left.

"You better not have let her pet you," I tell Moose, hoping he didn't betray me, too.

The more I process what I just saw, the worse I feel. Adam knew I was coming. He always knows where I am. He could have told Jessica to leave before I got there, but he didn't. He wanted me to see her. *They* wanted me to know she was there. They arranged the timing so I could see he's moved on.

The pain inside me is all-consuming, as if it's going to yank my soul right out of my body, leaving me empty.

I can't believe my life has come to this. Why can't Adam just believe me when I tell him I didn't do it?

CHAPTER 25

It's quiet at my apartment building when I arrive after noon, still reeling from the sight of Jessica inside Adam's house. There's no sign of anyone around. The reporters are gone.

I trudge to my front door with my suitcase and Moose's carrier. I have hours before dinner with Elliot. Hopefully, it's enough time to unpack and pull myself together so I'm in a good headspace for our first meeting.

When I slip my key into the lock and turn it, I hear a metallic clink. That's the sound of locking, not unlocking. I turn the key back, and the bolt slides open. My skin prickles. There was a lot on my mind when I left, and the ordeal of getting Moose into the carrier had me extra rattled, but I still can't believe I forgot to lock the door.

I peer inside my apartment and hear nothing. After pulling my suitcase in, and setting Moose's carrier down, I look around again. Everything appears the way I remember leaving it, but my heart is still pounding.

I can't just stand here. I have to handle this. Hunched over, I grab a golf club and check each room.

Nothing appears off in the kitchen. On the countertop, unopened mail waits next to a takeout cup I toss into the trash.

The bedroom and bathroom are the same. My towels are hanging lopsided on the towel bar.

I release Moose from his carrier so he can stretch and explore. He sniffs around the room with his tail up, acting as if he's never been here before. Does he smell something different?

Unable to shake my unease, I decide to speak to the woman in the apartment across the hall in case she saw something. Last week, I could brush this off and move on, but not now. The shooter is aware I saw him, and thanks to the viral video, he can find me.

I lock my door and walk the few steps to Ms. Berner's. There's music coming from inside. When I knock, the door creaks open a few inches. A short brass chain keeps it from moving any further.

Ms. Berner peers through the space. "Haley, dear! How nice to see you."

"Hi. I hope I'm not bothering you."

My eccentric neighbor wears a flamingo-pink velvet tracksuit with bright lipstick to match. At eighty-something years old, Ms. Berner has a distinctive style she carries well. Once a week she visits a beauty salon where they fashion her silver hair into a beehive updo that never lets a single hair escape. Behind large turquoise glasses, her eyes twinkle.

"This is a delightful surprise. Come in, come in."

"Thank you, but I can't. I've been away for most of the week and just got home. By any chance did you see someone go into my apartment while I was gone?"

She taps a pink manicured finger against the rim of her glasses. "No, I can't say I did. Was someone supposed to come?"

A small black cat weaves between her legs.

"Oh, you have a cat."

Ms. Berner looks down at the animal and smiles. "This is Sasafrass. He's new. He keeps me company."

"I have a cat, too. Moose. He doesn't like leaving my apartment. It was an ordeal to get him out."

"I could care for him when you go out of town. I'll feed him and give him some company."

"Oh, thank you. That's very kind of you."

"What are neighbors for? It wouldn't be any trouble."

Her offer removes my dependence on Adam for cat care. I'm so pleased that I almost forget to reciprocate. "I'd be happy to help you out as well if you ever have to go out of town."

"Thank you, dear, but it's rare that I travel. My hip's been giving me trouble."

"I'm sorry." I'm struck by a vision of myself years from now, alone in an apartment with a bad hip and only my cat for companionship. But Ms. Berner seems happy.

"Could I give you a spare key to my apartment?" I ask. "Just in case I ever get stuck at work, like if there's an emergency, and I can't get home to feed Moose. If it wouldn't be too much trouble."

"It's a wonderful idea. And I'd like you to have one of mine, Haley, so I don't have to worry about Sasafrass."

"Great. Well, I better get back and unpack my things. I'll drop a spare key off later."

As I turn to go, she calls after me, "Everything alright, dear? With your apartment? You seemed worried."

Ms. Berner must not follow social media. She doesn't seem to realize the reporters outside the building were here because of me and the viral video. I won't spook her by talking about the violent crime I witnessed. "I'm fine. Just had a strange feeling when I got home. It's probably nothing."

She presses an age-spotted hand over her heart. "You should always trust your instincts, dear. They're usually right."

Back in my apartment, I unpack my suitcase and consider Ms. Berner's advice. Instincts aren't always right. There are a lot of crazy things happening in my life right now. What seems like an instinct might simply be paranoia.

Who would I even call? Detective Millard? To say what? My door was unlocked, but I'm not positive I locked it? I have no proof of anything. I was frazzled when I left, just like I am now. That's probably the best explanation for my unlocked door.

The low-battery light on my phone comes on. As I grab my charger to power the device, I still feel uneasy. Again, I tell myself it's just a symptom of the emotional chaos I'm going through. But a voice inside me whispers that something isn't right. I'm afraid it's only a matter of time before I find out what.

CHAPTER 26

I gaze out my enormous office window at Chicago skyscrapers and their colored lights without seeing any of it. I'm lost in my own thoughts, and I'm grinning. I have a daughter. Haley. I still can't believe it's true.

Returning to my desk, I open the first file from the private investigator Lance hired. It's Carol's background information.

When she called my office, I didn't recognize her name or voice. But since our conversation, more memories have returned. I'm surprised by their vividness, and they're all pleasant. We were so young.

As if I have a bird's-eye view, I can picture us walking across campus in the dark. We're leaving a party and heading to my apartment. The anticipation I felt during that walk sends a thrill through me now. Carol's eyes were huge and expressive. We were drinking, and she laughed a lot. I wonder if she still laughs like that.

I remember us on my bed. Pulling her shirt over her head. A pink bra. Black bikini underwear. The mismatched set embarrassed her. I couldn't care less but teased her about it.

So strange how my brain held onto those small details. Is it normal, or does it mean something?

The thing is, Carol and I had a genuine connection. A spark of something that could have grown into more. We had potential.

I called her a few times in the weeks after we hooked up, but she didn't seem into me. Now I get it. She already had a guy. I was a breakup rebound.

What if I'd pursued her harder? Shown up with flowers or some other romantic gesture instead of letting her disappear? Would we have raised Haley together? Probably not. I'm not sure I would have handled the news of an unexpected pregnancy well. It's impressive that Carol embraced a baby at her age. It must have changed everything. Thirty years later, I couldn't be more grateful for her decision.

Which leads me to the second file on my desk. It contains everything I know so far about Haley.

Any man would be proud to call her his daughter. I already am. She's a nurse who saves lives, including someone I've met—Lauren Christensen. Both women boarded the commuter train around the same time, on that night of all nights. The timing and chance of it happening are incredible.

I've watched the video of Haley saving Lauren. Each viewing invoked pride mixed with horror.

The file in front of me contains photos from different periods of Haley's life. Haley's smile is a tad higher on the right side, just like mine. But it's a more recent photo that grabs me. She's wearing scrubs in a hospital corridor. The intensity in her expression—it's like looking at a prettier, female version of my face. A lump forms in my throat. I was supposed to wait for the paternity test results to come back before diving in too deep emotionally, but I already know the truth.

What will Haley think when she learns about *my* life? When she hears why my marriage ended?

Little about my personal life is available to the public because I refuse to give anyone leverage over me. So how much does she already know? Does she have a report about me like the one I have about her?

My alarm goes off, startling me. It's time. The anxious board members have already gathered. I have to present a Plan B, then make decisions that could forever change the face of an enormous, too-big-to-fail company.

I slide the files into my desk drawer and lock it up before heading out. My personal matters will have to wait.

At the far end of the hall, I push the conference room door open. The room falls silent when I enter.

"Let's not waste any time," I say, forgoing all pleasantries as I take my seat at the head of the table. "We have a situation requiring our immediate attention. We have some big decisions to make for Granite Global."

CHAPTER 27

I try to relax before meeting Elliot, but Jessica keeps flashing through my mind—her long legs, perfect hair, the confidence she exuded in my house. As if that weren't enough, I'm freaked out by the prospect of someone breaking into my apartment. It would help if the detectives found the shooter. That hasn't happened. I just checked with them.

I attempt to lose myself in my book, then realize it's the same one I couldn't focus on the night of the shooting. I slam it shut. My apologies to the author; it's not her fault, but I won't be picking it up again.

When I gather my things to leave, my keys aren't in their usual spot. After five frantic minutes of searching, I discover them in my hand. They were there the entire time.

At the restaurant, I'm as nervous as the first time I had to share my patient findings with the attending doctor during nursing school. I want to present myself well and gain approval. Tonight, all I can do is be myself. My best self. No one else, and nothing more.

The hostess leads me to a table Elliot reserved in the back. I smooth my hands over my skirt, even more nervous now than when I left my apartment. I can hardly believe this is happening.

My steps falter as I get closer to the table. It's not a stranger waiting. It's Lance. I hadn't realized he planned to join us. He sits alone, watching me approach.

"Haley." He stands to greet me in a tweed sports coat. "I'm sorry. Change of plans."

"What happened?"

"Elliot sends his apologies. An emergency came up."

"An emergency? Is he okay?"

"He's fine. It's work-related. A last-minute board meeting. He asked if I would meet with you, if it's alright?"

I wrestle with my disappointment, trying to imagine what sort of meeting would come up at the last minute and take precedence over seeing your daughter for the first time in thirty years. But what do I know? I'm not an important businessperson, and I'm not a member of any boards. At least he didn't cancel and leave me alone. Given today's events—Jessica strutting through my old home, and all my anxious energy about this dinner—I couldn't have dealt with getting stood up. I might have cracked and left the restaurant in tears.

"Sure, it's fine," I say, taking a seat. "Thanks for coming. I'm sure you had other things to do."

"No worries. My office isn't far from here. And I need to eat. But before we say anything else, there's something I have to clarify regarding an assumption you made. It's a little awkward now but we need to talk about it."

I know what he's going to say, and I'd rather spare myself the embarrassment. "It was my mistake. Nothing you did. I know who you are and your relationship to Elliot." I force a laugh. "We definitely don't need to discuss it."

"You sure? We're good?"

"I'm sure."

Lance studies me, about to say more. His phone buzzes on the table, and I'm relieved. Then the server is beside us, asking if we'd like starters.

Later, through gulps of wine, he steers our conversation, first asking about my trip back to the city, then about my mother's health. By the time our meals arrive, and I've almost drained my first glass of wine, I'm over the fact that Elliot isn't here, and I'm much more relaxed than when I arrived.

"How does your mother feel about you and Elliot meeting?"

"When we finally meet, I expect she'll want a play-by-play of our conversation." I smile because I know she will, and I don't blame her for it. "Overall, she's relieved Elliot and I finally know the truth."

"I can imagine," Lance says. "Family secrets can do a number on you."

Something in his tone grabs me. "Are you speaking from personal or professional experience?"

"Both. Let's just say my family's situation hasn't been a stable one." He takes a sip of water, seeming to debate whether to continue.

I stop eating and give him my full attention, silently encouraging him to share more.

"My mother and father divorced when I was still a baby. My father cheated, which ended their marriage. I barely know my real father."

This is the first piece of information Lance has shared about his own life, and it's surprising. I assumed he came from a family where everything was wonderful and came easily.

"After the divorce, my mother moved to be near her parents. My father remarried soon after and started another family. I have half-siblings I've never met."

"I'm sorry. Your mother must have been young when she divorced, if you were a baby."

"Yes, her second marriage here in Chicago didn't last long, either. She left... but let's not talk about that now."

Lance didn't have to share that information, but he did. I reciprocate by filling him in on the shooting investigation and how it's got me looking over my shoulder and double-locking doors. I tell him the detectives still don't have a suspect in the shooting, and the gunman probably knows I can identify him.

Lance rubs the back of his neck as he speaks. "The guy would be crazy to come after you. I wouldn't worry too much."

By the time we order dessert, almost thirty minutes have passed without me once thinking about Adam and Jessica. Lance is great company, easy to talk to, and I'm content. But not everything about this dinner is good. The information I'm holding back makes me feel like an imposter. I've had enough of it.

I set down my dessert spoon and dab my lips with my napkin. "I wasn't entirely forthright about my husband earlier."

He waits for me to continue.

I twist my rings. "If you're reporting everything back to Elliot, I might as well be upfront about this."

He laughs. "I'm not reporting everything back to Elliot."

"Still, what I didn't tell you is that Adam and I separated. It's pretty recent. I haven't even told my mother yet."

"May I ask why you're keeping the situation from your mother?"

"She loves Adam like a son and has always supported my relationship with him. I'm going to disappoint her in a big way." Right then, I remember how my mother picked up additional night shifts for months to help pay for my wedding. I feel extra awful about that.

"I might need a divorce attorney at some point," I add, attempting to lighten the mood with a half-joke. "You know one at your firm?"

Lance's expression is serious. "I can give you a referral if it becomes necessary. The best in the business."

"Thanks. I'll let you know if the time comes." I hope I'm joking, but that remains to be seen.

When the server brings the bill. Lance pays, but I'm not ready to leave just yet. I steer the conversation back to my biological father. "So, you mentioned a board meeting. Which boards does Elliot serve on?"

"Several." Lance takes another drink from his water glass.

"Any companies I've heard of?"

"Hopeful Horizons. It's a nonprofit that provides educational opportunities and healthcare to underprivileged communities. They have celebrity supporters, so I'm sure you've heard of them."

I nod, picturing their upbeat commercials with grateful children and families.

"Another is EcoSphere, an environmental conservation group."

"All non-profits?" I'm impressed by Elliot's involvement with two organizations that do so much good.

"He's also a long-standing board member of a Fortune 500. Granite Global Industries."

My breath catches. "Granite Global. Interesting." I try to keep the shock out of my voice.

"Elliot is the chairman of the board."

"He is? Wow! Which company's board meeting drew him away tonight?" I ask, making my question sound casual.

"Granite Global. The other boards meet outside Chicago."

The information chills me. Is there a link between Elliot's urgent meeting and the information Lauren was on the verge of exposing? Are Elliot and his fellow board members scrambling to cover up their crimes?

If Elliot is the chairman of Granite Global, he's potentially a very dangerous man.

He might also be my connection to the truth about the shooting.

CHAPTER 28

My buzzing alarm yanks me from fitful sleep. Where do I have to be? It takes me a second to remember. The answer is nowhere. I only set it to help get back into a routine. I don't have to go to the hospital today. My next shift isn't until tomorrow. Rather than appreciate another day off like my colleagues would, I'm disappointed. I wouldn't mind the opportunity to focus on something else and check on Lauren. Instead, for the next twenty-four hours, I'm stuck with myself, and I'm not sure what to do. Staying under the covers seems like a good idea. I slide my phone off the nightstand and scroll through marketing emails and new articles I can't read because I don't pay for a News Plus subscription. The headlines are enough to clue me in on what's happening in the world.

Eventually, I drag myself out of my warm bed and trudge to the bathroom. There are exactly two squares of paper left on the roll, and they're stuck to the cardboard. Great. I make a mental note to add toilet paper to the shopping list I should have created yesterday.

Moose meows with urgency beside his empty bowl. His breakfast is late, and mealtimes are the only instances when he appreciates my existence. I feed him the last packet of his special food, enjoying every second of his focus on me, then grab a lone apple from the fridge. Everything else in there needs to be thrown out except some condiments.

Crunching into the apple, I survey my apartment. Navy scrubs and compression socks overflow from the hamper. I'm on it. Mundane tasks and errands might bring back a sense of normalcy.

Once I've started the washing machine and created a to-do list, I put on a cute cap and take off in my car for the store.

The engine sputters as I'm nearing the center of the city. The car is too old to have warning messages, but the flickering dashboard lights indicate trouble. It's happening again. My car is malfunctioning. A little panicked, but not freaking out, I pull away from traffic and onto a side road. The car has just enough movement left to get me to the curb and into a spot clearly marked *no parking anytime.*

This was unexpected, since Adam said he got the car fixed. Did the mechanic mess up?

I try the ignition again. No response. Nothing. This is worse than before. The engine is dead.

After what I've been through, a broken car is nothing, but it feels like the last straw. I pound my fist against the steering wheel. After several good punches, the horn blares, making me jump in my seat.

A young couple stares as they pass on the sidewalk. I turn away. What on earth am I doing? My outburst isn't normal behavior. If any of my colleagues or patients saw, I'd be so ashamed. I just can't seem to triage the disaster my life has become.

Out of habit, I call Adam. The phone rings several times before going to voicemail. I hang up without leaving a message. This is my issue now. Then I remember the AAA card I always see when I'm searching for my credit card. We pay the yearly fee for exactly this type of situation.

"Triple A Roadside Assistance. This is Kevin. How can I help you today?" a monotone voice answers.

"Hi, my car broke down."

"Are you somewhere safe?"

"Uh, yes," I say, but scan the area.

"Can I have your membership number?"

I recite the number on my card, then look around again. I see nothing unusual.

"I'm sorry, Ms. James, your membership just expired."

After providing the information necessary to renew my card, I explain my situation again.

"I've got your location. We're experiencing high call volumes because of a major accident on the highway. All our tow trucks are deployed."

"About how long will it be?" I glance at the *No Parking Anytime* sign.

"Given the current situation, it could be up to three hours before we can get someone to you. Sorry."

I focus on staying calm. Often, I'm the brunt of people's frustration and helplessness at the hospital. I will not go that route. "I understand. It's not your fault." He knows, but it's probably nice for him to hear that I know it, too.

Three hours. I'm already shivering without the heat on.

Looking around, I realize I'm only a few blocks from last night's restaurant, which means, according to Lance, I'm also close to his law firm.

I scribble a note on the back of an envelope.

My car broke. AAA is coming. No choice but to leave it here.

With the apology note on my dashboard, I grab my purse and leave the car behind.

As I walk, my thoughts return to my dinner with Lance and the information about Elliot and Granite Global. Since then, I've wondered if the detectives are talking to Elliot. Are they aware Granite Global held an emergency board meeting? I thought about telling them, but I don't have much to go on yet. If only I'd gotten more out of Lance. Maybe this is my second chance.

By the time I reach the imposing glass building housing the law offices of Hartley & Hutchison, I'm determined to get some answers.

CHAPTER 29

Twenty minutes after leaving my broken-down car, I walk across the marble floors of Hartley & Hutchinson's lobby. The tip of my nose is probably Rudolph red as I approach the main desk.

"Hello, I'm here to see Lance Hutchinson," I tell the attractive receptionist.

She smiles, showing bright white teeth. "Do you have an appointment?"

I'm about to tell her no when Lance walks through the double doors on the other end of the reception area carrying a laptop bag. He's handsome in casual business attire with a charcoal-gray coat over his arm. He stops, and his eyes widen when he spots me.

"Oh, never mind. I'm good now. Thank you," I tell her.

As I head across the lobby area to intercept Lance, I dab my nose with a tissue.

"Haley?" He stops walking. "What are you doing here?"

"I was looking for you. My car broke down nearby."

"You need a ride somewhere?"

"I'm waiting for a tow. There's a delay." I shift my purse to my other shoulder. "I was wondering if you had a minute to talk about something that came up last night."

He checks his watch. "I have a few minutes before my meeting. There's a coffee place I like on the way. Come with me?"

"Sure. I could use something warm."

He shrugs his coat on, moving his briefcase from one hand to the other before we step outside. "So, car trouble, huh? What happened?"

I shove my hands deep into my pockets. "The alternator? I don't know. It just died on me. It's old, and I'm not exactly a car expert."

"I'm not either."

We weave through crowded sidewalks, everyone moving along with a sense of urgency. A man steps out of a café with a coffee in one hand and a phone in the other, while balancing a stack of folders and a laptop bag. He's struggling not to drop something. He looks the way I feel these days.

We pass a second coffee shop before we arrive at Coffee Roasters.

I turn to Lance. "You must really like this place to walk all the way here."

"Yeah. I do. They have excellent coffee." He holds the door open. "After you. Let's get warmed up. Then we'll talk."

We get to-go cups and sit at a table for two. The warmth and sweetness of my coffee are perfect, just what I needed.

Lance keeps his coat on.

"I have some questions," I say, eager to voice my concerns. "I'm just going to put it out there. There could be a connection between Granite Global and what happened to Lauren Christensen."

He frowns. "What makes you say that?"

"Just some things I've read. And heard."

I'm being vague, but only the detectives know what Lauren said on the train. "I was hoping you could tell me more about what's going on with that company. Why Elliot had an emergency meeting with the board, for instance?"

"Even if I knew, I wouldn't discuss Elliot's business dealings. You might be his daughter, but it's not my place to share his business."

Of course he can't share insider information. And attorneys have a legal obligation to keep their clients' matters confidential. But his response only fuels my suspicions. I wonder how much information he's privy to.

"I just need to know if I can trust him." I wrap my hands tighter around my coffee cup.

Something flickers across Lance's face. He opens his mouth as if to speak, then closes it again.

"Sorry." I offer a weak smile. "I understand."

"Sure is cold out there," he says, glancing out the window, in an obvious change of subject.

We talk about the weather for a minute before he says, "I have to head out. Are you going to wait here until the tow truck comes?"

"I might as well."

He picks up his laptop bag. "Good luck with your car."

After Lance leaves, I stay at the coffee shop to kill time. I organize my phone, deleting emails and photos. It's a small way to gain a sense of control over my life, and oddly satisfying, like decluttering a closet and getting rid of the clothes you haven't worn in years. When I reach duplicate selfies with Adam and see our smiling faces together, I leave them. I'm not emotionally ready to part with a single copy yet.

An hour slips by. My digital life is now a more manageable space. If only I could do the same with my actual life.

My phone battery is low again, so I grab the day's newspaper from a nearby table. There are no articles about the train shooting. The story has run its course. I read the entire paper, eat a maple-pecan protein muffin, and finally get a text from the tow truck dispatcher.

When I reach my car, a tow truck with flashing yellow lights is waiting. I sign the paperwork, then watch as they hitch up my vehicle. Seeing the front wheels raised, I experience a profound sense of sadness I didn't expect. It's an old car with dents and scratches because Chicago is not car-friendly. The cost of repairing it is likely more than its value. Last I checked, there were over one hundred and thirty thousand miles on the odometer. But right now, the car represents another piece of my old life and my control slipping away.

I take an Uber to my apartment, where I put a news program on the television just to hear voices in the background. Then I plop down on the couch. I never got the groceries I went out to buy this morning, which means I have no food for Moose's dinner.

I can ask to borrow cat food from Ms. Berner and replace it with a little something extra when I go to the store. I should get up, but I just sit there, doing nothing. My eyes grow heavy, and I drift off.

My phone rings, jolting me awake. Unknown number. It must be the mechanic calling me about my car.

"Hello?"

"Hello, is this Haley?" A deep voice comes through.

"Yes."

"This is Elliot. Elliot Rhodes."

I let out a little gasp.

"Am I catching you at a good time?"

"Uh, yes. I'm at home. In my apartment." This is the first time we've spoken. The first time I've heard his voice. He's no longer the hypothetical guy my mother had a fling with, the one I talk to Lance about. He's real now, and we're talking to each other on the phone. I get a little rush of adrenaline. It feels like my chest is vibrating.

"I understand you recently learned the same thing I did. We have a connection."

A nervous chuckle escapes me. "Yes. A connection. That's one way to put it."

Elliot laughs, too. "How are you doing with all of this?"

"Honestly? It's a little overwhelming. How about you?"

"It's a shock for me too, but not an unpleasant one. I look forward to meeting you in person."

"Good. Same here."

"I just had an unexpected opening in my schedule. Late notice, but are you available to meet later today? No pressure."

"Today?" The last-minute invite surprises me. I glance at the time on my phone. It's two o'clock, and I've only had a muffin for nourishment. "Would you be interested in an early dinner?"

"Sure," he says, and I can hear a smile in his voice.

We settle on a time and a nice restaurant. Scenic Plate. It's within walking distance of my apartment.

When we hang up, I'm eager to meet Elliot. I also hope my hunch about Granite Global is wrong. I don't want my biological father to be a ruthless criminal.

CHAPTER 30

Only one man is sitting alone in the restaurant. It's Elliot. He has thick, light brown hair and straight posture. I know he's my mother's age, yet I had pictured someone older.

Elliot stands as I near the table, a tentative smile on his face. He's taller than the father who raised me, and trim, dressed in olive-colored pants and a navy sweater. He's still handsome. I can see why my mother chose him for her fling.

"Haley?" he asks, though I can tell he already knows it's me.

I'm suddenly at a loss for words, gripped by the bizarre circumstances. Our dark eyes mirror each other in shape and shade. The similarities are striking. I resemble Elliot more than my mother. It's obvious I'm his daughter.

"Wow," I whisper with a mixture of awe and disbelief.

"Yes, wow," he repeats.

We stand there without speaking for a few more seconds, half-smiling as we take each other in. Elliot's eyes get glassy, making them brighter, and he swipes a finger across his cheek. I'm just as awed by the emotion building inside me.

He gestures for me to sit. "I'm glad to meet you."

"Same here."

These aren't the casual words someone might tell a new acquaintance. They're heavy with emotions that make me almost dizzy.

As I settle into my chair, I study his face again. He's studying mine. We laugh, amazed and still a little nervous.

The server comes, and we order drinks. A diet soda for Elliot, a glass of white wine for me since I can walk back to my apartment.

"So," Elliot begins, "I'd love to hear about your life, and what you like to do. Anything."

"Has Lance told you a lot about me?"

Elliot shakes his head. "Very little. It's better for us to get to know each other in person."

I appreciate Lance's discretion—though I wonder what he shared and what he didn't.

"I understand you're a nurse."

I respond with a smirk. "Everyone might know that now."

"Ah. Your viral video. Yes, that was something." Elliot raises his brows to stress his point. His smile is a little crooked and higher on one side. Just like mine.

I want to trust him, but there's still the question of Granite Global hanging between us, invisible to him, consuming me. I'd like to ask and get it out in the open. But what could I say? Ask him if his company is involved in attempted murder? If he's guilty, he won't admit it. If he's innocent, I'll have poisoned this moment with an accusation I can't take back. I'll have to be patient.

Our food arrives. He ordered steak and salad. I chose a pasta and chicken dish. As we eat, Elliot tells me about his interest in photography and tennis.

"Please tell me about your family," I say, thinking of my ancestors.

"My mother was born and raised in Pennsylvania. My father, New York. They've passed on." A shadow passes over his face. "I'm divorced. My ex-wife had a son, but I don't have any biological children of my own."

"Are you still on good terms with your ex-wife?" I'm asking because with my current marital situation, I'm curious about the end of other people's marriages.

Elliot coughs and places a hand over his mouth. He waves our server over to refill his glass. He's buying time. Finally, he answers. "Unfortunately, my ex and I haven't spoken in years. It's a long story. One I'd prefer to avoid tonight."

"That's fine. There's so much else to cover," I say, though I wonder what happened. I assume Lance told him Adam and I separated, and I don't want to discuss that either. I'd rather keep this first meeting focused on the positives in our lives, not the failures.

After the server clears our table, Elliot stacks his hands on the table. "I'm sorry I wasn't there for you growing up. If I had known."

"Neither of us knew. And I had a good childhood. But I'm glad we're meeting now."

Elliot smiles. "So am I. I'd like to spend more time with you. Soon. Would that be okay?"

"Yes, I'd like that."

"Could you come to my house for dinner? This Friday? I'm not much of a cook, but I know all the best restaurants for takeout."

"I'm not working then. Friday is perfect."

Elliot's face lights up. "Wonderful. I'll send you the address and details."

As we stand to leave, I consider hugging him. When I wait a little too long, the right time and the impulse passes. We're not there yet. Instead, we shake hands. He wraps both of his around mine, reminding me of my mother's touch and what it means to me. This is different, but things can change in time.

On my way out, I'm relieved at how well the meeting went. How easy it seemed.

I glance behind, and Elliot is still watching me. When our eyes meet, his smile is warm and paternal.

I wave goodbye, and something in my chest tightens. I want a relationship with him, and I'm choosing to trust him for now, even though he's the chairman of Granite Global. The company Lauren was investigating when someone shot her. The company that held an emergency board meeting yesterday.

He seems like a nice person, but it's possible I just had dinner with someone very dangerous.

CHAPTER 31

I open the apartment door with my elbow. All I want is to make a cup of tea and call my mother. It's been an exhausting day, mentally and physically. First the car fiasco, then the emotional excitement of meeting Elliot. I almost forgot to stop at the nearest convenience store on my way home, but Moose depends on me, and my single box of tissues will only last so long. I still don't have fresh fruit or vegetables, but I've got toilet paper and cat food.

When I drop my keys in the bowl by the door, the clatter resonates through my quiet apartment.

Moose stands atop the back of the couch, staring. I reach to pet him, and he runs off.

"You missed me that much?" I believe he loves me, but has a strange, non-existent way of showing it.

I'm stacking his food in the cabinets when my phone buzzes. I hope it's my mother, but Adam's name flashes on the screen. My stomach flutters. I'm uncertain whether it's hope or dread. I want him to explain Jessica's presence and tell me it wasn't what I think. With a sigh, I answer his call. "Hello,"

"You called me earlier." No "hello." No "how are you." Just straight to the point.

"Yes, I called you this morning. I had a problem, but I took care of it."

“Glad you’re problem free,” he says.

I laugh in disbelief. Has he already forgotten the train shooting? And that’s not the only “problem” I’m juggling. So many bizarre things are happening, and it’s strange that I’m no longer sharing those things with Adam the way I have for the past four years. He knows nothing about my mother’s earth-shattering admission and Elliot.

“I saw you were at a coffee shop.” Adam clears his throat and then adds, “For a long time.”

“My car broke down. Whoever fixed it didn’t do a good job. I couldn’t get it started, and all the AAA tow trucks were busy. It was freezing cold, so I waited in the coffee shop.”

“It’s probably time to get a different car.”

“Yeah.”

“And then you were at Scenic Plate for dinner?”

I don’t answer. He’s phrasing it as a question, but obviously, he checked my location and he knows where I was.

“You should pick up a few more shifts so you can buy a new vehicle rather than going out to eat so much.”

My mouth falls open. Anger flares in my chest. “I didn’t work this week because of the video and the reporters, because of what I went through. The hospital asked me to use some vacation days. I told you that. And I start back tomorrow.”

A new message hits my phone. It’s from Elliot about our Friday dinner plans.

“Look, Adam.” I try to stay calm and not raise my voice. “Whatever is up with you, it’s not okay that you’re still tracking me, then judging how I spend my time. If you don’t want to be my husband, you can stop monitoring my business.” Even as I say it, I’m disappointed about cutting off some of our last connections. That's not what I want. I'm just angry and disappointed.

There's a long pause on the other end.

"I still worry about you, Haley. It's a habit," he finally says, his voice softer now. "I didn't want us to break up. But how can I stay with you when I don't trust you?"

"I can't go through this with you again. I didn't do anything wrong," I say through gritted teeth. "I can take care of myself, and I'll figure out what to do with the car."

I hang up and shake my head. One minute he's thoughtful, and the next he's saying or doing things to hurt me. He's confused. I guess when you love someone, you can't just shut it off, no matter what you think they've done. But tracking my location and criticizing me? That's not love. It's control.

Despite our conversation, when I climb into bed later, I wish nothing had changed and Adam were here, snuggling up against me. Maybe I'll get used to being alone, but for now, it's as if I'm just biding time before I get the most important part of my life back.

CHAPTER 32

Things have been calm in the emergency room so far today. Plenty of patients have come in, but no true emergencies. I had one opportunity to peek into Lauren's room when I first arrived, but she was sleeping, still intubated.

At the nursing station between patients, when I get a chance to down a coffee, my mind drifts to Adam. Part of me wants to call and find out if he's calmed down. But I shouldn't have to manage his moods. He should call me to apologize.

The positive in my life is probably Elliot and the prospect of building a relationship with him. I wonder if we'll ever do father-daughter type things. Not the same activities I used to do with my father, obviously, since I'm not a child. But I could get back into tennis, and we could play matches together.

At the same time, I can't let myself get too close, not if he has anything to do with Lauren's shooting and whatever terrible thing she must have discovered at Granite Global.

"How is your mother?" Tamira asks as she grabs a patient chart.

"She's well. Only a month left of treatments."

"Good. Can't wait to have her back."

Tamira walks away and I toss my empty cup into the trash.

I haven't given my mother the scoop about my meeting with Elliot. I wanted to tell her in person when I visit her again tomorrow. Which reminds me, I haven't heard from the car mechanic yet.

"Nurse, can you grab me some gauze?" Dr. Burke's request brings my focus back to my job. We've worked together for almost seven years, so I'm used to the omission of my actual name when he speaks to me.

"Yes, Dr. Burke," I say before hurrying off to get the supplies he needs.

"You okay, Haley?" Cara asks, giving me a concerned frown as we pass each other. "You seem distracted."

I force a smile. "I've just got a lot on my mind, but I'm fine." I stop and pivot. "How are you, Cara?" I ask, realizing that although I'm wrapped up in my own problems, the world hasn't stopped spinning for everyone else.

"Oh, the usual. I just love working with Dr. Burke," she whispers. "In his mind, we all exist merely to wait on him."

I understand completely. Dr. Burke is a lot like Adam's grandfather. "Hang in there," I tell her.

When the next patient arrives, my heart breaks a little. She's a woman in her late twenties with a gash on one cheek, bruises on the other, and a split lip. Today marks her third visit this year.

"Hi, Missy. Can you tell me what happened to your face?" I ask as I help her sit on an exam bed.

She gives a weak smile, moving slowly.

"I fell down the stairs again. I was carrying too many things and couldn't see where I was stepping. I should have made a few trips instead of trying to get everything moved in one." She tries to laugh it off, but I'm not buying it, and there's nothing funny about this.

I lift her left arm to get a closer look at the bruises encircling her slender limb. "What about these? How did you get them?"

Missy winces as she looks down at her arm. "I must have caught myself on the railing when I fell."

It's all I can do not to plead with her. "Missy, we've treated you before for similar injuries. Are you sure there isn't something else going on? Someone hurting you, perhaps?"

Her face hardens. "No. No one's hurting me. I fell."

She's lying, but I can't accuse her of it. "I'll clean and dress this gash on your cheek, see if you need a few stitches. Dr. Burke will check for fractures."

"All right." She moves her hand to her side and winces. "I might have cracked a rib."

"We'll X-ray your torso." I keep my voice calm, maintaining control of my emotions the way I couldn't when my car stalled. "We have people you can talk to. Places you can go if your home isn't safe." This isn't the first time I've tried to address the root cause of her problem.

Missy's lips quiver. She might finally open up. Then she shakes her head. "I don't need to talk to anyone or go anywhere. But, um, aren't you the nurse who was on the train? The one who saved a lady?"

"Yes, that's me." I look away, making it clear that just like Missy, there are things I don't want to discuss.

After I finish treating her, I step out of the room and lean against the wall, closing my eyes briefly.

Cara approaches. "I saw the new ER tech wheeling your patient in. Let me guess. Another 'fall'?"

I let my disappointment show with a deep frown. "How can we help her if she won't admit what's really going on? It's going to keep happening."

"Just document everything and offer resources for when she's ready. There's nothing more you can do."

Cara's right, but I'm afraid that one day Missy might come in with injuries we can't fix. She might get beaten so badly, she'll never come here or go anywhere else again.

As I continue my shift, I pray Missy will find the strength she needs to leave before it's too late. That's what I would do if I were in her shoes. Wouldn't I?

The question sits uncomfortably in my mind. Adam tracks my location. He grills me about how I spend my time and money. But that's different. He never hit me.

It's probably always *different*, until it's not.

CHAPTER 33

Near the end of my shift, I enter room 407 to check on Mrs. Green, an elderly patient with pneumonia. She's sleeping, and each inhale produces a troubling wheeze. Without waking her, I take her vitals and update her chart.

As I turn to leave, something on her bedside table catches my eye. It's an orange pill bottle next to her water glass. Healthcare providers administer all medications, so it shouldn't be here. On closer inspection, there's no label. I shake out a few pills, bring them close to my face, and read the words etched on the sides. I'm familiar with this drug. It's a potent heart medication. A simple mistake with even one of these pills could be fatal, especially for someone in Mrs. Green's condition. I can't imagine how this bottle ended up on the table. A visiting family member or someone who works here must have left it.

I slip the bottle into the front pocket of my scrubs. I need to hand the pills over to my supervisor and report my find.

The intercom crackles to life. "Code blue in room 321!"

I join the rest of my colleagues who are running toward the emergency. Is it Lauren's room? My heart pounds as I jog through the door.

It's not Lauren. It's Mr. Johnson, a patient with congestive heart failure and several other comorbidities.

As I participate in the resuscitation efforts, relief washes over me, quickly followed by guilt. Yes, I'm glad it's not Lauren, but how dare I experience relief at another person's distress?

When Mr. Johnston is stable, and I'm leaving the room in a sheen of sweat, I see Cara coming toward me again.

"Haley, I'm glad I caught you before the shift change. Lauren Christensen is awake and coherent. She asked to see you."

The news gives me a burst of energy. "Great. Thank you for telling me," I say, hurrying away.

I'm already halfway down the hall when I remember I was supposed to do something. What was it? The thought slips away as I focus on reaching Lauren. I can't believe she's finally awake and ready to talk. I can't overwhelm her, and the police are probably on their way, but so many questions spin around in my head, each demanding attention. I want to ask if she recognized the person who shot her and if the attempt on her life might be related to her findings on Granite Global.

Depending on what Lauren shares, this could be a pivotal turning point not just for the investigation, but also for my relationship with Elliot.

It could mean the end of both.

CHAPTER 34

There are flowers and *get-well-soon* balloons all over Lauren's room. Extra tables were brought in to accommodate everything. Two unopened gift baskets with shiny cellophane wrappers fill one corner. It looks like a crowded florist shop.

Lauren is propped against the pillows. Her face is pale and drawn, but her eyes are finally open.

Kyle sits beside her bed, holding her hand. He hasn't shaved recently. He's wearing rumpled clothes as if he's been living here for days, but his worried expression has eased now that she's awake.

"This is Haley," he says.

There's recognition in Lauren's eyes. "I remember you." Her voice is weak, barely above a whisper, from lack of use and the tubes that recently came out of her throat.

I navigate through the flowers and gifts to move closer. "Are you in any pain?"

A ghost of a smile touches her lips. "No, the pain meds are doing their job. I've been better, but I'm here. Thank you for everything."

"You're welcome." I brace myself for what I need to ask. "Lauren, do you know who did this to you? Or why?"

Though she barely moves her head, the meaning is clear. "I didn't see the man. I barely remember anything."

I shouldn't press her, but she seems to be okay. Just a few more questions. "After you got shot, when you were still conscious, you said two words to me. Granite Global."

Lauren frowns. Beside her, Kyle sits up straighter.

"I don't remember saying anything," she whispers.

"Is there a reason you might have? Did you suspect they had something to do with your assault? Because the police still haven't found the shooter or a motive." I look at Kyle, just in case something changed with the investigation during my shift.

"That's my understanding as well," he says. "They don't have anything solid yet, but they're working on it."

I face Lauren again, waiting for her to explain everything.

She says nothing.

It's not my place to interrogate her, but she might have information that would clear up several things. I keep my voice gentle. "I've been wondering if you uncovered something about Granite Global when you were working on your story there. Maybe you learned something they don't want going public."

Lauren's eyes widen. "No. My report on Granite Global is positive. They have wonderful, progressive leadership."

I blink in surprise. "But… I thought… are you sure?"

Lauren cuts off my stuttering question. "I understand what you're thinking. Granite Global isn't the answer. They have no reason to hurt me."

Kyle agrees. "Lauren was writing about the company's environmentally friendly initiatives. They're a huge supporter of EcoSphere."

Ecosphere is another company Elliot works with, so that makes sense. I should be pleased and relieved by this information. It's great news, but I was so certain that it's hard to accept I was wrong.

"So, why did you say Granite Global?" I ask.

"If that's what I said, maybe I wanted to ensure my article got published." She looks at Kyle. "I'm sorry it wasn't about you, Babe."

Lauren and Kyle exchange loving smiles, but I'm confused. If Granite Global had no reason to silence Lauren, then who did?

Lauren's smile slips away, and her eyes close.

I turn to Kyle. "Have you thought of any other reasons this happened? Did Lauren's past work harm someone who wants revenge?"

Kyle shakes his head. "No. The media went wild with their retribution theories, but Lauren's reporting is mostly positive. I'm sure the police have reached the same conclusion by now."

"It's true." Lauren says, her eyes still closed. "I always focus on organizations doing great work, ones that deserve the spotlight."

"But the news called you a crusader. They mentioned whistleblowers."

"The media gave people what they wanted to hear," Kyle answers. "Try not to worry, Haley. Be glad Lauren survived and no one else got hurt. You've done your part already. Let the detectives figure this out."

"I will. I am. I'm sorry about all the questions," I stammer, looking from Kyle to Lauren. "I'm glad you're awake and doing well."

"No reason to apologize," Lauren says, her voice barely audible. "Wish I could tell you more, but maybe it was just a terrible, random act of violence."

I can't imagine why Lauren would lie, yet her accepting responses don't sit right with me.

When I turn to leave, I'm facing a massive bouquet. Its size sets it apart from the others. The flowers are open and fresh. A recent delivery. I move closer until I can read the card displayed in the center.

Dear Lauren. May your recovery be swift and complete. We look forward to your return and the bright future ahead. Your friends at Granite Global.

The message seems innocuous enough, but as I read it again, something in the phrasing sends a chill down my spine. 'The bright future ahead.' Is it a reminder of what Lauren stands to gain or lose?

I glance back at Lauren and Kyle. They're both watching me.

I lift my hand to say goodbye. "I'm so glad you're going to be okay."

"You will, too," Lauren answers. "If you can leave everything that happened behind you."

CHAPTER 35

It's going to cost more to fix my car than it's worth. I'd have to take out a loan just to get it running again, and I'm not doing that. I want to visit my mother again, and there's only one way to get there. It won't be easy getting back on the commuter train, but I can't let fear dictate my choices.

When I get to the station, I message her: *On my way. Be there in 40 minutes.*

I hit send, then stare at the platform. No turning back now.

The chaotic morning rush-hour crowd is routine for most everyone here, but to me, it's like a different world. My gaze sweeps the area searching for anything that might signal danger. This time, if I'm paying attention, maybe I'll sense trouble before it hits.

The train pulls in with a bone-rattling screech. I've heard it a hundred times, but today it makes me tense. The cars seem extra ominous, yet they look the same. I didn't expect to see blood stains or police tape, yet I thought what happened would have permanently altered the train station somehow.

The doors slide open with a soft hissing sound. I step forward with the crowd. *You can do this, Haley. It's just a train ride. People do this every day.* I force my feet to move. I'm practically holding my breath when I step inside. I've made it this far. Now I just have to survive the trip.

There are several seats available. I choose one in the back. From here, I can see the entire train car.

The doors close, and the train lurches forward. I grip the armrests, focusing on seeing my mother again. I'll help around the house, remove the dead plants from the front box, something I forgot to do last time, and most importantly, we'll talk all about my first meeting with Elliot.

"You're the nurse, aren't you? From the night of the gun shooting?"

I turn to the woman next to me. She's staring, waiting for a response.

"Excuse me?"

"I was here, too. In a different car. I didn't see it happen, but I saw the video. I remember you. First time back?"

I don't remember this woman, but thanks to her, I'm now seeing that night in vivid detail. Beads of sweat trickle down my spine as I try to think of something else. Anything else.

"Terrifying, isn't it?" she continues. "They still haven't identified the gunman. He could be on this train right now. Any of these people."

She is not helping. Not one bit. A tight ache spreads across my chest, and I turn away. I can't talk about the incident. I need to concentrate on the ride, as if I'm single-handedly guiding the train and my focus is critical to our survival. I clench my jaw, upper molars clamped against lowers.

When the train stops, my eyes pinball from person to person, scrutinizing everyone who boards. A man with a briefcase. The guy with the black duffel bag. This is what the shooter has done to me. He turned a simple train ride into a nerve-wracking ordeal. I should have seen a therapist for counseling before I attempted this alone, but it's too late now.

The woman who remembered me gets off before I do. She tells me goodbye and to take care.

I give her a curt nod as I grip the side bar. I have to focus, or we might not make it to the next station. Everyone's safety depends on my diligence. It's irrational, but exactly what's going through my head.

As we near my stop, and only a few minutes remain, I tell myself it won't be much longer. I try to think about something else, like Ms. Berner who agreed to feed Moose while I'm gone. My hands are shaking, and I'm on the verge of hyperventilating, but it's almost over.

When the doors open, I practically fall out of the train as I lunge for the platform. I stride toward the road at a frantic pace and leave the train behind.

CHAPTER 36

"Haley?" my mother calls from the family room.

"It's me," I answer, dropping my bag by the door and heading toward her voice.

She sits in a recliner, closing a book in her lap. She's wearing a thick sweater and a fleece coat over it.

I head across the room and give her a hug. "Want me to turn up the heat for you?"

She waves her hand in a dismissive gesture I've seen throughout my life. "No, thank you. And never mind me. How was the train ride?"

"It was okay," I lie.

"Good. I'm glad you did it. It's good to face your fears."

My mother sets her book aside. Her eyes sparkle. "Now, come on. I want to hear about your meeting. What's he like?" She leans closer, getting ready to hang on to every word as I imagined she would.

"He was nice. I liked him."

"Good. He was nice in college. Not one of those full of himself guys, even though he was good looking."

"He still is."

She laughs. "I finally took a peek at his photos online. There's a definite resemblance between you. Did you see it?"

A small smile tugs at my lips. "Yeah, it was hard to miss."

"Tell me everything you talked about. Did he ask you questions about yourself? Your life? Your work?"

"Yes, all of that. He kept steering the conversation to me. My childhood. College. Nursing. He had so many questions, and I ended up doing most of the talking. But I know he works a lot and plays tennis when he can."

My mother smiles. "He was on the tennis team in college. It's nice he still plays."

I watch her face, searching for any sign of lingering feelings. Maybe there weren't any to begin with, since he was just a one-weekend stand.

"He's not married. No kids," I say.

Comfortable silence stretches between us as we sit on the couch together. I'm thinking about Elliot, putting myself in his situation. He went most of his adult life childless, then learned he wasn't. It's an incredible gift without the work or sacrifice of raising a child. On the flip side, thousands of moments of simply being there forge an unbreakable bond of love. Elliot was cheated out of it. It's not the same for me. I already had a father, a man I loved and still love dearly.

"I was just wondering... " My mother adjusts a blanket over her legs. "Did he ask about me?"

Her question surprises me. "He did. Several times. He asked about your treatment. Specific questions about your cancer. If you were getting good care. I told him everyone at the hospital and the clinic loves you and you were getting the best."

She smiles and seems satisfied with my response. "It's wonderful you finally know the truth, sweetheart. And Elliot seems to be a good man."

We're quiet again, nurturing our own thoughts. I'm not entirely sure about Elliot. I consider telling my mother about Granite Global and my suspicions, but I hold back. After all, Lauren said my hunch was wrong. I should believe her, and I want to. I'm just not there yet.

"Do you have plans to see him again?" my mother asks.

"Oh, didn't I tell you? We're having dinner at his house tomorrow."

"You are?" Her mouth remains open for a few beats. "Is Adam going with you?"

I groan inwardly. I've been dreading this conversation, but I can't put it off any longer. Especially now that I've told Lance, who might have told Elliot. I have to tell my mother.

I fold my arms over my body, bracing myself for what comes next. "Mom, I have to tell you about Adam and me."

CHAPTER 37

Frowning, my mother grips the edge of the blanket. "What is it, honey? What about you and Adam?"

Instinctively, I dig the tip of my nail into my cuticles, releasing a sharp sting of pain. "We're separated. Have been for a while now."

"Oh, Haley," she whispers. "Why? What happened?"

I shrug, unable to meet her eyes. How can I explain he thinks I did something so horrific that he's incapable of loving me or trusting me anymore? It's too painful to say aloud. My mother loves me unconditionally, but I can't bear to share something so ugly with her. I avert my eyes and say, "It's just not working anymore. There's an issue with trust."

Mom takes my hand. "When did this happen? Is there someone else? Did one of you make a mistake? It happens. Couples get past it all the time."

"No one cheated," I say, though I don't know how long Adam's "friend" Jessica has been in the picture.

"Then surely you can work it out." My mother frowns. "Your father and I didn't do you any favors by getting along so well. You didn't get to see the way normal couples disagree. They argue. And it's okay. It's how some couples get through the hard times. Have you tried couples' therapy yet? That might help."

"No, we haven't. But it's not me. It's Adam. He doesn't trust me anymore. And how can you be with someone you don't trust?"

"Is he planning on moving out?"

I look away again because I'm so ashamed to be sharing this now, so long after the fact. "I moved out of the house and into an apartment three months ago."

My mother's hand flies to her chest. Silence reigns for a solid five seconds before she adds, "And I'm just hearing this now?"

I snap into defensive mode. After waiting thirty years to tell me about my father, she's in no position to judge me. But I won't go there. We aren't trying to one-up each other with our secrets. My mother has only ever wanted the best for me. I know this without the faintest doubt.

I take a deep breath. "I'm sorry. There's just been so much going on. I didn't want to burden you, and I was also hoping we could get through this. That if I didn't tell anyone, it would all go away soon. I thought he would come around, but now I'm not positive. It might be smart to move on."

Jessica's image invades my mind again. Adam may have already moved on. Or she might simply be a rebound fling, just like Elliot was for my mother years ago. Oh God, what if she gets pregnant? I'm spiraling now, thinking thoughts that don't do my mental health any favors. I need to pull myself together. Maybe I'll find someone too. My next thought arrives before I can stop it. Someone like Lance.

My mother squeezes my hand, her eyes burning with what I can only imagine is sadness. "I'm sorry, sweetheart. I'm sorry you didn't want to burden me. Please don't hold anything back. You are the most important person in my life. If you're hurting, I want to help you."

"I know. Thanks. I'm sorry I didn't tell you. I know how much you love Adam."

"Oh, Haley, what I love is you and Adam together. Remember when you got engaged? He surprised you with the proposal at a friend's lake house. Hired a photographer to capture all of it so we could share the moment with you. Those photos were beautiful. You two reminded me of your father and me."

Except my father didn't know the truth about one of the most important people in his life. If he'd known, would he have pushed my mother away just like Adam has done with me?

My mother isn't finished reminiscing. "And the surprise party he threw for your birthday... He wanted everyone there because he's so proud of you."

The memory causes a pang in my chest. "*Was* so proud of me."

Her grip on my hand tightens. "You've been there for him, too. Through all his struggles with work, and Frank. You were the family Adam never had." Her gaze finds mine. "Now don't you worry. Things happen. You'll work it out. You have to."

My mother's advice makes me wonder if I've given up too easily. But she doesn't have the complete story.

"Can I talk to Adam about it? Would you mind if I did?" she asks.

"I'm not sure that's a good idea. It's complicated."

She pats my hand. "Love is always complicated, sweetheart. But when it's right, fight for it. Do what you must to save it."

Relief comes with having revealed a part of my secret. I can breathe easier having shared some of the truth. However, the real reason I had to move out will remain locked away. No one else needs to know. Especially not my mother. It might kill her.

CHAPTER 38

I need to be in control of something. Anything. Even if it's just a well-stocked fridge and pantry. That's why I'm doing a major grocery shopping. I remembered to bring my reusable bags—which means my mind isn't entirely lost to worry.

My phone rings when I'm in the produce aisle, squeezing avocados to find the perfect one.

Detective Millard's name flashes on the caller ID.

"Hello?" I answer, placing an avocado back onto the pile.

"Mrs. James, we'd like to see you at the station. There have been some developments in the case."

I'm at once hopeful and afraid. "What developments?"

"I'd rather not discuss this over the phone. How soon can you get here?"

I glance at my shopping cart. There's not much in it yet. So much for getting stocked up. "I can be there in thirty minutes."

"Good. Ask for me at the front desk."

The line goes dead. 'Developments.' What could he mean? Have they caught the shooter? Found a motive? Or is it something else?

I pay for a few items: more cat food, apples, carrots, canned tuna, and a bag of chips—nothing requiring refrigeration, though it's plenty cold outside. The bus stop is across the street, and I arrive just as the next bus pulls to the curb.

Climbing aboard, I find an empty seat near the front. I thought I might be afraid on the bus, but I'm not. It's different. My mind is already at the police station. A chilling thought hits. What if this meeting isn't about Lauren at all? What if they've talked to Adam?

No, this is not about me. It's about the shooting. It has to be. Detective Millard is busy trying to find the person who shot Lauren. He wouldn't be calling because of Adam.

The bus stops just across the street from the police station.

I approach the front desk and wait behind someone who is filling out a form. Then it's my turn.

"I have an appointment with Detective Millard. He's expecting me."

"Ms. James?" A voice calls from behind me.

I turn to see Millard. As usual, his expression is stern. "Come with me, please."

Why do I feel like I should turn around and run back out the door?

With my meager groceries on the floor beside me, I sit across from Detectives Millard and Desai in the same room as before. Previously, Detective Desai made an effort to comfort me. A slight smile here and there. There's none of that today.

Desai starts our meeting off. "Thank you for coming in. Some additional details need clarification."

"About the shooting?" For some strange reason, now that I'm at the police station, I feel like a teenager who got called to the principal's office waiting to find out what I've done wrong.

Detective Millard doesn't seem as tall when seated, but he's still an imposing figure. "We've reviewed additional evidence from the assault. A video another passenger filmed on her phone. We have questions for you."

My heartbeat picks up its pace. "What did you see?"

Millard answers, "At the start of your commute, you sat for several minutes, speaking on the phone. Then you left your seat and moved to another. The move occurred just before Ms. Christensen boarded. Do you recall this?"

I remember Lauren boarding, the way she looked at me before taking the seat I vacated. "Yes, that's right. That's what happened."

Desai's eyes narrow, her pen poised over her notepad. "Why did you change seats?"

I remember the exact reason, though I don't understand why the detective is asking. "The man sitting across from me was staring and making me uncomfortable. I've been harassed on a train before. So I moved."

"What happened to this man?" Desai asks, her words sharp.

I shrug. "He got off when the shooter got on."

Millard's brow furrows, deepening the lines on his forehead. "This information didn't come up in your previous interviews. Why didn't you report it before?"

I shift in my chair, realizing I may have overlooked another crucial detail. Did I forget because it happened long before the gunman entered the train? Or did I block it out?

I shift forward, rubbing a hand down my thigh. "It happened while we were still at the other station."

"Every detail matters." Desai's slow and deliberate speech emphasizes that she's told me this before.

Detective Millard holds up a finger. "The information about you changing seats led us to consider a different theory."

I uncross my legs, accidentally toppling one of my grocery bags with my ankle. Two apples roll across the floor.

"What theory?" I ask as I bend down to tuck my apples back into the bag.

"You may have been the intended target all along," he answers.

I sit up. "What are you saying? The shooter meant to hit me?"

Millard holds my wide-eyed gaze. "It's a possibility we're exploring. You and Ms. Christensen are around the same age. Both with brown hair. You moved to another seat at the last minute. It's possible the shooter received specific instructions, and the situation changed without his knowledge."

I'm suddenly freezing, as if the temperature dropped fifteen degrees. "But I don't understand. It doesn't make sense. Why would anyone want to kill me?"

Desai answers first. "We're trying to figure that out. We hope you can help us."

"I'm not a renowned journalist. I'm nobody important," I add, though they already know who I am and what I do for a living.

"Was anyone following you that night?" Millard asks.

"Not that I noticed. Why?" My knee bounces beneath the table.

Millard leans in closer. "Whoever did this probably wasn't working alone. There was an accomplice. Think carefully, Ms. James. Who knew you were on the train?"

I frown, wracking my brain for possibilities.

Detective Desai follows up with, "There's no one who might want to harm you?"

Only one name surfaces. Adam. It's a crazy thought, one I never should have come up with. But he knew where I was. He has a reason to hurt me, but I'm not comfortable sharing that with the police.

"Do you remember who you were speaking to on the phone when you got on the train?" Desai asks. Her eyes seem sharper, more focused than before.

I fight the urge to spring from my seat and pace the room, or better yet, to leave. "I don't... I can't remember."

"We'd like permission to look at your phone records." Millard's tone leaves little room for refusal.

"My phone records? Why?" My voice quivers.

"For our investigation," Desai answers, her voice softened, a glimpse of her earlier compassion showing through. "Is there anything else about that day? Anything out of the ordinary?"

I remain silent. Conflicted. There's nothing I want to tell them.

Detective Desai shifts in her chair. "We apologize for asking personal questions, but it's important for us to have an accurate picture of your life. So, about your husband... the separation... was it amicable?"

I stare down at my groceries, then gather the bags together. "My husband wouldn't have me killed." I don't sound as confident or outraged as I should.

"Does he have life insurance on you?" Desai asks.

"Not that I know of. And he has plenty of money. He wouldn't... he would never."

I contemplate bolting to the nearest bathroom to get sick. I must look green because Millard's expression changes to one of concern.

"Is there something you want to tell us?" he asks.

I can't tell them why Adam left me. It could ruin my reputation, possibly end my career.

No one would want to employ a nurse whose husband suspects her of murder.

CHAPTER 39

I might have been the target. The shooter wanted to kill *me,* not Lauren. The more those words repeat in my head, the more I believe them. Millard and Desai said it's only a possibility. There's no proof. At least not yet. But that doesn't make me any less queasy and afraid.

Walking away from the police station, I try to remember all the people I've disagreed with or offended.

The first person who comes to mind is Mrs. Gardner, a hospital patient who accused me of stealing jewelry she'd left at home. She never apologized, yet I'm willing to bet that after leaving me a scathing review on the hospital's website, she didn't give me another thought.

Then there's Tiffany, a former colleague with an addiction problem. I wasn't the one who reported her, but she thought I was. When she got fired, she stared me down with glassy eyes and said: "You think you're so perfect, Haley, but you'll be sorry." After her threat, I looked over my shoulder for days. But the incident was two years ago, and last I heard from Cara, Tiffany was out of rehab and had a new job.

A car backfires nearby, and I nearly jump out of my skin, heart racing. I scan the area, half-expecting to see a gunman. There's no one there. It's just a car, I tell myself. Just a car.

I take an apple from my grocery bag and bite into it, avoiding the soft dent it got from falling out of my bag. The apple is unwashed, and it rolled around on the police station floor. I cringe, wipe the remaining skin against my shirt, and go back to eating it.

I try to come up with other possibilities, people who might want revenge, but that's all I've got. Two people in over three decades of life. Hardly a list of mortal enemies, and it's probably fewer than most people have. The short list brings me a small measure of comfort but also takes me back to the person who first popped into my head. Adam. The man I once trusted more than anyone in the world. Could it be him? I hope not. Again, I feel ill for contemplating the possibility.

I should talk this through with a professional who can help me make sense of my thoughts. Someone who can offer legal advice and counsel about what to tell the police about Adam. If they're going to question him, if he's going to share what he believes, it might be better if they hear it from me first. Or should I simply keep quiet?

With the grocery bag handles around my wrists, I toss my apple core into a nearby trash can and shove my hands into my coat pockets. Lance's business card is there. The one he gave Cara at the hospital when he was first trying to track me down. Before I can second-guess myself, I punch his number into my phone.

"Good morning. Hartley, Hutchinson and Associates, how may I direct your call?" a polite voice asks.

"Hi, I'm calling to speak with Lance Hutchinson."

"Hold one moment, please." After a brief wait with elevator music, she's back. "Mr. Hutchinson is currently in a client meeting. Can I take a message?"

I hesitate. "No, it's alright. Thank you."

Back in my apartment, I double-check the locks, put away groceries, and pet Moose until he wanders off.

I try Lance again, this time using the number he gave me when we met in person. It's a different number. Maybe his personal cell phone, so the call won't have to route through the receptionist. As it rings, I pray he'll answer. I'm not sure if I'm calling because I need legal advice, or because I just need a friend.

A few hours later, I'm at a coffee shop with Lance, who was gracious enough to meet me on short notice. I've got two pistachio macarons on a plate, and I'm contemplating what I'm about to share.

"How's your mother doing?" he asks before I can speak. "Last time you mentioned she had another round of chemo coming up."

"She's hanging in there." I'm touched he remembered.

"And work? Are they being understanding about everything?"

He does this every time we're together. He asks questions, listens to answers, remembers details. He's giving me the kind of attention that makes a person feel appreciated. But how much is real? Is this Lance the person, or Lance the attorney still vetting me for Elliot?

The creases across his forehead deepen. "You said this was urgent. What's going on?"

I eat my second macaron. Finally, I say, "It's about the assault investigation."

"What about it?"

"The detectives have a new theory. *Potential* theory. I was the target. Me. Not Lauren."

Lance lets out a low whistle. "Why do they think you were the target?"

"I switched seats right before Lauren got on the train. She took my seat."

He scoffs. "That's all? It doesn't seem like much."

"I imagine they're going to dig into my personal life a bit more now. They'll want to interview people who know me and find out if anyone wants me dead." I force a laugh as if it's funny but regret it right away. Totally in poor taste. It's only because I'm nervous. I clear my throat and begin again. "My issue is that I wasn't exactly forthcoming with them when they asked if I could think of anyone who might have a motive."

I glance around the shop. It's nearly empty. The barista places mobile orders on the counter. Two students huddle over laptops on the opposite side of the seating area. An older man in workout gear focuses on his phone.

A chill runs down my spine as I remember the detectives' words from my first visit to the station. Anyone could be a potential threat. Even the people I least suspect. Does that include Lance? If I can't trust him, I don't have anyone to talk to right now, and I'm desperate.

I scoot my chair closer to the table and lower my voice. "Look, I need professional advice. There's something I haven't told anyone." I push my plate to the side. "Any chance I can retain Hartley & Hutchinson and attorney-client privilege for some amount of money I can afford?"

Lance studies me, then asks, "Do you have a dollar?"

His reasonable offer surprises me. Perhaps he's already billing Elliot for every ten-minute increment of time spent with me and doesn't want to double dip. The thought reassures me. If it's true, he's an ethical attorney.

As I fumble in my purse for a dollar, the barista calls out an order for someone named Samantha, but otherwise, it's quiet.

After rummaging around in my purse, it's clear I don't have any cash. "Do you accept credit cards?"

The corners of his mouth curl up slightly. "Sorry, I'm not that high-tech." He takes a twenty-dollar bill out of his wallet and hands it to me. "Consider this a loan."

"I guess your fees went up." With a wry smile, I take the money and make a show of putting it in my purse, taking it out again, then handing it back to him.

His face is serious. "What sort of advice do you need?"

I press my lips together, buying a few more seconds while gathering courage. "I told you I'm estranged from Adam. We're not living together. But I didn't tell you why. What I'm about to share—" I stop and decide to start off with a different explanation. "I'm afraid of what might come out if the police talk to my husband."

"Why would they talk to him if you're not together?"

"Because Adam knew I was on the train. He even knew what I was wearing because I had seen him earlier that day."

"But surely you don't think Adam would... " He doesn't finish, but it's clear where his question was headed.

I cover my face with my hands, ashamed of what I'm about to say next. "I hope he didn't. The thing is, Adam might have a motive."

Lance's gaze sharpens. "What kind of motive?"

"Revenge."

CHAPTER 40

A bell rings at the front door of the coffee shop, just like it did when we entered. A man with a black quilted jacket backs through the door. Adam has that coat. Same height. Same hair color. Every muscle in my body tenses as I stare. Why is he here?

He turns. It's not Adam. I exhale as he walks toward the counter and grabs a to-go order, never once looking our way.

Lance is waiting. "Why would your husband want revenge?"

I take a small sip from my coffee cup before answering. "It involves his grandfather. Frank."

Lance remains silent.

"Frank was a total narcissist," I say, words tumbling out. "Everything revolved around him. He always needed something from Adam. Treated him like an employee. Didn't matter if it was six in the morning, or if we were out celebrating with friends. Frank expected Adam to drop everything and show up."

"Did Frank treat you the same way?"

"No, he ignored me. Acted as if I was an inconvenience, but he resented sharing Adam."

"That must have been rough."

"I tried not to dwell on his behavior, but yes, it was difficult. There's no doubt Frank's expectations placed a strain on my marriage."

"Did Adam try to do something about it? Set boundaries with his grandfather?"

I clasp the collar of my shirt, gripping the fabric between my fingers. "No, it was never that simple. Adam felt indebted to Frank for raising him. Frank's controlling behavior was all Adam had ever known. He thought it was normal, though I tried to tell him it was toxic and manipulative. But Adam couldn't see it, or didn't want to. It's hard to accept that the person who raised you is flawed, I guess."

In contrast, my mother always put my father and me first, even after her long nursing shifts. Unlike Frank, she expected little in return. No wonder I struggled to understand Adam's relationship with his grandfather.

"So, Frank's behavior eventually destroyed your marriage?" Lance asked.

"No. Not at all. Everything was pretty much okay between Adam and me until Frank died."

Lance tilts his head, waiting for me to explain the rest.

"One night, Frank had what *he* called an urgent problem. He needed Adam to come over immediately. Adam was leading a client meeting and messaged me. I had just gotten off work and was on my way home, so I went instead. I rushed over, expecting a health problem."

I look around the coffee shop, a little self-conscious that I might have raised my voice and someone has overheard, but I don't stop talking. I'm on a roll now. "Frank was rude from the moment I arrived. 'Where's Adam?' he said. I asked him what he needed and if he was okay. His answer floored me. Even knowing how he was, I thought he was joking. But he wasn't."

"What was the problem?"

I let out a huff of breath. "He'd accidentally pushed the source button on his TV and couldn't figure out how to switch it back. He was freaking out about missing a football game later that night. To him, it was a federal emergency. No awareness of how selfish he was. Still, I kept quiet, figured out how to get his cable back. When I finished—not a single thank you or apology from him. He shooed me out the door. I'd had a long day. I was tired and worried about my mother, who had just received her cancer diagnosis. I snapped."

Lance hasn't moved since I began telling my story. "You snapped? What does that mean?"

"I told Frank the world didn't revolve around him, and he could act more appreciative of all the things Adam did for him day in and day out."

I lift my eyes to the ceiling, remembering Frank's furious red face. How spittle ran down his chin when he shouted, "How dare you? Who do you think you are? No, let me tell you. You are nothing! I've never understood what Adam sees in you."

Seated across from Lance, I fight back tears as I recall how Frank lashed out, said things he probably didn't mean.

"Unfortunately, shortly after I left Frank's condo… he died." I close my eyes and take a deep breath. "Now Adam is convinced I had something to do with it."

I open my eyes to Lance staring at me, his face full of questions.

"Adam thinks I poisoned Frank or gave him something to cause a heart attack."

A few beats of silence pass before Lance asks, "And… did you?"

"No! I would never," I exclaim with a grimace. "But Adam doesn't believe me."

Lance leans back, putting distance between us at the table. I see doubt in his eyes.

"But *why* does Adam suspect you? He must have a reason."

"I was the last person to see Frank alive, and Adam knew how I felt about Frank's behavior. He keeps pointing out that Frank was in great health for a man in his seventies."

Lance cocks his head. "Regardless of the man's health status, it's not unheard of for someone in their seventies to die unexpectedly. There must be another reason."

When I don't elaborate, Lance asks, "Was there an autopsy?"

"Yes. The results were inconclusive. The coroner couldn't identify one specific cause of death and ruled it natural causes."

"I sense there's a but coming," Lance says.

"No, there isn't. No but. There was zero evidence of foul play," I say, omitting the one other tiny thing that connects me.

Lance separates his hands, palms facing the ceiling. "Then you don't have anything to worry about, do you?"

"I shouldn't, but it doesn't look good. My husband suspects me of murdering his grandfather. I'm a nurse. If the detectives speak to Adam, if he tells them why he left me... "

My hands are in my lap now, my thumb digging against the nail bed on my little finger and troubling the skin there. "I don't want Adam's suspicions to become public information. And after seeing that video and my few days of fame, I'm worried everyone will hear about it. I may have already lost my husband, but I could also lose my job, my reputation."

Lance watches me. I can't tell what he's thinking.

"Should I get ahead of the matter and explain all this to the detectives? Tell them there's a reason Adam resents me? Or do I keep quiet and hope he does too?" Worry creeps into my voice. "I don't want to get in trouble for withholding information, but I can't bear the thought of those accusations going public."

"Right." Lance cups his hands. "Generally, it's best to stay quiet. Don't disclose anything. In this case, I'm not sure."

His tone suggests my situation is worse than I imagined. My vision blurs as tears well in my eyes.

"Haley, are you okay?"

I blink to hold my tears back and press my lips together.

Lance reaches across the table toward me.

Without thinking, I take his hand.

He stiffens and yanks his hand away. Only after his jarring reaction do I realize he was aiming for the paper napkin above my plate.

"I'm sorry. I didn't mean to... I'm sorry." My face burns with embarrassment. I can't explain why I touched him.

"Thank you for listening. I appreciate your time," I manage to say, avoiding eye contact. "Please don't share any of this with Elliot. If he hears why Adam and I separated, it should come from me. I'll tell him myself when I see him again."

Lance seems taken aback, even more so than when I touched him. "What do you mean?"

I don't understand the question, but I answer. "I'll tell Elliot about Adam the next time I see him."

"The next time? You already met with Elliot?"

"We had dinner a few days ago. He didn't tell you?"

"No, he didn't." Something changes in Lance's expression. Is he surprised? I can't tell, and I'm too mortified to analyze it.

"We're meeting again on Friday for dinner at his house."

Lance checks his watch, then scoots his chair back. "I've got to return to the office. Let me consult a colleague about what you've told me. I'll get back to you with your best course of action."

He drops a tip on the table and leaves first.

Outside, I pull my coat tight around my body and zip it to my chin. My insides feel strange. Not quite nauseous, but wrong, like I have low blood sugar, which I definitely don't have after a sweet coffee and two cookies.

What have I done? Not only have I shared my most embarrassing and painful secrets with Lance by telling him my husband thinks I'm a murderess, but I also made a complete fool of myself by reaching for his hand.

As I walk down the sidewalk alone, my paranoia kicks into overdrive. What if Lance tells Elliot about my confession? Or my pathetic attempt at comfort or connection? But he can't tell anyone about our conversation. We exchanged money. Which means I've got attorney-client privilege. That has to count for something.

I thought discussing my predicament with an attorney would give me confidence about how to proceed. Instead, I'm more confused and uncomfortable than ever.

CHAPTER 41

Two days have passed since the detectives informed me I might have been the real target. They don't know yet. There's still no solid suspect or motive for the shooting. That doesn't make me feel great about my current situation.

It's also been two days since I asked Lance for advice. He said he would get back to me but hasn't yet. He's an important attorney who must have other clients like Elliot, and urgent situations tying him up with lawyerly duties. Yet I've been uneasy since our last conversation.

With a sigh, I flop down on my bed and pluck tufts of Moose's gray hair from my duvet cover. Collecting his fur and discarding it usually brings me mindless satisfaction, but not today. Why did I unload my problems on Lance? He's Elliot's lawyer, not mine, and he's certainly not my psychologist. I cringe, remembering how I touched him and how he pulled away. He looked so surprised. Maybe even disgusted. It wasn't good.

My nagging sensation intensifies. Something else in our conversation keeps nudging my subconscious.

I scoop up my phone and type another message. "Hey, Lance, just checking in. Hope everything's okay."

Before sending it, I read what I've written and groan. It doesn't sound like a message for my attorney. I delete it.

Now that Elliot and I have met, Lance's job as intermediary is done. He's no longer vetting me. There's no reason for us to see each other again. Maybe that's why he's not responding.

Except I paid him for a consultation. Unless it was a joke to him—handing over the twenty I handed back.

I roll onto my side, tossing a small clump of gray hair into the trash bin. Lance's silence shouldn't hurt this much, but it does. When did I start caring about his presence in my life? Elliot hired him to talk to me, and that's what he did. Yet somewhere along the line, I began thinking of him as a friend. If I'm being honest, potentially more, way off in the future, if things don't work out with Adam.

I push myself up and go to my closet, where I grab a clean set of navy scrubs for my shift.

At the hospital, I throw myself into my work, grateful for the distraction. Lauren is gone. She's home now, with private nursing care.

In the brief, quiet moments between patients, I check my phone to find Lance still hasn't responded.

At the end of my shift, I type a final message. "Lance, if I said something wrong or made you uncomfortable, please accept my apology." I hit send and put my phone away. Staring at it won't make him answer any faster.

On my way home, as I'm analyzing interactions and conversations, a fragment of my last conversation with Lance resurfaces. It's the question he asked me. "Did you do it?"

That's odd, and I think it's what's been bothering me.

Everything I know about attorneys and their clients comes from television, movies, and novels—probably not the most reliable sources, but it's all I have. According to those sources, attorneys never ask whether their client is guilty. It has something to do with plausible deniability. Yet Lance asked me outright if I was involved with Frank's death.

The implications stack up in my mind. Did he ask because his priority is protecting Elliot's interests? Is he going to tell him? And if he does, will it matter? Would it destroy any chance of having a decent relationship with my biological father before it even begins?

I force myself to take slow, even breaths. All I can do is wait.

CHAPTER 42

I still haven't heard from Lance, and I can't stop thinking about it, even before my dinner with Elliot.

The driver Elliot sent drops me off at his house and pulls away. I'm alone on the quiet street. I glance in both directions before heading up the front path.

The house is a modern white brick mansion that makes my childhood home seem like a small cottage. Reflective glass windows stretch two stories high. Landscape lights illuminate perfect flowerbeds. There isn't a stray leaf in sight.

Instead of my usual orthopedic shoes, I'm wearing nice leather boots with a small heel. I'm not used to them, and already they're annoying me. My steps are more careful than usual. I chose a sharp, modest outfit. I dressed to feel confident, but I also want Elliot's approval.

As I approach the arched double doors, my worries get triggered. What if Lance told Elliot everything from the coffee shop? Who would want a relationship with a woman suspected of murder? Elliot might wonder if he's next.

I pause at the door. The next few moments will reveal everything. If Elliot acts distant or distrustful, then Lance told him.

As I press the bell, another thought surfaces: I might not be the only one with secrets. What if Elliot and Granite Global are responsible for the attempt on Lauren's life? No—I have to trust what Lauren told me. Otherwise, I'll ruin what could be an important and special evening.

The door on the right swings open, and there's Elliot, beaming. "Haley! Come in!"

There's no trace of the standoffishness I'd prepared for, no hint of suspicion or distrust in his eyes.

We still don't hug, but he takes my coat with a beaming smile, then ushers me inside with a gentle hand on my upper back.

"I hope you're hungry. I might have gone a bit overboard with dinner preparations."

His enthusiasm is infectious, and I'm already more relaxed. "I'm starving," I say, realizing it's true. With everything that's been going on, I've been skipping meals and merely nibbling on occasional snacks.

Elliot ushers me into a spacious living room with soaring ceilings and a wall of windows. Through them, I see a beautiful backyard. My mother would love it.

I take in the modern furnishings and a few pieces of artwork. The overall effect is beautiful. Like a showroom. Almost too perfect.

"It's gorgeous," I tell him.

"Thank you. I had help from a designer when I moved in." Elliot smiles. "Help is an understatement. If this place looks good, she's the reason. Please make yourself comfortable. I have dinner in the oven, but it's not quite ready."

Above the mantle is a painting of a beautiful woman in her forties. "Is she family?" I ask.

"My ex-wife. Jules."

I'm surprised her photo hangs on his wall, but I don't press further. We settle into armchairs, still smiling at each other.

Since our first dinner, Elliot has prepared more questions about my life: hobbies, sports, what sort of books I read, and what I watch on television. It's clear he's been thinking about me.

My answers come easily. They're all pretty factual, and it's just nice that he's so interested. I study him as he talks and gestures in response to what I'm sharing. How can I not stare when I see so much of myself in him? Like the dimples that form when he smiles.

My previous nervousness has disappeared. My concerns about Granite Global are fading. I don't want to be all doom and gloom and suspicious when this is going so well. Truly, it's incredible that we're together now. I'm grateful my mother finally shared her secret with us and didn't take it to the grave.

Eventually, I turn the tables, asking Elliot about his upbringing. He's sharing a story about his parents when his phone rings. He glances at it, his smile temporarily vanishing.

"I'm sorry, I need to take this. It'll just be a moment."

Once he leaves the room, I get up and stroll around. Framed photos on a gallery wall catch my eye.

The first one is Elliot and Jules. Now that I see them together, it's clear Jules was older than Elliot. Not a lot older, but enough that I notice the fine lines around her eyes and on her neck. A boy of about fourteen stands between them. Elliot said he has no other biological children. Perhaps the boy is Jules' son from a previous marriage.

Another photo shows Elliot in a tuxedo. From the images, I can piece together bits of his earlier life. I'm so engrossed, I startle when he clears his throat behind me. I didn't hear him come back into the room.

"Sorry about the interruption. My attorney has to drop by later tonight. I hope you don't mind. It won't take long."

Lance is coming. My initial reaction is, *oh, no,* and I'm nervous all over again. This could be extra awkward. Lance has ignored my messages, and even after days of analyzing the situation, I can't come up with any reasonable explanation for ghosting me. Will he apologize, or will we both act as if it never happened? I want to avoid making a scene in front of Elliot. If Lance apologizes, I'll accept it graciously. If he says nothing, I'll do the same.

The dinner is delicious. The main dishes came from a local restaurant, and the salad and rice dishes Elliot prepared himself. With decades of life to catch up on, we linger at the table after finishing large slices of an incredible chocolate cheesecake with fresh raspberries.

A doorbell chimes through the house, interrupting my list of places I've traveled. I'm surprised to see hours have passed since I arrived.

"Must be Lance," Elliot says before excusing himself.

Muffled voices come from the hallway, barely reaching the dining room. Their hushed conversation continues for at least a few minutes while I squirm in my seat. What if Lance makes an excuse and leaves without seeing me?

When I hear their footsteps moving in my direction, I sit up straighter, smooth my hair behind my ears, and cross my legs at the ankle.

Elliot returns, but he's not with Lance. Instead, he's accompanied by a man I've never seen before. He's tall, about Elliot's age, and his face is smooth, skin perfect except for a raised scar across his right temple.

Elliot smiles. "No need for introductions. You two know each other."

Confused, I stand from my chair. "I'm sorry, but I don't—"

"This is our first time meeting in person," the man says, extending his hand to me. "Hello, Haley. I'm Lance Hutchinson. It's nice to meet you."

Blood whooshes at my temples as I stare at him. "Your name is Lance Hutchinson?"

He nods, still smiling, though it's slipping a little as he registers my odd response and the surprise I'm not hiding well.

I turn to Elliot. "Do you have two attorneys named Lance? Is there a Lance Hutchinson, Jr. at the firm?"

Elliot shakes his head. "No, Haley. I only have one attorney."

"I'm the one and only Lance at the firm," the stranger adds.

A sickening sensation floods my body. How could this be? If the only Lance Hutchinson is standing a few feet away from me, then who have I been talking to all this time? Who have I been sharing my life story and personal problems with?

CHAPTER 43

I'm frozen in place, battling a wave of nausea as I gape at the man who claims to be the real Lance Hutchinson. I plant my hands on the edge of the table to steady myself. Everything seems distant, like I'm watching a scene from the Twilight Zone. I'm the stunned character trapped in an alternate reality where nothing makes sense.

"I don't understand." My gaze darts between Elliot and the stranger. He's at least a decade or two older than *my* Lance Hutchinson.

Elliot's brow furrows. "Haley, what's going on?"

I straighten, wringing my hands. "I've been talking to Lance. For weeks now. In person." My voice sounds as frightened as I feel.

The newcomer blinks and tilts his head to the side. "I'm sorry, Haley, but we've never met before now."

"I met someone with the same name. Elliot's attorney. But not you."

Elliot rubs his chin. "I assure you, this is Lance Hutchinson. We've been friends since college."

The room spins. I have to swallow the panicked sensation crawling its way up my throat. "Then who have I been meeting with? He knew so much about you, about me. He was helpful." My stomach lurches, the dinner and cheesecake threatening to come up. I'm so freaked out I emit a strange bark of laughter.

"I'm not sure I understand." Elliot's brows draw together.

Lance crosses his arms. “It sounds like someone has been impersonating me.”

“Start from the beginning,” Elliot says, frowning. “Tell us everything about this person.”

I blow out a long exhale. Breathe. Just breathe. “He contacted me the day before the train incident, before I even knew about you. Then he came to the hospital where I work and—” My hands tremble. Memories of Lance, my Lance, flash through my brain like clips from a horror movie trailer. “I met him at my mother’s. He said he represented you.”

“He showed up at your mother’s house?” Elliot asks.

“Yes. We invited him in. He asked questions so you could learn more about me. After that, we met for coffee twice, and we had dinner together when you had to cancel our first meeting.”

Elliot frowns. “I never canceled a meeting with you.”

“You did. For an emergency board meeting. Don’t you remember?”

“I’m sorry, Haley, but I promise I didn’t. We’ve only ever had two meetings planned. Last week for dinner, and now tonight. I canceled neither.”

A shudder wracks my body. I can’t wrap my head around this. My grasp of reality is slipping away. I trusted Lance. I can’t believe how much. The things I told him. Things I’ve never told anyone else.

Goosebumps rise on my arms. But then I recall something that yanks me out of my daze. A few days ago, after my car broke… when I was downtown. I walked up to the reception desk at Hartley & Hutchinson and asked for Lance. He was there. He works at Hartley & Hutchinson.

Which begs the question—who is lying to me now? Is it the man I believed to be Lance? Someone I thought I befriended over the past two weeks, though he did eventually ghost me. Or is it the two men in this room? I barely know Elliot. The other man is a complete stranger.

I stand, eyeing them as terror courses through me. I have to escape from this house and get away from them, so I can figure out what the hell is going on, and yet I'm afraid to turn my back. Afraid to move. Another chill makes my shoulders quiver.

Elliot and his friend keep staring at me. I sift through the situation again to see if I'm losing my mind. The Lance I met is most definitely an attorney at the law offices of Hartley and Hutchinson.

My recollection expands. More memories. Downtown. Broken car. I walked to the law office. But that's where I just got it wrong. That's the part I misremembered. The receptionist never notified Lance to say that I was there. He happened to leave only seconds after I arrived. No one ever verified his name. But he *was* there. I didn't imagine him.

"He works at the Hartley & Hutchinson Law Firm," I blurt. "I'm positive he does."

"We believe you, Haley." Elliot speaks slowly, as if he's talking to a frightened child. "Can you describe this man to us?"

"He's tall. Around 6'2". Dark hair. A mole right here." I point to the spot on my face, then close my eyes, conjuring up an image of my Lance so I can give them more. That's all I've got to describe him. "He knows so much about you. Your past and present."

A silent exchange passes between Elliot and Lance.

I'm the one frowning now, bothered because just like my mother and Maria, they have their own way of communicating without words. "We need to call the police. Detective Millard."

Elliot stops me. "Wait. Please don't call the police. It's best we handle this matter privately."

"Why wouldn't we call the police? Do you know who he is?"

"We'll find out," Elliot says. "What's important right now is helping you. I can't imagine how unsettling this must be."

"We need to keep you safe," the new Lance adds.

"Safe from whom?" I demand as a fresh geyser of fear erupts inside me.

No one answers, but Elliot extends his hand toward my shoulder.

I step back and away from him. My uncertainty is suffocating. I need answers.

"Trust me on this," Elliot says. "We'll sort this out. I promise. Stay here for the night. I'll prepare the guest room."

I don't feel safe here, but I don't expect I'll feel safe anywhere. After a stretch of silence, I respond with a simple, "Okay."

None of this makes sense. What motive do any of these people have to lie to me? Who can I trust? These two, or my Lance, who they claim is an impersonator?

The answer, I fear, might be no one at all.

CHAPTER 44

The guest room door clicks shut behind me. I'm alone in a large space with soft white walls, a white rug, beige linens, and neutral décor. Everything looks staged and unused, like I'm the first guest to stay here.

My hands shake, sloshing chamomile tea over the side of the cup Elliot made me. Before it spills, I set the full cup on a table and place my purse beside it.

Unable to stay still, and not at all tired despite the hour, I pace the hardwood floors around the bed. Is this happening, or am I having an incredibly realistic nightmare? Bit by bit, my world has shattered like glass. Each broken shard reflects another horror, secret, or lie.

My phone rings. It's Adam. After our last conversation, I can't deal with him now.

I'm not sure what's happening downstairs. Last thing I knew, Lance went into Elliot's office, while Elliot insisted on making me tea. I should have stayed with them. But then again, do I want to know what they're talking about? A creepy saying pops into my mind: *If we tell you, we'll have to kill you.*

My fear is multiplying. First, I was afraid of a hitman lurking in the shadows. Then, my suspicions turned to Adam. But this new mystery is as confusing as it is chilling. Which is the real Lance, and who's lying to me?

A creak comes from the hallway. I stay still, listening. Footsteps retreat before the house settles back into an uneasy silence.

Hurrying to the door, I push the handle down, making sure I'm not locked in. The door swings inward. Thank God I'm not trapped. If that's something I'm worried about, maybe staying here wasn't a good idea. Should I call for a ride and leave?

I decide to trust Elliot.

I step into the en-suite bathroom with a large rainfall shower and deep soaking tub. The collection of toiletries on the marble countertop grabs my attention. Everything I need is here: a new toothbrush still in its packaging, toothpaste, makeup wipes, and facial moisturizers. Each item is my preferred brand. The same ones in the medicine cabinet at my apartment. It could be a coincidence. The brands aren't unusual. But it's as if someone prepared this bathroom specifically for me.

I'd better make sure someone besides Elliot and his attorney knows where I am. I wish I hadn't told Adam to stop monitoring my location. But even so, my mother is the only person I fully trust now.

The power on my phone is low as I type a text.

I'm staying in Elliot's guestroom tonight because it got late. I'll tell you about it tomorrow. Just wanted to say I'm here.

She probably won't get the message until the morning. I'll have to borrow a charger before then, or my phone will die.

Looking for a spare cord, I scan the room again. A corner bookcase holds a variety of genres. I run my fingers along the spines, pulling out a few of the books. Classics alongside contemporary bestselling fiction. All the books are in immaculate condition. Crisp dust jackets on the hardbacks. Uncracked spines on the paperbacks. One book is unlike the others. Its spine is creased, with a few pages dog-eared. The title is *The Gaslight*

Effect. It's a psychological thriller I might choose at the bookstore. But considering my current situation, I shove the novel back into place.

The sound of an engine comes from outside the window. A sports car pulls out of the driveway, its headlights cutting through the darkness below. There's a Porsche symbol on the back. It must be the attorney. I'm glad he's gone.

A thumping noise echoes through the house, making me turn away from the window. A door closing on the first floor? With my heightened alertness, every sound seems sinister, as if I'm in a haunted house jumping at creaks and shadows.

Elliot hasn't come up to give me an update. He must think I'm in bed. I should try to sleep. I hope the situation won't seem as awful in the daylight. But if I'm staying, I need to borrow a phone charger.

I leave the room and step into the long, dark corridor lined with closed doors. It appears he's shut the house down for the night.

"Elliot?" My heart beats faster than normal. "Elliot?"

Still no response.

I reach the corridor's end without finding a wall switch, but my eyes are adjusting to the low light. Gripping the banister, I head down the wide staircase. Each step feels risky. At the bottom, I stop and listen. Nothing. If Elliot retired to his bedroom, I don't know whether it's upstairs or down.

In the near darkness, I navigate around furniture, trying to make out the large forms. I spot a lamp and switch it on. I'm near the framed photographs.

I move closer, taking in another image of a younger Elliot with his ex-wife. They're with the same boy from the photo I saw earlier. He's a few years older in this one. He's shot up several inches and has the awkward look of puberty. There's something familiar about his expression, but it's the dark mole beside his eye that makes my mouth fall open.

A sudden noise makes me snap around.

"Elliot?" I call, straining to hear and wondering if anyone else is here with us.

When no one answers, I continue moving through the house until I find Elliot's study. The door is ajar, and I slip inside like an intruder, which I am.

As I scan the room for a spare charger, curiosity gets the better of me, and I approach his desk.

Under the beam of my phone's light, I see documents and business reports. One catches my eye. The letterhead reads *Granite Global Industries.* Words jump out at me: *Urgent. Priority to be dealt with ASAP.*

Floorboards creak.

I pivot, my heart pounding faster. The doorway is empty, but I could swear I saw a shadow move in the hallway.

"Elliot?"

I set the document down and return to the hallway. Pale blue light comes from a partly open door. I move toward it in slow motion. Every instinct screams to turn back, but I can't. I need answers. I need to figure out what's going on. Not to mention the phone charger.

My hand trembles as I open the door wider.

A large control panel with switches and dials blinks silently. Rows of monitors dominate the far wall, each displaying a distinct part of the property. One screen shows the guest room I just left. The bathroom and bed aren't visible—good to know—but the bookcase, chair, and side table are. I can see my abandoned mug of tea and the purse I left behind. Did anyone watch me when I was in there pacing the room?

Other screens show different rooms I recognize. The kitchen, dining room, and the living room. One monitor displays the driveway; another, the back garden.

As I take a step toward the wall of monitors, movement on one screen startles me. I raise my hand, and so does the figure on the monitor. It's me, in real time, standing in this very room.

What kind of person needs this sort of security system? What is Elliot so intent on protecting?

I bend over the desk, investigating a trail of wires in search of a phone charger. The monitors hum, but not as loud as my breathing.

A hand clamps down on my shoulder.

CHAPTER 45

Someone's hand covers my mouth, and a powerful arm pulls me closer with a force I can't overcome. I smell cologne and recognize the scent. It's him. The man I thought was Lance.

"Don't scream," he hisses, his breath hot against my ear. "You need to come with me. We have to get out of here and talk."

I whirl around, finally escaping his grip. I'm about to shout when his hand covers my mouth again. "Please, Haley, don't scream. I won't hurt you."

He releases his hand, and I can speak again.

"You lied to me, didn't you?"

He glances toward the door, then back at me. "Come with me now, and I'll explain."

"No. Why would I? I don't trust you."

"Please, Haley."

"I'd be crazy to go anywhere with you."

"You're going to hear me out. Because I have this." Without letting go of my arm, he lowers his gaze.

My eyes follow. His hand rests over the handle of a revolver at his hip.

That changes everything. Images of the leaking holes in Lauren Christenson's chest choke me with fear, and I can't respond. Does Elliot know this man is here? Did he see him enter the house? Are there security monitors in other rooms or only here?

I glimpse the monitor showing Lance and me. We're standing so close, someone might think we're in a romantic embrace.

He leads me through the house, his body pressed to mine, his leather jacket rubbing against my arms. My urge to scream is strong, but something besides the gun holds me back. Is it possible that in some twisted way, this man is trying to help rather than hurt me?

Outside, without my coat, an icy wind bites into my skin. The cold and my fear combine to make me shiver so hard my teeth chatter.

"Get in," he orders, nudging me at the passenger side of a black SUV. "Slide behind the wheel. You're going to drive."

My knees nearly buckle as I scoot from one side of the SUV to the other with a gun on me. He gets into the passenger seat beside me.

"Where are we going?"

"Somewhere private." His voice cracks on the last word. He runs a trembling hand through his hair, then checks the side mirror. Strange that he looks so nervous when he's the one with the gun.

"Please don't hurt me."

"I'm not going to hurt you. Just drive." The anguish in his voice surprises me. He looks as if he might be sick.

"What's your real name?"

"Carter."

The name means nothing to me, but his distress is unmistakable. Is he upset about something, or nervous because he plans to kill me? I clutch the steering wheel tighter.

We drive without speaking. Carter's head swivels between me, the road, and the rear window. Sweat beads on his forehead despite the cool air.

My foot hovers over the brake. One quick stop, throw open the door and run. But the gun... Even though Carter looks more likely to throw up than shoot, I can't risk it. Staying alive is my top priority. Besides, underneath my terror, I'm desperate to make sense of everything.

Carter breaks the silence. "Turn right at the next intersection."

I go for the blinker but turn on the wipers instead. He leans over and shuts them off.

The route takes us deeper into the darkness. Massive trees press in on both sides. The paved road becomes gravel. We're headed into the woods.

"Here," he blurts. "Stop here."

I ease onto the shoulder, the crunch of rocks loud under the tires.

"Let's get out for a few minutes," he says, wiping a hand across his forehead. "I need some air."

I stumble out on shaky legs, keeping my eyes trained on Carter's every move.

To my surprise, he tucks the gun away.

"You're cold, and I'm sorry. Please, just let me explain." His voice is softer as he removes his leather jacket. It's the voice I came to know over the time we spent together.

What he does next is even more surprising. He drapes his jacket over my shoulders. I'm torn between refusing any gesture of kindness from him and pulling it tighter around me to ward off the freezing temperature.

I walk backwards, increasing the distance between us, but I don't run. My curiosity is as strong as my fear.

The car door remains open. Light streaming from the interior illuminates Carter's face and the dark mole beside his right eye.

"You're in the photos in Elliot's house, aren't you?"

He rakes his hand over his head. "My mother was married to Elliot. For a short time, I was Elliot's stepson. I thought you knew."

"Well, I didn't." If I hadn't seen the pictures, I'd be shocked right now.

A twig snaps in the darkness behind us. I turn toward the noise.

Carter peers into the woods, then back at me. "Sorry I showed you the gun. I promise I had zero intention of using it. I brought it to protect you. But then you weren't cooperating. We had to talk somewhere alone and away from Elliot's house."

"Why?"

"Because you're in danger."

CHAPTER 46

Another sound comes from the dark woods. An animal? It hardly matters right now. I'm more afraid of what I can see than what I can't. The man who manipulated and tricked me is standing in plain sight, and he has a gun.

"Why did you track me down and pretend to be Elliot's attorney?"

"It's complicated."

"Obviously, or I would have a clue about why."

Carter looks over his shoulder, more worried about whatever is out there than I am. "For the record, I never told you my name. When I met you and mentioned where I worked, you just assumed I was Lance. I said I came to see you on Elliot's behalf, but I never told you I was his attorney."

I stare at him, thinking he's crazier than I imagined. "Yes, you did."

He folds his arms. "No. I didn't."

Is that correct? I guess it's possible, but I don't know. It hardly matters. "You had plenty of chances to set the record straight, but you continued to deceive me and let me believe you were Lance Hutchinson."

"I tried to tell you at the restaurant. I said you'd made an assumption, and it was awkward now. You said you knew who I was and understood my relationship to Elliot."

"What? I... that's not what we were talking about...I thought..." My words trail. I'm trying to relive the conversation and see if he's not as guilty as I think, but how can I be sure of anything right now. When I recall the feelings I was developing for Carter, I want to retch. He's what? An ex-half-step-brother? We're not related by blood, yet it still seems creepy.

"And I do work at Hartley & Hutchinson. In IT. Elliot got me the job. He's been good to me, even after he and my mother split up."

"That doesn't explain why you asked me so many questions. Why did you?" I shove my hands onto my hips.

He sighs, his breath misting in the cold air. "I overheard a conversation at work. Elliot Rhodes might have a daughter he never knew about. It was pretty *convenient* for a daughter to suddenly show up with everything that's happening at Granite Global."

"What's happening with Granite Global? And how would I have known about it?"

He shakes his head. "I can't tell you, but I had to find out if you were real or part of someone's scheme."

I cross my arms in defiance. "You thought I was running a scam? Seriously? I told you I didn't even know Elliot existed until the day before you showed up at my mother's house."

Carter shrugs. "I went about it all wrong. I can see that now, but I couldn't let you and your mother manipulate him." Carter moves closer. "I had good reason to suspect you at first."

Is any of this true? Or is it another trick? I back away, my mind racing. "Did Elliot know you were meeting with me?"

Carter shakes his head. "No, I planned to explain everything to both of you before you met him. Then I lost my chance."

I scoff.

"There's more, Haley. I haven't totally figured it out yet, can't prove it, but you're still in danger."

How can I believe a word he tells me after what he's done? I study his face. Is he playing me again? I couldn't detect his deception before, so I probably can't now. He said it was all to protect Elliot. That doesn't even make sense. Elliot can take care of himself. He has people like the real Lance looking out for his interests. So why would Carter do this?

An explanation creeps in. Elliot still has photos of Carter on display. They might be close. Is Carter an heir to Elliot's wealth? The only potential heir until I came along? If so, Carter has a vested interest in finding out if I'm legit. He also has a motive for wanting me gone.

Oh, my God. The train shooting.

I was the target.

Carter has a motive.

Light appears on the road behind us. Headlights.

When Carter turns to look, I sprint away from him, toward the trees.

"Haley, wait!"

I don't slow as I crash through the underbrush. Branches whip at my face and arms, pull at my hair, and tear Carter's coat from my shoulders. I crash through someone's yard and hear Carter behind me. I don't look back.

My lungs burn as I dart behind the next house, where I'm hidden by a tall privacy fence.

Still moving, I pull my phone from my back pocket. The screen is black.

"Come on, come on." I shake the device, but the battery is dead.

I peer around the fence, hoping I won't see Carter.

In the distance, a car is coming this way.

I run toward the road, begging the driver to stop.

CHAPTER 47

The car approaches fast, glaring headlights expanding and blinding me. I wave my arms in a frantic motion and take a giant step onto the road.

"Stop! Please, stop!" I'm desperate enough to get into a stranger's car at night. No, when the car pulls over, I'll ask them to call the police.

The car isn't slowing. It swerves left, crossing the center line to avoid me, then speeds past. Its taillights disappear into the night.

I spin around. I don't see Carter. The road stretches empty in both directions. I'm not familiar with this area. I have no wallet. My phone is dead.

A rustling sound comes from behind the tall bushes across the street. I don't wait to find out what it is. I dart behind a privacy fence and through the yard to another road. My boots slap painfully with each step. I wish I had my running shoes.

The first house is dark. The occupants might be asleep. Or away.

"Haley! Where are you?"

Carter's voice makes me shudder. If I run to the front of the house, he'll see me or hear the knocking. If no one lets me in, I'll be trapped on the porch. His first attempt on my life might have failed—if he's truly the one responsible—but I can't risk him succeeding.

Frantic, I crouch and hide behind a three-sided fence concealing garbage bins.

"Haley!" Carter shouts again.

A dog barks. Then another.

I try not to move or even breathe.

The calling stops.

The dogs go quiet.

I count silently inside my head to track time. After a few minutes, I come out from behind the bins and alternate running with fast-walking, staying close to the tree line.

What might be only fifteen minutes seems like an eternity. My teeth chatter. Feet aching, I rub my hands up and down my arms as I move. My face is numb.

Finally, I spot blue and green lights in the distance. A gas station and convenience store. I move faster. The closer I get, the more paranoid I become. I look over my shoulder, half-expecting to see Carter emerge from the shadows and charge in my direction. This is the scene from the movies where the fleeing character seems so close to safety, only to get grabbed at the last second. The part where the audience jumps out of their seats shrieking. My shoulders rise, bracing myself for the dreaded moment to strike.

There's no one behind me when I lunge for the convenience store's door. A bell chimes when I enter as if I've made it across the finish line of a race I never signed up for. I spin around and peer through the glass door. If Carter is out there, I don't see him.

Inside the store, a young man with long, stringy hair sits behind the counter, scrolling on his phone.

With one hand on my racing heart, I try to catch my breath and stop panting. "I need help."

He stares at me.

"Can I use your phone? Please?"

He picks an ancient landline phone off its base and slides it across the counter.

Keeping my eyes on the front door, I dial the only number besides my own that I know by heart—my mother's. It rings and rings. Please pick up. My chances aren't good. She might sleep through the call. If she wakes up and sees an unknown number, she'll probably ignore it.

"Hello?"

Hearing my mother's sleepy voice is like reaching a life preserver in a dark ocean. "Thank God you answered."

"Haley? Is that you? What's wrong? What time is it?"

Detecting the fear in her voice, I try to sound normal. "I'm sorry to wake you. My phone died, and I need a favor."

"Are you still at Elliot's?"

"No." I look around for a clue to my current location. My gaze lands on a small sign by the register. "I'm at Nolan's Gas 'N Go."

"Oh, sweetie." My mother sounds fully awake now. "What happened?"

"I'll tell you later. But I'm okay."

"Then why are you at a gas station all by yourself? How did you get there?"

"I promise I'll explain everything later, but first, I need to get back to my apartment. Will you request an Uber for me?"

The cashier, who has been listening to my conversation, gives the store's address.

I don't hang up until my mother confirms the Uber is coming. I can't wait to get into my apartment and lock the door.

I sink into a chair by the counter where I can see the front entrance. This nightmare is far from over. Carter is still out there. And I still don't know the truth. Is he trying to kill me, or was he trying to protect me?

CHAPTER 48

My Uber driver keeps glancing in the rearview mirror. I'm disheveled and coatless. He must wonder if I'm too drugged or drunk to register that it's freezing cold outside.

"Can you turn up the heat?" I ask, and he does.

I smooth my tangled hair and touch something crunchy that shouldn't be there. Lurching forward, I fling it away, then see it's just dried leaves from my run through the woods.

I catch the driver looking at me again. "I'm okay." I tell him, or perhaps it's an attempt to reassure myself. I'm still trying to process what happened.

The ride drops me off in front of my apartment building. I clamber out of the car. When I go for my purse, I realize I don't have it. No purse. No keys. I've left everything at Elliot's house.

Tears of frustration sting my eyes. This night has been insane. I need it to end. Then I remember delivering a spare key to Ms. Berner a few days ago. My first stroke of luck in days.

It's past one a.m. I feel sick about waking her at this hour. I'll probably scare her, but she's my only option. She's about to regret exchanging keys with me. Plus, I've already borrowed cat food and asked her to feed Moose. A basket of baked goods and new cat toys is in order, maybe a gift card to wherever she gets her nails done.

I press her buzzer. No response. I press it again, shuffling my feet and rubbing one arm. The cold is unbearable.

A gravelly voice finally crackles through the intercom. "Who's there? Stop ringing or I'll call the police!"

"Ms. Berner. It's Haley from across the hall. I'm so sorry to wake you. I don't have my keys. Could you please let me into the building, then let me use the spare I gave you for my place?"

"Haley? It's you?" She starts off sounding relieved, but her tone changes to irritation. "Good Lord, girl. Do you know what time it is? I nearly had a heart attack."

"So sorry, Ms. Berner. I wouldn't bother you if it weren't an emergency."

"You young people enjoy gallivanting from bar to bar, but I go to sleep at nine pm."

I'm too numb with cold to correct her. "It won't happen again, I promise." I wait, shuffling my feet and hugging my body until the door buzzes open.

"Come on up. And I'm going to need a minute to find where I put your key."

Five minutes later, after profuse apologies and promises to make it up to her, visions of a gift basket peace offering forming in my head, I'm at my apartment. I nearly sob with relief when I get the door open.

Inside, I lock the door, double-check it, and plug in my phone. As fast as I can, I grab two blankets and wrap them around my body to stop shivering.

Once my phone has enough power, I send a message to my mother so she won't worry.

I'm home. Sorry about waking you. Talk tomorrow. Thank you for helping me.

My phone rings. It's Elliot.

I don't answer; he keeps calling. While my phone was out of commission, I missed multiple calls from him. When I finally answer, it's only to prevent him from sending the police to my apartment.

"Haley? Oh, thank God. When you left your things at my house and didn't answer your phone, I was worried. Are you okay?"

"Yes, I'm not hurt." My body isn't, aside from the blisters my boots caused.

"I watched the security footage from earlier. I know who you left with."

Who I left with? Strange way to phrase it. Sounds like I took off for a late-night burger with a friend.

I close my eyes. "It was Carter. Your stepson. He never actually said he was Lance, but he certainly let me believe he was."

"I'm sorry about the miscommunication, Haley."

"Miscommunication?" I let out an incredulous huff.

"I promise I'll handle the situation. Where is Carter now?"

"I got away from him. I don't know where he is now."

"Where are you? In your apartment?"

I don't answer.

"I need to see you. To make sure you're okay and talk face to face. I'd feel much better if you were at my house where someone can keep an eye on you. I'm sending a driver to pick you up."

"Don't send anyone. I have to call the police."

"Please don't. Let me handle this. I'm ordering you a ride as we speak. A car will be there in less than ten minutes. A gray Honda Civic. The driver's name is Mike."

"I'm not leaving my apartment, Elliot. I can't go anywhere right now."

"Haley, you shouldn't be there alone. You must be afraid. Let me look after you until we resolve this matter."

I'm not comfortable leaving, but I need to retrieve my purse with my license and credit cards. I can't function without those. Or is returning to Elliot's house too risky? I'm so confused.

"I need time. I'll call you back tomorrow." I hang up, needing to wrap my head around the crazy evening and all that I've just learned. Despite Elliot's plea to handle the situation, I've already decided to call the police. Detectives Millard and Desai need to know about Carter and his potential motive.

Leaning against the wall, I sort through what to tell them first. Carter's deception, or how he abducted me from Elliot's house? It's all incredible, and I don't want my story rushing out in a jumbled panic that makes me sound unhinged.

As I'm going over what to include, I freeze. Something isn't quite right. Did a door just click?

Goosebumps prickle my skin.

"Moose?" I whisper, rising to my feet. "Hello?"

I've been through so much tonight. I might be imagining things.

"It's just Moose," I murmur aloud to convince myself.

Another click. It's neither Moose nor my imagination.

Silence follows.

A figure emerges from the shadows.

There's someone in my kitchen!

I scream.

CHAPTER 49

Someone is in my apartment.

My heart races, but my body is paralyzed. I consider lunging for my phone or the golf club behind my bedroom door. The golf club is closer. I regain control of my wits, dash to grab it, then whirl around.

"Haley? What are you doing?"

"Adam?"

He steps out of the darkness and comes into focus.

Dropping the golf club, I stumble toward him. "Oh God. I was so scared."

He wraps his arms around me, and I cling to him, trembling. I let myself sink into his embrace, setting aside all the complications between us. I'm so grateful Adam is here, holding me tight.

Once my fear ebbs, I feel incredibly foolish. I can't believe I thought Adam tried to kill me. I thought he was responsible for the shooting, when all along, it must have been Carter.

"Shhh, it's okay," he whispers. "I've got you. Tell me what happened."

Through hiccups, I say, "Carter abducted me. He wants to kill me."

Adam's body tenses. "What? Slow down, Haley. Who is Carter?"

I try to calm myself before pouring out the entire story. There's so much he doesn't know yet. I share the news of my biological father and eventually reach the part about Carter. "He's Elliot's stepson."

"Wow, you've really stepped into it, haven't you?" Adam says, guiding me to the couch.

"Why would Carter deceive you?" he asks as we sit.

"Elliot is well-off. Maybe Carter was worried about Elliot's money, a future inheritance."

"This is huge, Haley. You have to tell the police right away."

I was going to do exactly that, but now that Adam is here, I feel a little better. I have time to sort things out. Something Carter said has stuck with me. The part about me being in danger, and him trying to help.

I rest my head against Adam's shoulder. "It's not an emergency now. It's late, and I'm tired. I'll call the detectives in the morning."

He lifts my chin. "You should call now. Tell them everything."

I open my mouth and yawn for a full five seconds. Not only am I tired, but Elliot told me not to call the police. He was very clear about it. If I disregard his wishes, it might be the end of our relationship. It would be over before it barely got started. That might be for the best, but I can't bring myself to do it yet. I need to sort things out tomorrow when I can think clearly.

"Come on, Haley. I came all the way here."

I pull back from Adam so I can look at his face. "Wait. What are you doing here? Why were you in my apartment?"

Something shifts in his expression. "Why am I here?" he repeats in a low voice.

I move away from him and stand up. "How did you get in?"

Adam also stands, looming over me. "You gave me a key so I could check on Moose."

I make myself sound calm, not accusatory, despite warning signals going off inside me. "I didn't ask you to check on him today."

"I called you earlier. You didn't answer. I came to wait for you."

"Inside my apartment in the dark?"

"I had a headache, turned the lights off, I must have fallen asleep. I was waiting for you to come home."

"Why?"

"Detectives questioned me today. The ones working the train case. They asked me for an alibi and had a dozen questions about our relationship. What did you say to them, Haley?"

"I told them we were separated. Nothing else."

He narrows his eyes. "I'm having trouble believing you. The police questioned me as if I were their primary suspect. They want to pin the train shooting on me."

"They've questioned me several times, Adam. That's what they do. They try to rattle people."

He raises his voice, speaking faster. "No. You must have told them something. And why haven't you called them about Carter yet, when he's obviously the one you should be afraid of? He just abducted you, for Christ's sake! I don't want them looking into my business when I've done nothing wrong. You're the one who hurts people."

"I do not hurt people, and I did not hurt your grandfather."

Adam removes something from his pocket. He shakes an orange bottle, rattling the pills inside, then thrusts it in my face. "Looks like an unmarked container. Last I knew, you didn't take any medication. So, why don't you explain what they are and why you have them?"

I take a better look at the container. Hard to do when he's holding it so close to my face. It's the bottle I found next to a patient's bedside. The one I meant to give my supervisor. Then my shift got busy, and Lauren woke up. I accidentally carried the pills home with me.

I stare at Adam. "Where did you get that?"

"Found it in your bathroom. Did you use these to poison my grandfather?"

"You have no right to search my bathroom now, and I didn't kill Frank! We've been through this. He died of natural causes."

Adam's bitter laugh makes his handsome face look cruel. "Natural causes? Is that what you call it when you slip something into an innocent person's drink?"

"The autopsy didn't find anything!"

"The autopsy was inconclusive. Obviously, you knew what you were doing. And let's not forget about the coconut oil on his water glass."

I can only shake my head. That tiny little finding is what has Adam convinced. Yes, there was a trace of coconut oil on Frank's water glass, and no traces of it anywhere else in Frank's house. I don't remember touching Frank's water glass with my bare hands when I was there, but I was so upset about his request and then our argument. It's possible I forgot.

Fear clouds my thoughts. A few minutes ago, I was leaning into Adam for comfort, so sure Carter was my biggest threat. Now I'm confused again. Adam's face is contorted into a snarl. He's been nursing his suspicions and his grudge for months. The detectives' questions might have pushed him over the edge.

"Adam, please." I move farther away. I can't keep doing this, and yet I am. We're locked in a stalemate of accusation and denial. Even if Adam's suspicions disappear and he apologizes, the trust between us has shattered. "Frank frustrated me, but I also loved him. And I would never hurt anyone. It's the complete opposite of what I do."

"I need the truth about my grandfather."

"He died, just like thousands of people do every day all over the world. He was watching a football game, drinking, and probably shouting at the refs. I'm sorry it happened; I really am, but I'm the one who should be angry. How dare you keep accusing me!"

Adam glares. "I know you hated him."

"I hated the way he treated you. There's a big difference."

"You thought you were helping, didn't you? Freeing me from his control?"

"It wasn't like that." I inch backwards, toward my bedroom, where my phone is charging. "There's nothing new to say. Enough is enough! You need to leave."

A dangerous glint flickers in his eyes. Before I can jump away, he lunges forward. His hand closes around my arm with bruising force.

I gasp. Adam has never laid a hand on me before.

Twisting, I wrench my arm free and stumble backwards before righting myself and dashing toward my bedroom.

Adam is faster.

He slams into me, driving the air from my lungs. We crash down together. My forehead connects with the floor. Bright shapes explode behind my eyes.

He has me pinned down and immobile. I can't breathe.

"I'm sorry, Haley." His voice is oddly calm considering what he's just done, what he's still doing. He digs his fingers into my wrist and presses my hands to the floor above my head. "I can't let you go. Not until you confess."

I struggle to draw a breath. This can't be happening. "Get off me," I hiss. "I won't confess to something I didn't do."

A loud buzz from the intercom system catches both of us by surprise and allows me to scramble out from under him.

A man's voice cuts through the static. "Haley? It's Mike. I've been waiting in my car. You ready to go?"

Mike? I can't think of anyone named Mike until I remember. He's the driver Elliot called.

"Yes!" I shout, using the intercom in my bedroom. "Don't leave. I'm coming. One minute. I just have to pack a bag."

"Who is Mike?" Adam snarls. "How many men are you seeing?"

I hurry to grab my phone, charger, and a few other things. "I'm leaving. I have to be alone and think things through. Take Moose, because I might not be back for a few days."

"You need to tell the detectives..."

"Tell them what?" I ask, cutting him off. "Carter must be responsible because you'd never hurt me? You just blew that defense out of the water."

Gasping for breath, I can't even think about what might have happened next. How far would Adam go to get me to confess?

I truly can't believe the situation I'm in. It's now an equal toss-up between Adam and Carter as to who wants to kill me more.

CHAPTER 50

During the drive to Elliot's house, my mind is blank, barely registering the eighties music filling the car or the Red Bull can in the driver's console. Mike. His name is Mike. I'm numb with exhaustion. Everything seems distant and surreal.

My gaze drops to my wedding rings. I slip them off and put them in my pocket.

When my ride stops at Elliot's house, the front windows are ablaze with light. Elliot is waiting outside.

"I'll turn on the security system and the motion detectors," he says, helping me out of the car.

I'm so tired as I trudge up the path to his house. At least I've got comfortable shoes this time.

"I'm so sorry," he repeats. "You must have been frightened."

"Yes, I was." I assume he's apologizing for Carter's lies and my abduction. He doesn't even know what just occurred with Adam in my apartment.

"What did Carter say when you were with him?" Elliot asks.

"Not much before I ran off. I don't understand his game."

"It will all be okay. We'll sort this out," Elliot leads me toward the kitchen. "Here, I'm going to make you some decaf tea. The box claims it's a calming blend. Then you should get some sleep."

I sit at the kitchen table on a leather banquette bench, wrapping my arms around myself, while Elliot microwaves a mug of water with a tea bag inside. It's the second cup of tea he's made for me in the past few hours.

"I'm going to turn the security system on now. With you and Lance here earlier, with all that happened, my usual routine was out of whack."

He returns right after the microwave beeps. "The doors are all locked. The system is on."

When he finally sits across from me, he glances at his watch and adjusts his cuffs.

"What's your relationship with Carter like? Are you close?"

"He lived with me and his mother for a few years when he was younger. I treated him like my own son." Elliot's voice softens. There's pain or regret in his expression. "I loved him and still do. It broke my heart when Jules left me and took him with her."

I remember what Carter told me at the restaurant. His father cheated. His mother remarried in Chicago. That marriage didn't last long either. He was talking about Elliott.

"Why did she leave?" After today, with my life already in danger and this bizarre situation with Carter, I'm bolder with my questions and less concerned about politeness.

Elliot frowns. "Somebody convinced Jules I cheated on her. She claimed she had evidence but never shared it with me. Never gave me a chance to convince her I hadn't. After she moved across the country and cut off all communication, she wouldn't let me see Carter."

"But you see him now?"

"He called a few years ago about moving back to Chicago. Through Lance, I helped him get the IT job at Hartley & Hutchinson. Carter and

I are close now. We have a weekly lunch meeting. I've done my best to stay in his life. I paid his college fees. Made sure he had everything he needed."

"So, why was he interviewing me? Why didn't he tell me who he was from the start? What was the endgame?"

"I don't know. Tomorrow is Thursday. The day we meet for lunch. We'll sort this out then. In the meantime, I'd appreciate your patience and not calling the police. I consider Carter family. I'd prefer not to ruin his life without hearing his side of the story."

I wrap my hands around the warm cup. "Elliot, he didn't just deceive me. It's possible he tried to kill me."

"Tonight?"

I'm still holding the mug, letting its heat spread through my fingers. Not drinking. This conversation is way more than I'm willing to go into right now, but it's important for Elliot to understand. "I don't know what he might have done if I hadn't run from him. But that's not what I'm talking about. I mean, when Lauren Christensen got shot on the train. I changed seats at the last minute. Lauren took mine. The detectives say it's possible I was the target."

I let the news sink in for a moment before saying, "What if Carter arranged a hit to get rid of me, to secure your inheritance or your house or whatever it is you have?"

Elliot leans back against his chair, his shoulders slumping. "Haley, that's not reasonable."

"After everything that he's done—tracking me down and interviewing me—does it seem like that much of a stretch?" Yet even as I ask this, I remember Carter putting his jacket around me and apologizing. He needed to tell me something. If only I'd stayed long enough to hear it. But no... escaping him was the smart decision.

Elliot scoffs. "I'm not old, Haley. I'm fifty-three and in perfect health. No one is going to benefit from my death in the near future. At least I hope not."

I can't help thinking Elliot might be Carter's next target. Get rid of me first, then Elliot.

He's silent for a long moment. Maybe he's thinking along the same lines as I am. Finally, he speaks, sounding just as tired as I feel. "The idea of Carter wanting to kill you is preposterous. But I can't explain why he deceived you. I will find out. And I promise you're safe here."

I hold my tea up, letting the heat mist my chin. "What happens now?"

Elliot leans forward, his eyes meeting mine. "You'll get some much-needed rest, and then we'll figure this out."

I want to believe Elliot is in my corner, but how can I trust him or anyone now? I have doubts about everyone in my life. My gut is still bugging me to notify the police, but I can barely keep my eyes open. I need sleep, rather than staying up into the early morning hours recounting my terrible evening while the detectives take notes and ask more questions. Besides, I'm sure they won't appreciate being woken up for something that can wait until morning.

"Let me make this right, Haley. I may not have known about you for most of your life, but now I'll do anything to protect you."

I set my tea down. "We're not off to a good start. It's been a little rocky, hasn't it?"

He offers a sad smile. "Yes, it has. But we'll get past this."

His words are comforting, but the rational part of my brain reminds me I barely know him. The last person I trusted turned out to be lying, and he's part of Elliot's inner circle.

"I'll get answers," he says. "Now finish your tea."

I offer a weak smile, but I haven't taken a single sip, and I don't plan to.

When I return to the guest room, I lock the door from the inside, then lie down and shut my eyes. I'm exhausted, but I can't let my guard down. Carter is somewhere out there. So is Adam. And I'm now locked inside Elliot's estate. Elliot is powerful, probably used to getting exactly what he wants. He's the kind of man who can make problems disappear.

CHAPTER 51

Something is going on with the bedsheets. They're different. So soft and smooth. Then I remember I'm in Elliot's guestroom. Everything comes back. Carter forcing me into his car. Adam's assault. Returning to Elliot's house because I didn't know what else to do.

My wrist is sore. Purple bruises surround it. Adam caused those.

Can my life get any more frightening?

A soft knock at the door precedes Elliot's voice. "Haley? Are you awake?"

"Yes."

"Good morning. Are you a breakfast person?"

"Sometimes. Coffee for sure." My throat is dry and hoarse, probably from running and gasping for breath in the cold last night.

"Good. Come down when you're ready. We'll talk."

"I'll be down in a few minutes."

Before getting out of bed, I check my phone.

The first message is from Carter. He's still listed as Lance Hutchinson in my contacts.

I'm sorry about last night. I can explain everything. Please give me a chance.

I ignore it, just like he ignored my calls and texts when he realized I'd met with Elliot.

There are several missed calls from Adam. As I read the notifications, another text from him pops up.

Haley, please. I'm sorry. Can we meet to talk?

Both men are suddenly sorry and need to talk to me. Well, I have no desire to see either of them.

I can still feel the weight of Adam's body on top of me, pinning me down. Carter also made me afraid, but Adam... it's worse... I've known him so much longer. His change in behavior came as more of a shock. A total blindside. Did he always have a violent side to him, or did he just crack?

Another text from Adam follows. *I went too far because I was upset. My behavior was out of line. Please accept my apologies.*

I don't respond. If only it had never happened, but I can't erase it from my mind, nor should I. When victims of domestic abuse come into the ER, I always empathize with them. Yet, I never truly expected to experience that shock and betrayal myself.

Incredibly, Adam's physical assault is probably not the worst thing that's happened to me in the last three weeks, but thinking about it, which I can't seem to stop doing, makes my stomach twist in knots. I'm worried about trusting him with Moose. What if he takes his anger out on the cat?

I type a message. *How's Moose?*

Time passes. I start to worry. Then the response comes. A video of Moose curled up on the couch next to Adam's hip, looking as content as ever. He's purring as Adam strokes his fur.

The same man who attacked me, who accused me of murder, is sending me sweet videos of our cat. I zoom in on the image, studying Moose's peaceful face, and tears prick at the corners of my eyes. It's as if everything has changed. Before last night, I wanted Adam back. I wanted Jessica to disappear, and my old life restored. I don't want that now. Maybe I'll never want it again.

After wiping tears from my eyes, I simply type: *Take good care of Moose. Brush his teeth with the coconut oil or at least sprinkle some on his dinner.*

Adam likes my message and responds: *I will.*

He doesn't enjoy brushing the cat's teeth. Not that I do either, but it's always been my job. On the few occasions when I've asked Adam to do it, he always grumbled. There's no question he is trying to get back on my good side now. But why? He still believes I'm capable of unthinkable things. He doesn't trust me. So why is he trying now?

My answer comes in his next text.

Did you tell the detectives about Carter? He's the one they should be hounding. Not me.

I stare at it, frustrated that everyone is telling me what to do.

I told Adam to stop following me, but I'm not sure if he did. With a few swipes and a tap, I turn off my location so he can't see where I am. Before, I always wanted the safety net. I wanted Adam to know where to find me in case something happened. That's when I worried about what strangers might do to me.

Now I'm more afraid of the men I know.

After a quick shower, I change into running pants and a sweatshirt and make my way down the long staircase to the first floor. There must be cameras in every room, as evidenced by the monitors I saw, but they're hidden well. I can't find even one.

The house seems different in the daylight. Less threatening now that I can see there's no one lurking in the corners. I make a mental note of the switch panel at the bottom of the stairs, higher than expected, in case I ever find myself alone here in the dark again.

The smell of freshly brewed coffee comes from the kitchen. I need it so badly. I'll have to set my trust issues aside.

Elliot wears a black apron over his pants and sweater. "Good morning, Haley. I hope you're hungry."

I take in the spread he's set out on the table. A plate heaped with scrambled eggs, a bowl of fresh fruit, pastries and donuts, bacon, and bagels with cream cheese and jam. I'm famished, but I can't believe he's gone through so much trouble for the two of us. Perhaps he hasn't.

"Are you expecting anyone else?"

"No, it's just you and me. Breakfast is my favorite meal. I wasn't sure what you liked, so I made some of everything."

"You sure did. Wow. Thank you."

He pours two mugs of coffee. I take a sip of mine, and it's amazing.

Elliot sets his mug down. "I was up all night thinking and talking to Lance. I have a course of action to propose."

As I listen, I reach across the table for a bagel. When my sweatshirt sleeve rides up, I retrieve my arm quickly to hide my bruises.

"I'll see Carter today for lunch," he continues. "I'll find out why he misled you and why he insisted you leave with him last night."

I stay quiet, pulling my sleeves down.

"The second item is the train assault investigation, and the detectives' suggestion that you were the target. The not-knowing factor doesn't sit well with me. I'm sure you and Lauren Christensen are struggling with it more than anyone else. I'd like to hire a private investigator, or an entire firm, whatever is needed, to figure it out."

"But the police are already investigating."

Elliot picks up his fork, though he has yet to take a bite to eat. "And have they found anything yet?"

I hate to admit it, but from what I can tell, they have not.

When my only answer is a shrug, Elliot continues. "Weeks have passed. They're instilling more fear than confidence in those affected by the ordeal. Private investigators mean additional resources and a fresh perspective. I've already asked Lance to get it done."

"Why Lance?"

"He knows the right people to call. They'll want to meet with you, though. Ask you the same questions the police must have asked. It might be traumatizing. I wish it weren't necessary, but it is. Are you okay with that?"

"I'll tell them anything I can if it will help catch whoever is responsible."

I'm grateful for Elliot's proposal. It makes me think Granite Global can't possibly be involved. But what will he do if the investigators uncover evidence implicating Carter?

"Your courage is admirable," Elliot says, finally putting food on his own plate. "And there's just a few more things." He sets down the serving spoon and looks at me. "Consider staying here for a few days. Or longer. However long you feel comfortable. I'd enjoy your company, and you won't have to be alone while you're going through this."

"Oh."

He laughs. "You'll need to think about it, of course." He leans toward me. "There's one more thing I'd like to propose. Why don't we bring your mother to stay also? I have several guest rooms to choose from. I know she's currently undergoing chemotherapy, and I can help her with it."

His offer really surprises me. It's unexpected, but also thoughtful. Not crazy. A good idea. Elliot's place isn't far from the treatment clinic. But the decision isn't up to me, and I'm not sure how my mother will react.

"It's kind of you. But won't we seem a little intrusive? You must have work things to keep you busy during the day."

Elliot's expression softens. "Haley, right now you're my priority."

Suddenly, I'm a little overwhelmed. "Thank you. I just need to think about it for a bit. And talk to my mother."

"I understand. Tell me after you discuss it, and then I'll call her." He pats my hand. "For your safety, I'd prefer you to decide soon. But the offer stands indefinitely. You're both welcome here anytime."

As we finish our breakfast, I consider my situation. A few weeks ago, I didn't know this man existed. I never imagined I'd have another father. Now he's asking my mother and me to move in until the authorities or his private investigators figure out who was behind the train shooting incident.

If Elliot harbors any resentment for keeping my birth a secret, he's hiding it well, and I admire that. We can't change the past. We can only control what happens next, what we do with this new knowledge. Elliot acts as if he doesn't want to waste another minute of the time we have. He wants me in his life, and my mother is part of that equation. He wants his future to include us.

That's what I want to believe so I can stop being paranoid and start trusting him.

Over breakfast, he tells me about his college tennis team days and his tennis injuries. I share adventures from the time I spent traveling around

Europe with a friend, a college graduation gift from my parents. It's normal conversation, which is a relief. When we're finished, a surprising amount of food is gone. I push my chair away from the table.

"I'm going to refill my coffee and take it upstairs with me if that's okay."

"Haley, please. Consider this your home while you're here. You don't need to ask my permission."

"Thank you." As I reach for the coffeepot, my sleeve rides up again. I quickly pull it back down to my wrist. Not quick enough.

"What happened to your arm?" There's a stern tone in Elliot's voice that wasn't there before.

My first instinct is to brush it off. "It's nothing," I mumble, but even I can hear the lack of conviction in my voice. I sound just like my patient in the ER, denying the truth.

Elliot stands, coming around the table. He's not going to accept my lame excuse. "You didn't have those marks yesterday. Did Carter give you those bruises?"

There's an internal debate going on in my head about what to admit, but it doesn't last long. I blow out a long breath, then answer, "Carter didn't hurt me. It was Adam."

Elliot's expression shifts from concern to anger. "Your husband? Is that something he's done before?"

"No, he hasn't. Never." It's very important he believes me.

"What happened?"

"He was waiting inside my apartment last night. Apparently, the police questioned him about the train incident. They treated him as a suspect. He wasn't happy about it."

Elliot's eyes widen. "Why would they suspect your husband? Because you're separated, or is there another reason?"

I just want to take my coffee upstairs and try to relax, to forget about all this awfulness for even a few minutes. But if Adam's accusations are going to come out, it's better Elliot hears about them from me.

We sit back down, and I tell him the same story I recently told Carter. Adam suspects me in his grandfather's death. When I finish speaking, Elliot claps his hands into a tight ball, and I'm clenching my jaw just as hard.

"I didn't hurt Frank," I say.

Elliot grimaces, as if my words affected him. "I told you about my ex-wife. That she believes I cheated on her. She never gave me a chance to explain myself, never questioned what she'd been told. I didn't cheat. I never would. But once someone plants a seed of suspicion... I know what it's like to be accused of something you'd never do." He trails off, shaking his head. "Do the police really think Adam could be behind the train shooting? That he tried to kill you because of his suspicions?"

"I don't know. The thing is, I never thought he would lay a hand on me until he did last night. And Adam always knew my exact location." I glance at my phone on the table. "That's no longer the case. I've turned off the share function." I press my lips together, shocked because I'm starting to believe it's possible my husband hired someone to kill me. "I guess he has a motive. And the means to pay for it. And now this." I hold my arms out to display the marks around my wrists.

"That's the last time Adam is going to hurt you." Elliot lifts his phone and taps the screen. He waits a few seconds. "Lance? It's me. I need your help with a restraining order. As soon as you can get it."

Elliot and I fill Lance in on the situation, and just like that, the restraining order is underway. I'm relieved and appalled. It happened so quickly.

Is it too much or warranted? I never imagined my marriage could end up where it is today.

Elliot frowns after the call. "I hoped to meet Adam, but after this, it's best I don't. We're going to make sure he can't come anywhere near you without facing repercussions." He leans down and pulls me into a gentle hug. It's a little awkward at first, but long overdue and exactly what I need right now.

"Thank you."

"You don't have to thank me. You're my daughter. I'm going to take care of you."

CHAPTER 52

I'm alone outside on Elliot's patio in my winter coat. It's chilly, but there's no wind, and I'm not having a private phone conversation inside the house. The security cameras might also record sound.

I turn my phone over in my hands, wrestling with what to tell my mother. I want to spare her the ugly details of my current life. When I finally told her about the separation, I didn't share the catalyst. But after confessing to Elliot, keeping the truth from her is wrong. If she learns about Adam's accusations from someone else, she might never forgive me. Well... that's not true. She'd forgive me for anything, but she deserves to hear it from me.

In considering Elliot's offer to stay at his house, I'm mostly thinking about her well-being. Carter knows where my mother lives. He could show up and threaten her. So might Adam. Elliot's house, with its alarm system and all of us here, is the safest place for her right now. If Elliot hires a good private investigator to get to the bottom of the train assault, we might not be here for long.

I press her name at the top of my favorites screen.

"Haley? Are you home?"

I can tell she's concerned and has been worrying about me since last night. I should have called right away.

"No, I'm at Elliot's house again."

"You went back this morning?"

"I came back last night and slept in his guest room. Listen, Mom, is this a good time for you to talk? I need to tell you something. Several things."

"Yes, anytime is a good time if you need me. You know that, dear. What is it?"

"It might take a while. And please don't freak out."

"You're scaring me. What's going on?"

"Okay." I swallow. "When I got to my apartment last night, Adam was there. He pushed me down and hurt my wrists. But I'm okay."

"What?" She sounds shocked. "He hurt you? Why?"

"He was angry. He's been angry with me for months. Since his grandfather died."

"But you don't know why?"

I'm digging my thumbnail into my index finger and tearing the cuticle, so I stuff my hand into my coat pocket to stop myself. "I do. I just couldn't bring myself to tell you before."

"What happened, Haley?"

"Adam thinks I'm somehow responsible for his grandfather's death. Remember, I told you I went to see Frank the day he died, and we argued?"

I hear a sharp intake of breath before my mother speaks. "He thinks you killed Frank?" she whispers, as if she can't bear to say the words aloud.

"He suspects me and can't seem to get over it."

"It must be his grief. He needs someone to blame."

"Yeah, well, he blames me. After Frank's death, he started looking at me strangely. Then he wouldn't look at me at all. He couldn't. Then he began voicing his suspicions, asking questions. Next thing I know, he'd found me an apartment, paid the first three months' rent, and told me I had to move out."

"But Frank died of natural causes."

"I'm sure he did, but Adam is convinced the tests missed something."

"That's preposterous. Oh, Haley. Why didn't you tell me?"

My voice cracks as I struggle to explain why I kept something so important from my mother. I feel sick about it now. "It's humiliating. How could anyone think I would do such an awful thing? Especially my husband!"

"Adam isn't the man I thought he was if he believes that. I mean, good God, does he realize you carry spiders out of the house in a tissue rather than stomping on them?"

I nod even though she can't see me. "So, there's more.... because Adam assaulted me, Elliot and his attorney helped me file a restraining order. If Adam comes near me again, he'll get arrested."

There's another gasp before my mother simply says, "Oh."

Her shock and anger don't surprise me. They're part of the reason I didn't want to tell her and make her upset.

"Why did you call me from the gas station last night?" she asks. "Did it have something to do with Adam?"

My hand is back out of my pocket, and I'm pinching my cuticles again, procrastinating another few seconds.

"There's more." I take a few breaths before launching into the tale of Carter's deception.

The story renders my mother speechless again.

"The man who was at my house?" she finally asks. "He's Elliot's stepson?"

"Yes. He never said he was Elliot's attorney, but for good reason I assumed he was. He didn't go out of his way to set things straight."

"What does Elliot say about it?"

"He wants to hear Carter's side of the story. They're meeting today. Meanwhile, with everything so crazy right now, I'm worried you might not be safe there alone."

"I'll be fine, Haley. I'm only worried about you. Does Elliot think Carter poses a danger?"

"He says he doesn't."

"Hmm."

"So, here's an idea." I try to sound upbeat. "Elliot asked me to stay at his house for a while until everything dies down." My choice of words makes me cringe. *Settled down* would have been a better option. "Elliot says it's best if you stayed here, too. There's plenty of room."

"Elliot suggested I move in?"

I'm surprised at her tone. It's not dismissive like I expected. "He did. It's a wild idea, but he thought it would be good for all of us. He said he could help with your chemo. The treatment center is closer to here than your house. His place is enormous. And beautiful. You'll love the gardens. Even at this time of year, they're special."

"It would be nice to know him better, and a relief to be closer to you right now. I won't worry about you as much if we're together."

Her acceptance and the brightness in her voice catches me off guard. "You're okay with the idea? I mean, you're considering it?"

"After everything you've just told me, yes, I'm going to consider it. Let me think about what it would mean exactly."

"It won't be weird for you?" I ask. She'd be moving in with someone she barely knows at one of the most vulnerable stages of her life. Except I'll be with her, and she has only a few weeks of chemo left.

"Yes, it might be weird," she answers. "In fact, I'm sure it will be. But we're all adults now. Weird is something we can work through. After all this time, it's something we need to do. Talk. Get to know each other properly."

"Okay. Elliot told me to speak with you first, and depending on your reaction, he'll contact you."

As we end the call, I'm relieved. I've finally told my mother everything, and soon we might live together under one roof. While I never imagined life playing out this way, it's the safest situation for all of us right now. Why not accept Elliot's help when he seems so keen to provide it?

It's unreal. In a matter of days, my mother might be here, too. This is by far the strangest chapter of my life, but at least we'll face it together.

CHAPTER 53

"Can I get you anything to drink, Mr. Rhodes?" the server asks.

"We're good for now." My gaze goes to the water glasses he just filled.

"I'm fine, thanks," Carter echoes as he fidgets in his seat across from me.

We're in a quiet corner of my club, where privacy is guaranteed. It's where we always sit. After what happened with Haley, I wasn't sure if Carter was going to show up. He keeps looking around as if he's afraid I've tricked him. I would never do that. If what Haley told me is true, I'm disappointed and confused, but I still love him.

Before we order our meal, I take a direct approach and say, "I've met Haley. Is it true you pretended to be Lance?"

Carter flinches. "I never told her I was Lance. I said I was speaking on your behalf."

At least he isn't trying to deny it.

"What were you thinking?" I ask, keeping my voice low.

He unfolds his napkin, letting the silverware fall to the table, then wrings the cloth between his hands. "I'm sorry, Elliot."

I lean back in disbelief and yet grudging admiration for his audacity. Lance is fifty-two, with weathered skin from too much time on his sailboat. He's had some work done on his face—Botox for sure, and something with the skin around his eyes. In contrast, Carter is only thirty-three and has zero legal training, but he carries himself well and dresses like a professional. The standards for business dress have relaxed in recent years, especially for people like him who work behind the scenes in IT. But Carter wears sports coats and shirts that look custom-made. He and Lance have excellent clothes in common.

Carter's gaze goes to the front of the restaurant again before settling back on me. He's never had a problem looking me in the eye. No, he has. Once. He stole a Hawaiian shirt from the mall, trying to impress some older boys. I had to retrieve him from the security office. Fortunately, they didn't want to press charges. But he was twelve then, wanting to fit in at his new school. I was disappointed but understood what drove him to make such a poor decision. This is different.

"Why the gun?" I ask.

"I had it with me, not to use it. I just wanted to talk to her, to explain why I tracked her down."

That still doesn't make sense. "How did you find out about Haley?"

Carter twists the napkin tighter. "I overheard someone at the office saying a woman had called you and claimed you had a daughter. You hired a PI through the firm."

My jaw tightens with disgust. Someone at Hartley & Hutchinson discussed my personal life with little discretion. Not Lance. It must have been an associate or an investigator. I imagine someone in the firm's break room gossiping beside their fancy espresso machine.

Now that I've met Haley, I regret using a PI to dig into her background. I want to explain my decision, why it seemed necessary, so I start with, "Lance recommended I hire an investigator to make sure—"

Carter interrupts me. "I don't blame you for investigating her. That's what I was doing. I thought she was a con artist. I was worried about you."

"You don't have to worry about me. I've got people for that."

"Yeah. Lance. Anyway, I took the water bottle she drank from. I was going to get it tested against something of yours—see if the DNA matched."

"She's my daughter. I could tell after seeing her pictures."

"I know. I never got it done. And the more time I spent with her, the more I realized she was legit. And she's nice."

Carter's expression takes me back to the day his mother packed her things and left. I hear the same sadness in his voice now. Does he think Haley is replacing him in my life? He's not a child, but he might have seen Haley as a threat to his relationship with me. A threat he could sabotage. It's awful, but is it possible?

"I have to say… it's hard to understand what you did."

"Maybe you don't know people as well as you think," Carter mutters. "People can surprise you. Even those you trust." He looks away and shifts in his seat.

"Is there something else, Carter?" I can tell that there is.

He sighs. "No, that's everything. About misleading Haley… I wish it never happened."

"I'll salvage things and encourage her to forgive you. It will take time for her to trust you, I expect. But I want both of you in my life. You're like a son to me. Nothing can change that." I smile, but it's brief. "Carter, I have to ask you this, and for your own good, tell the truth."

He looks up, his face pale. "What?"

"Did you have anything to do with the shooting on the Chicago commuter train a few weeks ago?"

He recoils as if I've slapped him. "What? No. Jeez. God, no."

"I'm meeting with a PI firm today. As long as you're not involved, I'm hiring them to find out who is responsible."

"Yeah, do that," he says. "It's a good idea. For Haley's sake." Carter picks up his napkin and twists it tighter.

CHAPTER 54

I sit at the head of the conference table at Hartley & Hutchinson, drinking coffee from a china cup engraved with the firm's logo and waiting for the private investigator to arrive.

Lance taps his folder with a pen. "Reeves is ten minutes out. Before he arrives, we should discuss what Carter did. It's serious, Elliot."

"I agree." I take a deliberate sip of coffee before speaking again. "But there's something you should know first. It affects Carter's situation and your firm."

Lance's eyes narrow. "Go on."

"I'm not pleased with how Carter discovered I had a daughter. I should have had the opportunity to tell him myself. My terms. My timing. I had it all planned out and was looking forward to it. Instead, Carter overheard someone discussing it here. Apparently, my personal situation was the subject of gossip in your office."

Lance's mouth presses into a thin line. It's a reaction I've observed many times over the years. A tell he's never been able to suppress.

I set the cup down. Our eyes meet, and understanding passes between us, as I knew it would. Carter impersonated Lance to some extent. That's grounds for termination at any firm. But the confidentiality breach about my personal life would damage the firm's reputation if it got out. As a senior partner, Lance will do anything to avoid the problem.

Crossing my arms on the table, I lock eyes with Lance. "Perhaps it would be in everyone's best interest if both these unfortunate incidents were to remain unmentioned."

Lance stares back, unblinking. "It would."

That's all we have to say. We just cemented an agreement between friends who have been through so much together, sealed with nothing more than a look and the promise of mutual benefit. Clean and simple.

A knock comes from outside. We both turn toward the conference room door.

"Come in," Lance calls.

A lean man in his fifties enters wearing a suit and tie. He has the alert eyes of someone who notices everything. Jack Reeves runs the top private investigation firm in Chicago.

"Nice to meet you," I say as we shake hands.

Reeves takes a seat, never smiling. "You want to know if Haley James was the intended target of the commuter train shooting."

"Yes," I confirm. "If the crime wasn't random, I need to know who is behind it and why."

"Reeves is a former attorney," Lance explains. "His team provides meticulous documentation for their work. I can scan everything and share only major developments. Of course, you'll have full access to all the reports and findings whenever you want them."

Under other circumstances, I'd accept Lance's offer to play the middleman, allowing me time to handle my business matters and get to know Haley and Carol better. His billing rate is steep, but I can afford it, and he's always given me a discounted friend rate. In return, I've been extremely generous to him. It's why he's currently a substantial shareholder of

Granite Global stock, just like I am. This situation is different. "Given the personal nature of this investigation, I'd like to see everything."

We devote the next twenty minutes to discussing the train shooting and what the police have learned to date. Reeves has already done extensive research and clearly has connections to the ongoing investigation.

We're finishing up when Reeves faces me. "Mr. Rhodes, I should warn you. When my team investigates people's lives searching for motives, we often uncover things people prefer to keep hidden."

"I understand."

"And you're prepared for whatever we might find?"

My throat tightens as I consider the possibility of Carter's involvement. The danger to Haley or Lauren may still exist, and we need to figure out who is responsible and their motive. I refuse to believe Carter is guilty, but after he misled Haley, I'd be insane not to harbor some doubt. Solving this case is the best thing for all of us to move forward.

"Yes," I assure him. "I'm prepared."

As Reeves stands, I have a change of heart and consider calling off the entire investigation. But I stop myself. It's best to let Reeves do his thing. The truth usually comes out. In this case, because I have the resources to dig it up.

As I leave the offices of Hartley and Hutchinson, I worry I've set something in motion I can't control.

CHAPTER 55

The wind lifts the end of my scarf when I cross the street to the hospital, eager to start my shift. In the emergency room, I'm Nurse Haley James. I know what I'm doing. I have the skills and experience not to second-guess everything around me.

There's a lot happening today. My mother is moving into Elliot's house. Though it's temporary, I'm still surprised she agreed. I wonder how they'll act around each other and what they'll talk about.

As I approach the emergency room doors, I stop walking and freeze. Adam is waiting with a deep scowl on his face.

"A restraining order, Haley? Really?"

I thrust my arms forward to show him the bruising he caused, but my coat covers the discoloration. "That's right, Adam. A restraining order. You need to leave. You can't be here."

"Did your *new* father convince you not to trust me?" He takes a step toward me, reaching his arm.

I move away.

"Look, I told you I was sorry. I never meant to hurt you. You know me. I've never laid a hand on you before. I was upset. But I would never—"

"Stop," I interrupt. "You hurt me, and whether or not you *meant* to, it's not going to happen again, because I won't let it."

He presses his fingers against his temples. "Haley, the police suspect I hired a gunman to kill you. You have to tell them it's not true. You know I wouldn't."

I laugh. "I should just take your word for it? Yet you can't believe me when I tell you I'd never harm your grandfather?"

"That's different," Adam argues, his voice rising.

"What? How is it different?" I snap, surprised by my conviction now. Heads turn in our direction, and I lower my voice. "You chose to believe the worst of me. You let your suspicions destroy our marriage. And then..." My voice breaks. "You attacked me, Adam."

"I didn't attack you, Haley. I grabbed you. You tripped and fell over, and I ended up on top of you. I said I was sorry. It shouldn't have happened, but cut me a little slack for a one-time mistake. A restraining order is going too far. And coming on top of these allegations from the police, it's undeserved. Are you trying to destroy me?"

I stare at Adam, the man I've loved for years. Until recently, I would have done anything to regain his trust. Not anymore. "Leave now or I'm calling security."

He glares at me. For a terrifying second, I think he might lash out again. But then his shoulders slump. "I just wanted the truth, Haley. My grandfather didn't die of natural causes."

As he turns away, a deep sadness overwhelms me. This is truly the end of us.

I'm trembling as I hurry through the ER doors. Inside, I lean against the wall for a moment, staring straight ahead as I catch my breath.

Cara comes toward me. "Are you okay?" she asks. The look on her face tells me she knows I'm not. But there's too much going on, and I don't have enough time to share it.

I straighten. "Yes. I'm okay. Thank you."

I've become quite the liar myself.

Later, as I'm treating a child with a broken arm, and then a man with chest pains, I keep glancing over my shoulder. I half expect to see Adam striding toward me in blatant disregard of the restraining order. The possibility he wanted me dead, and still might, won't leave me alone. I have to focus. I can't make mistakes here, and mistakes happen when people are distracted.

When I check a patient's vitals, something I do multiple times throughout each shift, I go back to the night in my apartment and wonder if I misunderstood "the assault." Did I trip? Is the restraining order an overreaction? Elliot called Lance, setting everything in motion so quickly. Then I remember the bruises and can feel Adam's hands grabbing me. I have to shake off the sensation. No, I tell myself, don't attempt to rationalize his behavior. The restraining order was smart. Especially if Adam wants to kill me.

"BP's 140 over 90," I report to Dr. Burke, my voice shakier than I'd like.

"Nurse James!" The urgent call from outside the room makes me whip around. In the split second after hearing my name, my mind floods with terrible possibilities. I imagine someone bursting through the double doors with a weapon. I have to protect the patients. Get everyone down.

"We need you in Trauma Two."

It takes a second to realize I overreacted. I have to get a grip on my emotions.

CHAPTER 56

Elliot picks me up when my shift ends. I scan the parking lot before hurrying through the frigid air to his car.

"Hi, thanks for getting me." I buckle up beside him, already appreciating the heated seat. I'm dying to know about his meeting with Carter and if my mother is settled. "How did today go?"

"Busy day. Met with Carter. He admits to misleading you."

I didn't realize part of my story was ever in doubt. Did Elliot think I was lying? Or delusional? Frowning, I ask, "What did he say about it?"

"He's sorry. There was a misunderstanding, and he didn't go far enough to correct it. He was trying to protect me. We're hoping you can forgive him."

Before I can ask more questions, Elliot continues. "I met with the PI I hired to investigate the shooting. His team will figure out what the detectives haven't."

"Good. I hope so." Regardless of what Elliot just told me, in my mind, Carter and Adam are the top suspects.

"I brought your mother to the house and helped her settle in. She'll be comfortable there."

"I'm sure she will." It hits me again how weird this is. My mother is at Elliot's.

When we pull into his driveway, she's sitting on the front porch, bundled in her winter coat. We join her, and I give her a hug. Elliot watches us.

My mother beams, and just like that, we're all more comfortable. The three of us. Me and my two sources of DNA.

"I was just enjoying looking at your yard. Haley told me it was beautiful. It must be something in the spring and summer," she says as the cold air stings my face.

"Thank you. The place is too big for just me, but I love it." Elliot rubs his hands together. "Let's go in."

Despite the strangeness of it all, as we head inside together, I'm grateful for this unconventional new family experiment. Adam is no longer a part of my life, but I'm not alone. This new chapter with Elliot is a good thing for now, though I've been wrong before.

A familiar scent fills the kitchen. It smells like my mother's bourbon salmon recipe.

"Dinner is almost ready," she says. "How was the ER today, Haley?"

"Fine, but you shouldn't be cooking meals for everyone. That wasn't part of the deal. You're supposed to be resting."

"She didn't cook... not exactly," Elliot answers. "She told me what to do, and I hope we'll all approve of the results. Sure smells like I got it right."

"Oh." They did this together. Interesting.

"Go upstairs and change so we can eat," she says with a smile.

When I've changed out of scrubs and I'm seated at the kitchen table, Elliot serves our meal.

The vibe between them reminds me of a first-date atmosphere. They're being extra considerate with each other. A nervous politeness.

My mother looks lovely wearing a blouse I gave her last Christmas. When she opened the gift, she said it was so nice she'd save it for special occasions.

Her hand accidentally brushes Elliot's. They're both quick to smile and apologize.

"So, what did you do together while I was at work? Besides the cooking lesson?" I ask.

"We've been getting reacquainted," Elliot answers.

My mind goes straight to the way they first got "acquainted." Not something I want to think about. I cringe and have to look away.

"Your mother is quite the storyteller. It's clear you were doted on your entire life," Elliot tells me.

"Yes. I suppose I was. By both my parents. I was lucky."

Elliot slides a serving of salmon with rice and asparagus toward me. "You had quite an imagination."

I groan. "Oh no. What did you tell him?"

He laughs. "I heard about how you cared for your pet rabbit and hamsters. You kept a notebook of observations. What they ate each day, how much they drank. You weighed their poop."

"I was an only child. They do strange things." I raise my eyebrows and laugh. "They treat their pets like people."

My mother lifts her hand. "Yes, but it was more than that for you. The way you looked after them. I've known you would make a wonderful nurse since you were a toddler."

"I had the best to learn from."

"Some things are meant to be." Elliot smiles, but there's regret for not being there to see things himself.

In any other situation with people acting the way these two are, I might feel like a third wheel. But there's no chance of that tonight, not when Elliot is so interested in making up for lost time. Not when my mother is shamelessly bragging about what a wonderful daughter I am.

After dinner, we move to the living room, where I stop before another photo on the wall beside the mantel.

"My mother," Elliot says from behind me. "She passed away five years ago."

I turn to him. "I'm sorry."

His smile is thoughtful. "You have her eyes."

I see it. Elliot has her eyes, and I have his. The resemblance between the three generations is striking.

Mom joins us, resting her hand on my shoulder. "Your mother was beautiful, Elliot."

"She would have loved both of you." He sounds wistful. "I wish you could have met."

I glance at my mother, the woman who prevented Elliot's mother from meeting her grandchild.

Elliot's phone rings, and he excuses himself.

My mother sighs. "I hope he'll forgive me."

"Seems as if he already has." I shrug. "I can't pretend this isn't strange. It is. But not bad."

"Considering everything that's happened recently, being together now is important. It's good you and Elliot are getting to know each other."

When Elliot returns, his expression is serious.

"Everything okay?" I ask.

"Just work stuff. Nothing to worry about," he says, but I can see the concern in his eyes, the wrinkles now creasing across his forehead. Worried is exactly how he looks.

"How about starting the movie now?" he suggests.

We settle onto the large couch with our feet on the ottomans and a movie playing.

Despite some emotional ups and downs, this is nice. Easier than I thought it would be.

Out of the corner of my eye, I watch my mother and Elliot sitting close together. She breaks into a smile at a joke on the screen. She's comfortable and already behaving as if we're a family. Beside her, Elliot's expression doesn't change. Like me, he's got something else on his mind.

I hope one of us isn't keeping secrets that could destroy everything. The stakes are higher because I'm not the only person who could get hurt. Now I have my mother to look out for.

CHAPTER 57

Eating tortilla chips from a large bag, I stand alone in my security monitoring room, scanning the screens, making sure the house is secure. This is how I used to eat a lot of my meals. I'd realize I'd worked right through lunch and dinner and needed something quick to keep my stomach from growling. Then I'd snack while continuing to work. With Carol and Haley here, there's been less work and less snacking on random foods. I've had more nutritious meals around a table with engaging conversation.

Two of the monitor screens are black. One is Haley's room. The other is Carol's. I turned those off days ago to allow my guests their privacy.

Haley is working a late shift tonight. She switched with a coworker so she could go to her mother's chemo session tomorrow. They have a wonderful relationship. Their closeness and concern for each other shows in everything they say and do. Carol was obviously a wonderful parent.

She must be in her room resting because I don't see her anywhere else on the property, and I'm pretty sure she wouldn't go to sleep without first telling me goodnight. I have the urge to turn the monitor on just long enough to make sure she's okay.

The doorbell chimes. I'm not expecting anyone. The monitor positioned at the front door shows Lance in casual clothes holding a bottle of wine.

I leave the bag of chips in the kitchen as I make my way to the front of the house, wondering if he's already heard something back from the private investigators.

"Hey. Come on in," I say, stepping aside at the door.

"I just left the club and thought I'd swing by."

Carol appears behind me in the hallway. She was on my mind only seconds ago, yet I'm still surprised to see her. It's as if she existed only in the private world I've built with her and Haley. Separate from business, from Lance, from my past. Now those worlds are colliding.

"Carol, I'd like you to meet Lance Hutchinson, my friend. Also, my attorney. The real Lance." I attempt a laugh but immediately regret the comment. It's not funny. I don't know what I was thinking. "Lance, this is Carol, Haley's mother."

Lance's smile widens as he extends his hand. "It's a pleasure to meet you. Haley clearly gets her beauty from you."

Carol's cheeks color. "That's kind of you. And this isn't the first time we've seen each other."

"It isn't?" I ask.

Her eyes light up. "You and Lance were together the night we met, and Lance and I were in a political science class together one semester."

Lance draws back his chin. "Your memory is impressive."

"It's strange the things that come back to us after so many years," Carol says. "Do you remember my friend Maria? She was in the same political science class."

"Can't say I remember the name, but maybe if I saw her," Lance answers.

As I observe their exchange, I'm caught off guard by an unexpected twinge of jealousy. The emotion startles me. Why should I be jealous if

Carol remembers Lance from college thirty years ago? It's not as if they had any sort of relationship beyond classmates.

"I'm so sorry about your wife," Carol tells Lance. "I remember hearing about it and feeling so terrible for you."

He lowers his head in a show of respect for the wife he adored and tragically lost. "Thank you. It was a long time ago, but I appreciate your mentioning it. I never want Becca to be forgotten."

My mouth falls open. In seventeen years, Lance has shut down every conversation I've started about Becca. He's changed the subject, left the room. Not wanting to cause him more pain, I took his cue and eventually stopped talking about her. Was that a mistake on my part?

"I come bearing a gift." He lifts the bottle of Cabernet. "Shall we open it and catch up?"

Carol's eyes twinkle. "A little won't hurt."

I fetch glasses while Lance uncorks the bottle.

"So, Lance," Carol begins, accepting a half-full glass of wine, "you and Elliot have stayed close since college?"

"We went to law school together, too."

Carol turns to me. "You're an attorney, Elliot?"

"I got my degree and passed the bar but went into business instead."

"Elliot was a brilliant law student," Lance says. "Graduated at the top of our class. With minimal effort, I should add."

Carol gives me an impressed look, a slight smile with one eyebrow raised more than the other. I distinctly remember the moment I first noticed her in college.

"Is that true?" she asks.

I shrug, smiling despite myself. "Lance exaggerates."

He gives my shoulder a friendly slap. “He’s always a modest one. Don’t let him fool you.”

“Oh, I won’t,” she answers.

Yet Carol deceived me for thirty years, and I can’t change that fact.

She finishes her wine, then excuses herself with an apology about being tired.

After she leaves Lance’s charming expression disappears, and he’s serious. “What’s going on? Why is she staying with you?”

CHAPTER 58

With Carol gone, the mood in the room has changed. I take a generous sip of the Cabernet, then settle back into my chair.

"Carol and Haley are staying here for a while," I tell Lance while swirling my wine. "I feel better having them close. I can look out for them."

"If I'd known, I wouldn't have dropped by unannounced."

I wave off his apology. "No, I'm glad you met her. Again." I pause, the wine loosening my memories. "Back in college, I wanted more than just one weekend. Thirty years later, and she's still... let's just say I remember what I liked so much about her. I wish she'd given me more of a chance back then."

Lance watches me over his glass. "Can't change the past. Seems like you're getting a second chance now."

Something in his tone makes me straighten in my chair. "Did you stop by for a reason? Something on your mind?"

"It's about hiring Reeves. I've had some reservations. I'm concerned we might open a can of worms."

"Why?"

The room seems to grow darker as Lance speaks. He changes position in his chair, then runs his finger along the rim of his wineglass. "I've been hearing things about Carter at the firm."

"What things?"

He lowers his voice. "Rumors about his behavior. A few missed meetings. Money problems, possibly."

"That doesn't sound right." I made sure Carter had no debt coming out of college. He's worked since his graduation. I'm aware of his salary. More than enough to afford his car and his condo.

"One of his colleagues says drugs might be involved. Nothing confirmed, but if Reeves digs…" Lance speaks as if he's reluctant to share this information.

The excellent wine turns bitter in my mouth. This is news to me. Carter didn't appear to be taking drugs, but an addiction would explain his strange behavior with Haley.

"I sure hope they're wrong, but if there's any truth to it, any good prosecutor could spin his troubles into motive. A desperate man, suddenly learning about a new heir to your fortune…"

I stare into my glass. Lance has echoed Haley's suggestion.

"I'd rather we handle it internally before Reeves uncovers it. For Carter's sake. For your sake. And the firm. Perhaps we don't want the PI team to investigate every potential suspect. We could tell him to focus on Haley's husband first. The restraining order. The assault in her apartment."

"We're not doing that." Although I want to protect Carter, I'm not okay with sending Reeves after Haley's husband. If Adam is guilty, Reeves and his team will figure it out for themselves.

Lance pours the rest of the wine into his glass. "The other option is we call off the investigation."

"No. I appreciate you thinking about this and coming here, but I'm going to let Reeves do his job. I'm paying him to separate fact from fiction."

"Just making sure we're prepared for every possibility. Not mentioning Carter's deceit and impersonation attempt is one thing, but I can't keep an employee who is using drugs. Not if it reaches the attention of the other partners."

"I understand."

We finish the wine, but the mood is strained.

Later that night, I sit alone at my desk, finishing the same bag of chips. Jack Reeves's words from our earlier meeting echo in my mind. The part about uncovering things. Would I rather know if someone I love is guilty or live with doubt? It's tricky. I believe I'd rather know, only because I hope the truth will bring relief. If it doesn't, well, I'll have to handle the situation.

I've reached the crumbs at the bottom of the bag, and I need to talk to Reeves. It's late, but I expect the PI keeps unconventional hours.

He answers after two rings.

"Elliot Rhodes here. Listen, about your investigation... anything that relates to my stepson, Carter... anything you find about him, tell me first. No reports to anyone else. Just me."

"Understood, Mr. Rhodes."

I should end the call there, but there's more weighing on my mind. "I have another matter that needs careful handling."

"Go on."

"This stays between you and me. Don't hand it off to your team. Don't share it with Lance or anyone else at his firm. I'll pay whatever premium is necessary for absolute discretion."

The silence stretches between us. Finally, Reeves says, "I'm listening."

"Look into the death of a man named Frank James. His death certificate should say he died of natural causes, but someone believes otherwise. Could you find out if there's anything suspicious about his death that might have gone undetected?"

"Give me his name with his birthdate and date of death, so I'm looking into the right person."

"I will. Again, anything you find comes directly to me. In fact, I don't want a written report. No record of this work. No one else can know about this. Understood?" I rarely repeat myself in this way, but this is important. I want to make sure my instructions are clear.

Again, I hope I haven't unleashed something I'm going to regret forever.

CHAPTER 59

After work, I find my mother on Elliot's patio, wrapped in one of the new plaid blankets Elliot bought.

"What are you drinking?" I ask, glancing at the mug in her hands.

"Apple cider. Elliot took me to lunch after my treatment, and we stopped for fresh cider on the way home. I can heat a mug for you."

"I'm okay. Thanks. Maybe I'll have some later, and I can get it myself. Everyone at the hospital asked about you, as usual. Tamira and Cara and even Dr. Burke wanted to make sure I told you."

"I miss them, too."

"Elliot went all out." I point to the tall heat lamp beside us and the new stadium blankets. All recent additions, because Elliot noticed how much my mother enjoys being outside, even in winter. How considerate is he?

"How was the treatment?" I ask.

"Same as usual," she answers, looking relaxed as her gaze drifts over the backyard.

Her chemotherapy is almost finished, the worst is nearly over. Soon, we'll get the next set of scans. We'll discover the chemo's effectiveness and determine the next steps in her treatment plan.

"Mom," I say, breaking the peaceful silence. "Being here has been good for you."

"Oh, most definitely. It's like I'm taking an extended stay at a beautiful hotel." She smiles, her eyes on the dormant flower beds beyond the patio. "This yard. I get so many ideas just looking at it. Imagine in the summer."

Is she thinking about living here in the summer? That seems like a very long time and probably not what Elliot had in mind. "Pretty sure Elliot already has a gardener who takes care of the property. He worked with a designer on the inside."

"Doesn't surprise me. The interior is amazing. Elliot has excellent taste. He always has."

"How would you know?"

My mother waves her hand. "Only from what I remember. The way he dressed in college, and certainly from everything we've seen since we've been here. He might not have designed the home, but he hired the right designer and approved the choices."

"What do you think of him now that you've spent more time together?"

"He's a wonderful man."

I keep staring, imploring her to expand because she must have more to share than just a surface level, polite answer.

"I have to admit, I didn't know him very well in college." She flashes a mischievous grin before turning serious again. "He's successful now, obviously. Hard working. Maybe brilliant in a business sense. But there's a sadness about him. I see it sometimes."

"Yeah, I do too. Has he ever told you anything about his previous marriage?"

Mom's eyes widen. "No. And I wouldn't ask. I only heard it ended with an ugly mess. Something about infidelity, I believe. She left him."

I turn to face my mother, waiting for her to do the same. "If you haven't kept track of Elliot since college, and haven't spoken to him about his marriage, how do you know anything about the way it ended?"

"I said I didn't go searching for information. But we had some mutual college friends. Every so often, I'd hear something about Elliot. News spreads when it's gossipy."

I scrunch my mouth. "Elliot doesn't strike me as the type to cheat on anyone."

"I don't think he is the type now. People change. His marriage ended a long time ago."

"But you never saw him until recently?"

My mother is silent.

"Did you?" I ask again.

She looks away. "I did once. Years ago. He was at the hospital with Lance when I was working. They weren't on my floor, but I heard what happened. They'd gotten into a car accident. Lance's wife died. A shocking tragedy, and not the right time to catch up or even say hello, I assure you."

I straighten. "Wait. They were all in the accident? The one that killed Lance's wife? Elliot was there too?"

"Yes. Like I said, a terrible night."

I stare at the garden, processing this.

"Excuse me, ladies."

We both turn to see Elliot coming toward us. He's wearing a cashmere sweater with a coat over his arm as if he's on his way out. It's Thursday. The day he meets with Carter for lunch. I'm still upset about everything with Carter. Elliot hasn't mentioned his name lately.

"I'll be gone for the rest of the afternoon, but I want to have dinner together, if it's all right with both of you," he says.

"Sounds lovely," my mother answers. "What should I make?"

He waves his hand. "Unnecessary. I'm going to bring something home. Haley? Are you able to have dinner tonight with us?"

"Sure."

"The lighting is perfect right now," Elliot says, raising his phone. "Would you mind if I took a photo? You both look beautiful."

He takes the photo, then says goodbye, leaving us alone again.

"So, have you spoken to Adam since you've been here?" my mother asks.

I check my wrists to confirm the sickly dark yellow discoloration is gone. "No, I haven't. Lance advised me not to reach out to him on account of the restraining order. But I want to get Moose back soon."

"Do you miss him?"

From her tone and lack of smile, she's asking about Adam. I look out at the garden, avoiding her gaze. "Yeah, I miss Moose."

My mother huffs. "Your cat was never very affectionate with you."

"I still love him."

She's right about Moose. He's never shown me love or devotion, but he never accused me of murder, either. And though he has scratched me on many occasions when he didn't want to leave the house, he never made me feel as if my life was in danger.

CHAPTER 60

It's late afternoon when I get home and spot Carol through my office windows. She's alone outside and still reading on the patio. Was she out there all this time? I'm glad I bought the heat lamp and blankets. I'm paying attention to her wants and needs, trying to make her feel at home.

I'm surprised at the pull I feel. Carol deceived me for three decades and kept my daughter from me. I should resent her. Instead, I want to join her on the patio, ask what she's reading, make plans for dinner. I want to—

My phone rings. Jack Reeves. I answer right away.

"Mr. Rhodes, is this a good time to speak?"

"Yes, have you found something?"

"I have."

A sickening sense of dread spreads through me. I hired Reeves and his team to get information, and he did. It's too late to back out now. "Is this about the other matter I asked you to investigate? Frank James' death?"

"No, it's about the shooting."

I don't know if I'm relieved or not.

"Where should we meet?" Reeves asks.

"Come to my home office. I'll send you the address."

I have a bad feeling about what he's going to tell me, and an hour to prepare for it. Needing to ground myself, I join Carol outside. She looks up from her book and smiles. "You're back already."

I sit beside her. "Yes. Someone's coming over soon. A business matter. Shouldn't take long. I just wanted to say hello, see if you're warm enough."

"The lamp is perfect. I love it out here."

"Good. What are you reading?"

She turns the cover of her gardening book. "I like dreaming about spring and all the possibilities. I hope you don't mind a suggestion." She points to the garden beds on the right. "Lavender would look beautiful along the south fence. The afternoon sun is perfect for it."

"Sounds nice. Maybe you could show me where to plant it when the timing is right."

Her smile grows, and for the next forty-five minutes, I forget about Reeves and what he might share.

Jack Reeves sits on the other side of my office desk. The door is closed.

"What did you find?" I ask, bracing myself.

"Someone was following Haley."

"Yeah. I hired a PI through Hartley & Hutchinson. He wasn't supposed to tail her. That's not what I had in mind, but perhaps he misunderstood."

Reeves shakes his head. "I'm not talking about the person you hired to do a background check on Haley and her mother. This was someone else. Another person was paid to follow Haley and report on her whereabouts before and including the night Ms. Christenson got shot."

"How did you learn that?"

"The PI who tailed her is an acquaintance of a friend. He told me. The thing is... he's not someone you find in a normal advertisement."

"Oh, Christ," I mutter. "A hitman?"

"Among other things."

My blood runs cold, but I have to ask the next question. "Who hired him?"

"He doesn't have the information, wouldn't have told me if he did, but I traced his payment to an account owned by a firm you're familiar with. Hartley & Hutchinson."

Oh, no. My body goes rigid, and coldness fills my core. Carter.

"It's the kind of account they'd use for business they don't want anyone to know about."

"Who has access to it?" I ask, bile rising into my throat.

"Hard to say. Could be partners, could be someone lower doing the dirty work to allow others plausible deniability."

I stop, fixing Reeves with a hard stare. "Can you find out who made the payment?"

"I can try."

When the PI leaves, I'm left with the crushing realization that the detectives' new theory was correct. Haley, not Lauren, must have been the shooter's target.

Before I can stop myself, my imagination is off and running with a horrifying alternate reality. If Haley hadn't switched seats. If the bullet had found her instead of Lauren. There were no other medical professionals on board. She could have bled out alone on the floor. I would have learned I had a daughter and never got to meet her. I could have lost her right after discovering she existed.

Reeves is good. He's getting closer. He'll dig up the horrifying truth and drag it to the surface. What he uncovers might force me to choose.

Carter told me he wasn't involved. He's also proved to be exceptional at fooling people.

Two instincts battle within me. A fierce desire to keep Haley safe. And a primal need to protect Carter.

CHAPTER 61

I wake to voices downstairs. Elliot and my mother are talking in the kitchen. She's laughing at something he said. At my apartment, mornings were silent except for Moose's occasional demands for food. I like this change.

Daily, Elliot reminds us we're welcome here and we can stay as long as we need. We're waiting for the detectives or Elliot's private investigators to find the gunman and the facts about the train shooting.

It's only been two weeks since we moved in, but it seems longer. I don't miss my apartment, but I do miss Moose. Every time I hear a soft sound or catch movement in my peripheral vision, I expect to see him padding around the corner. One morning I thought I heard him mewing outside my bedroom door. I got out of bed to check, but the hallway was empty. I have this persistent, sad feeling he needs me, and I've let him down.

I put on sweatpants and a sweatshirt and head downstairs in my socks, drawn by the wonderful scent of coffee. It's become my daily ritual. Elliot's brew is far superior to anything I've ever had at my house or at the hospital. It's the combination of carefully roasted beans and the quality of his machine. Maybe I shouldn't get used to it. I don't take it for granted.

In the kitchen, my mother and Elliot are chatting at the table. She's wearing a robe over pajamas, and Elliot has workout clothes on.

"Morning, sweetheart," she says, her smile bright. No one could ever tell she's undergoing chemo.

"Morning." I return her greeting as I pour myself a cup of the excellent coffee.

My mother is still watching me. "You're off today, right? What are your plans?"

Facing her, I lean back against the counter. "Go for a run. Then read. Unless there's something I can do to help around here."

Elliot gets up from his chair. "You'd better bundle up good for your run. And there's nothing you need to do here except relax."

"Thanks. I'm going to take advantage of that. But let me know if you change your mind."

As I head back to my room with my coffee mug, I stop by the stairs. Something is different on the wall. A new addition. An image of my mother and me. The photo Elliot recently took on the patio.

I scan the symmetrical arrangement of photos again, trying to determine what's missing. It's a picture of Jules, Elliot's first wife. She's been replaced.

We're becoming part of Elliot's life, his home. It's been so easy living here. I feel safe. As if Adam and Carter, the violence on the train, and all the associated complications can't come past these walls. And yet, they're the reason we're here.

I haven't talked to Adam since I saw him outside the hospital before my shift. With Elliot and my mother keeping me occupied, he's out of sight and out of mind for now, as much as possible.

I start up the stairs, and my phone rings from inside my sweatshirt pocket. An unknown number scrolls across the screen. The reporters stopped calling weeks ago, so it's not likely to be one of them. It's probably just spam, and yet, rather than hit the button to eliminate the call, I let it keep ringing.

As I stare at my phone, a peculiar sensation washes over me. I can't explain it exactly. A premonition? Somehow, I know the peace I found here is about to shatter.

CHAPTER 62

I refill Carol's coffee cup, then my own. Offer her another slice of brioche. Haley has left to get ready for a run, and we're alone.

"You've never seen a professional tennis match?" I ask.

"Only on television."

"I plan to attend Wimbledon this year. You should come with me."

Before she can respond, a heart-wrenching cry echoes from the stairwell.

I'm on my feet before I realize I've moved. Carol's eyes meet mine, wide with alarm.

We're rushing toward the stairs. I want to help Haley and shield Carol from whatever we're about to find.

Haley sits on the bottom step of the staircase, her face ashen and her eyes vacant. She's clutching her phone. Her coffee cup is beside her. A small puddle of brown liquid surrounds it.

"What happened?" My voice is soft with worry. It's rare that I speak to anyone this way.

Haley stares straight ahead and whispers, "Adam was arrested for attempted murder because of the train shooting."

Carol gasps.

Haley grabs the stair railing. "He's at the police station. I have to see him. And he needs an excellent attorney."

"But the restraining order," I say.

Haley's eyes flash with emotion. "I can't abandon him. He needs me. And I have to get Moose. I have to pick him up at the house and take him to my apartment."

"Your cat? You can bring him here. What does he need? Food? Litter box?"

Haley nods, but I'm not sure if she's hearing us.

Carol puts an arm around our daughter's shoulders. "We're going to help Adam."

"Yes, we're here for you. And him," I add, meeting Carol's eyes over Haley's head. "Whatever you need, we're here."

I like how that sounds. The 'we' part.

Haley looks at me for the first time since we found her on the stairs. "Thank you," she whispers.

I squeeze her shoulder, then stand. I know something they don't. The detectives are wrong. It wasn't Adam. The real villain is someone with access to a shady expense account at Hartley & Hutchinson. But Reeves is still investigating, and we're not certain of anything yet, so I'll just support Haley and Carol in whatever they decide. The first thing I'm going to do is get the best attorney money can buy.

I call Lance from my office.

"I need an excellent criminal defense attorney. Someone who has handled attempted murder charges. It's for Haley's husband. He was just arrested."

"Adam? The one we got a restraining order against?"

"Yes, the same one," I say with a sharp tone. "Who else would it be? She only has one husband. He needs representation."

"Why are you helping your daughter's estranged husband? Especially given the charges?"

"Because Haley asked me to."

"What evidence do they have against him?"

"We don't know anything yet. You're my first call."

"I'll contact Thomas Becker. He's excellent, especially with circumstantial evidence cases."

While we're waiting for Lance to make arrangements, a detective from the train shooting investigation calls Haley. The conversation doesn't last long.

"They're executing a search warrant at Adam's house," she says, her face pale. "Detective Desai told me."

We barely have time to hear the rest when Lance calls back.

"Thomas Becker is heading to meet with Adam now. He's the best," Lance assures me. "If there's any way to create reasonable doubt, he'll find it."

"I hope this won't go to trial." I'm concerned about the prospect and what it would mean for Haley, what it would do to her.

Later, after we've changed into presentable clothing, I'm driving Carol and Haley to see Adam when the attorney, Becker, provides an update. I put my phone on speaker so everyone can hear.

"The police search found something," he says. "A prepaid phone hidden in Adam's dresser. Several texts discussing 'taking care of the problem' and 'making it look random.'"

My stomach tightens. I'm no fan of Adam since I learned he assaulted Haley, but after the information Reeves gave me, I didn't expect this. "Who was he communicating with?"

"The other number's another burner."

"That doesn't make sense," Haley says from the backseat. "Adam's not stupid. Why would he keep the burner phone? Why not destroy it?"

I'm thinking it's because the job isn't finished, but I don't say that aloud. "It could mean anything," I say instead, glancing at Haley in the rearview mirror. Though it sounds to me like he's guilty. And if he is, Carter is off the hook.

Becker continues. "They'll try to build a case saying Adam had the means and the motive to put a hit on his wife. The motive being revenge, based on his suspicion that Haley murdered his grandfather."

Haley is shaking her head. She didn't want that information to get out, and now it has.

"But I didn't do anything to hurt Frank," she says.

"Whether you harmed Adam's grandfather is irrelevant to the case against Adam," Becker answers. "If Adam believes you did, that's motive."

Haley makes a soft whimpering sound, and Carol reaches for her hand. "It's going to be okay, honey."

I grip the steering wheel tighter. As the evidence mounts against Adam, I wonder if I'm letting my desire to protect my daughter cloud my judgment. Was it in her best interest to hire an excellent defense attorney? If Adam hired someone to kill Haley, I don't want him to get away with it. I want him to rot in jail.

CHAPTER 63

Adam approaches me in the visiting room. He's wearing a faded gray jumpsuit. Dark circles surround his eyes, and stubble covers his normally clean jaw. There's a permanent snarl on his face. He looks like a stranger, someone to be afraid of in a dark alley.

But it's still Adam. The man my cat prefers. A man who slept to my right every night and held my hand whenever we binged a new series together. He's also the same man who recently pinned me down in my apartment, frightening me enough to get a restraining order. He recently accused *me* of murder, which is ironic now. But the police arrested him, and with his grandfather gone, I'm his only lifeline.

He sits behind a thick Plexiglass divider. Most of me wants to reach through it and hug him. Yet in a small way, I'm glad it separates us.

Adam picks up the phone on his side of the glass. "Haley. You came." His voice is gravelly, the way it gets after he's shouted for the duration of a football game. "This charge is BS."

"Of course I came. And we got you an excellent lawyer. Becker is one of the best."

Adam leans toward me, so close his forehead bumps the glass. "You have to believe me. I didn't do this. I would never."

I whisper, "They found evidence at your house." I give him a look, pleading for a good explanation.

"The burner phone isn't mine. I swear. And the other so-called evidence is ridiculous. Part of it was that I was tracking you. I mean come on! Everyone on a shared phone plan can track each other. They say I called right before the shooting to pinpoint your location, as if I haven't called you a thousand other times this year." Adam bangs his fist once against the glass. "Here's the real kicker—they had pictures of the bruises on your wrists."

My mouth drops. "How did they... I didn't..." I stop, remembering when Elliot documented my injuries as part of the restraining order.

"That's not doing me any favors, Haley." He glares. "I told my attorney about Carter. You've told the police about him, right?"

It's a challenge to meet Adam's eyes. "I haven't yet."

"Haley, what the hell?"

My body tenses, yet I reach my hand toward him, only catching myself and pulling back halfway to the glass. These conflicting impulses are driving me mad.

Adam narrows his eyes as he gazes past me. He's spotted my mother and Elliot at the back of the visiting room.

"You brought your mother here? Who is that guy with her?"

Elliot stands with his arms crossed, watching us.

"That's Elliot."

"Is he protecting Carter? Is that why you haven't contacted the police yet?"

"Elliot is helping me to support you. His attorney friend got you the lawyer."

Adam grips the phone so tight his hand turns white. "I'm not a criminal, Haley. And I had nothing to do with that train shooting."

I want to believe him. But after everything we've been through lately, how can I be sure he's not telling me what I want to hear?

"Someone is setting me up. It has to be Carter. So hell if I'm taking Elliot's help. I have to get my own attorney."

"We'll figure this out. The hearing is in two days. Don't switch lawyers."

A guard signals our visit is over.

"You're a fool to trust them," Adam says. His parting words.

Leaving him like this, my chest feels hollow. I'm numb with sadness when we exit the detention center. It's impossible to think clearly. Hopefully, this is as low as things can get for us. I can't take any more.

My mother wraps her arm around me, and I lean into her. Outside, Elliot walks ahead of us, phone to his ear, talking to Adam's attorney. I catch only bits and pieces. I'm sure he'll fill us in later.

I can't unsee the image of Adam in the ugly jumpsuit behind the glass. Whatever has happened between us, in my heart, I can't believe he wanted to kill me. And if he did, then there's something physically or chemically wrong with his brain. A neurological malfunction? A brain tumor? Yes, perhaps it's been something like that all along. That could be why he's so convinced Frank didn't die of natural causes, why he's obsessed with his theory, and why he asked me to move out. It's the only thing that makes sense to me.

Adam deserves the benefit of an excellent defense. Thanks to Elliot, he has one.

What Adam said about Elliot and Carter framing him is ridiculous.

Isn't it?

Then again, I once thought Adam trying to hurt me was ridiculous, too. And no matter what Lauren claims, something about Elliot's involvement with Granite Global keeps bugging me.

I still don't know who to trust and who to fear. I'm not sure of anything anymore.

CHAPTER 64

It's late afternoon, and my mother is taking a nap. Seeing Adam in jail exhausted us. I should rest too. Instead, I've been pacing my room for the past hour. I'm driving myself crazy trying to understand things even the detectives don't have a handle on yet. Carter told me I wasn't safe. Adam thinks someone is framing him. What if he's right?

My frantic thoughts return to Elliot's connection with Granite Global. The flowers in Lauren's room with the strange note. The recent urgent meetings. These doubts won't go away on their own. I must face them head-on.

I head downstairs to Elliot's office. Through his partially open door, I see him at his desk, staring at his computer monitor. I lift my hand to knock.

What am I doing? Accusing Elliot of conspiracy? Of attempted murder?

I have to ask and hear him say no. I have to hear it and believe him. I owe that to Adam.

I rap twice on the door.

Elliot glances up from his computer. His face softens when he sees me. "Everything okay?"

I shake my head. "I have to ask you about Lauren Christensen."

He removes his reading glasses, giving me his full attention. "What about her?"

I force myself to meet his eyes. "The night she got shot. Before she lost consciousness, she said something. Granite Global. She was writing a piece about the company."

"Go on."

"You're the chairman of the board. You've had a lot of urgent meetings lately. The kind of meetings a company has when it's facing a serious problem."

He's just staring at me, waiting. He doesn't get what I'm implying.

I keep going. "A problem like the prospect of harmful information going public and ruining the stock prices or whatever."

His eyes widen. "You still think the target of the train shooting was Lauren? And someone at Granite Global is responsible?"

I wring my hands. "The timing. All the secrecy. And until someone finds the shooter, or identifies the person who hired him, we don't really know who the intended target was. The detectives said it *could* have been me. But maybe it wasn't. Now Adam is in jail, possibly for something he didn't do. I just had to get it out there, to ask you."

"Haley, I wasn't involved. You have my word. My promise. And I strongly doubt anyone at Granite Global was."

"How can you be sure it wasn't someone else?"

"There wasn't anything damaging for Lauren to discover. I met with her myself. She was a pleasure. Her coverage was positive. And Granite Global is a huge company. One journalist's article can't do much damage, no matter what."

"Investigative journalism has destroyed plenty of companies." I can't name a single one, but it must have happened. "Seems it would depend on what she uncovered."

Elliot is quiet before saying, "Let me show you what's going on." He unlocks his desk drawer with a key and pulls out a thick folder. "These are the merger documents we're finalizing." He opens the folder and slides it across the desk. "This is the reason for my urgent meetings. Granite Global is acquiring another large public company. The negotiations have to be kept secret."

I scan the documents. They look legitimate but mean little to me.

"To prevent market manipulation, very few people can know. It's not something I should share, but I trust you won't tell a soul or run out and buy stocks, which would get us both in a lot of trouble." He smiles.

"Oh. I won't." I keep staring at the documents. "I'm sorry I suspected the company. And thank you for telling me what's really going on. I promise I won't breathe a word of it."

"Don't be sorry. After everything you've been through, I understand why you might be suspicious. I wish you'd told me earlier. I could have put your worries to rest sooner rather than later. "

I'm grateful he doesn't seem offended. I feel lighter. Relieved. But as I look at Elliot, I see something in his eyes. It's what I would think if I were in his shoes. As I've harbored doubts about him, he might have his own doubts about me. Questions about my role in Frank's death. Maybe he's been wanting all this time to ask me and just can't bring himself to do it.

I look him square in the eyes without blinking. "I didn't kill Adam's grandfather."

CHAPTER 65

Haley pushes scrambled eggs around her plate, then stares into her coffee. Carol watches with a pained look. She internalizes her daughter's worries. Or she's equally unsettled about what happened to Adam and what it all means.

Adam believes I'm part of the reason he's in jail, and I'm plotting against him. He's refused to work with the attorney I got and hired a new one. The rejection doesn't bother me. I was only doing this for Haley.

Neither Haley nor Carol has spoken much since we sat down. I want to say something comforting, but every phrase that comes to mind sounds hollow.

"I have some work to do, but I'm not leaving the house," I finally say. "I'll be in my office if you need me."

"Thank you, Elliot. You've been wonderful." Carol's frown briefly lifts, and the gratitude in her eyes makes me feel warm despite everything.

"Thank you," Haley murmurs without looking up.

I'm still thinking about them as I head to my home office and the work I've been neglecting. For the past decade, because of my solitary life, I've had no distractions, nothing to cloud my judgment or prevent me from working long hours. But family changes availability, especially when their lives are in chaos. I've been spending more time with Carol and Haley than I have working.

When I log into my email, confidential messages regarding Granite Global's acquisition have multiplied overnight. The board members are arguing about the stipulations in the contract. They're waiting for me to weigh in and help settle matters. But someone as preoccupied as I am probably shouldn't be making these kinds of decisions.

I'm trying to focus on contract terms when I get a text from the PI: *I've got something new to share with you.*

An hour later, he's in my home office again with his usual serious expression.

"Mr. Rhodes, you're not going to like this."

I clench my teeth. "You found out who hired someone to track Haley?"

"Yes."

We're standing on opposite sides of my desk. He won't sit until I do, but I can't right now. I'm too on edge.

Reeves sets his laptop bag on my desk but doesn't open it. His hesitation unnerves me.

I cross my arms. "Tell me what you found."

"A commonality in the payments from Hartley & Hutchinson."

"Okay," I prompt, trying to keep my voice neutral. "And?"

"I found another payment authorized from the same IP address."

My throat is dry as Reeves hands me a square of paper. I unfold it and read the name written there. I laugh aloud in disbelief. "This has to be a mistake."

"It's not a mistake," he says. "I've documented the evidence for you."

My vision narrows. I lean on my desk for support. "Show me."

Reeves unzips his bag, removes a folder, and sets it on the desk.

Still standing, I sort through the documents, feeling more lightheaded with each passing minute. He's presented the evidence in a methodical, chronological way. I can't misinterpret the information.

"But the evidence against Adam? I told you what the attorney has. A burner phone with messages about 'taking care of the problem'. How do you explain that?"

"Someone is setting him up. My guess is…" Reeves gazes toward the paper. "What do you want to do with this information?"

"Nothing yet. Who else knows?"

"Just you."

"Good. Keep it that way until I tell you otherwise."

A minute after Reeves leaves my office, I still haven't moved.

I can't believe I got played.

And now, I have to find out why.

CHAPTER 66

Elliot sends me a message while I'm on break in the nurse's lounge. I haven't seen much of him in the past two days. Even when he's at the house, he's spent most of the day holed up in his office. Usually, his texts include questions about groceries or information on dinner plans. He'll tell my mother and me that someone is coming to clean or do maintenance. But there's no information like that in this message.

We need to talk when you get home. It's important.

I can't imagine what it's about, and I'm a little nervous. He's been acting strange. I'd think he was avoiding me if I didn't know about the big merger keeping him busy.

When I get back to his house, I follow voices to the kitchen. Nothing could have prepared me for who I find at the table with Elliot and my mother.

Carter.

The last time I saw him, I escaped through the woods, terrified. Now he's invading what I've come to think of as my safe space. I grip the back of a chair and glance at my mother, hoping for some explanation of what's happening. She gives a slight head shake, equally confused.

"All of you need to hear this," Elliot says. "Sit down, please, Haley."

That's the last thing I want to do. I don't trust Carter. But after all Elliot has done for us, how can I refuse?

When we're all seated, Elliot speaks again. "I hired a private investigator to look into the train assault. He did what I asked and recently presented me with some very disturbing information." He turns to me. "You *were* the intended target, Haley. A hired hitman was following you that night."

The detectives were right. I should be spooked by the confirmation, but it's strangely calming. One less thing to second-guess. "Did they tell you who hired the hitman?"

My mother speaks at the same time. "Was it Adam?"

Elliot looks at each of us. "It wasn't Adam."

Relief floods through me. Adam is innocent. He didn't try to kill me. He doesn't hate me that much. The rest of his life won't be spent in jail. But then: "Who?" My gaze swings to Carter.

He's kneading his knuckles. "I know who it was."

"You couldn't," Elliot says, grimacing as if he's in actual pain.

Carter breaks in. "It was Lance."

"You knew?" Elliot gapes. "I thought you looked up to him."

Carter shakes his head. "I've never trusted Lance. Not since I moved here to work at his firm. Not after what he did to my mother."

Elliot makes a fist with one hand and places it over his chest. "He did something to Jules? What are you talking about?"

"When I was ten, someone came to see her. I was supposed to be in bed, but I heard them arguing. He told her you'd cheated, and he showed her *proof*." Carter makes air quotes. "He said you had a history and would never change. He gave her money to leave."

"What?" Elliot's hand goes to his mouth.

"He made her promise never to tell where the information came from. I didn't know who he was then. But years later, when I started at Hartley

& Hutchinson… that's the next time I saw him. It was Lance. Your best friend."

"He lied to her," Elliot says. "I never cheated on Jules."

"Even if you had, I never trusted him after that. What kind of friend does that to another?" Carter turns to face me. "I think Lance framed Adam."

Now I'm the one covering my mouth with my hands. I knew Adam wasn't stupid enough to keep a burner phone in his dresser with incriminating texts. "We have to clear his name."

"I already gave the PI's information to Adam's attorney," Elliot says. "I expect they'll be releasing him sometime today."

"Good, good." I rock forward and back in my seat. "But why would Lance try to kill me? Why would he want me dead?"

Elliot hesitates, and there's no way to miss the pain in his eyes. "I didn't realize until now. I think Lance wants to hurt me for something that happened a long time ago. Something I can't undo. It was an accident."

"The car accident," Carol whispers. "Lance's wife. You were there when she died."

Elliot drops his head. "It's my fault. All of this is my fault."

CHAPTER 67

I keep my eyes on the door, waiting for Lance to arrive. We're meeting in my office because I can't bear to have him in my home. My stomach is in knots.

I still can't quite believe my best friend was actually my worst enemy. Lance has always been the person I turn to when I need clarification. This is the most significant of those times. He has some serious explaining to do.

He knocks once and enters. "What's going on? Is this about Adam? Becker told me he'd found a new attorney. He's going to need a good one with the evidence they've collected."

"We need to talk about evidence, but none that points to Adam." I hand him the documentation from Reeves.

Lance opens the file and glances at the contents. He's smart and processes information quickly.

"Reeves has copies of everything. Now I understand why you wanted me to drop the investigation."

Lance studies the evidence again. "Have you spoken to the police?"

"Not yet. I'm meeting with the police and Adam's new attorney right after this. I had to see you first. After all we've been through, I'd do anything for another explanation. But that's impossible." It's strange how calm I sound despite the emotions battling inside me. "No more manipulation. You tried to kill my daughter."

Lance smiles, but it's cold and calculated.

"And there's zero evidence Carter has money problems or drug problems. You made that up so I'd drop the investigation, and it almost worked. Why would you do all this? Why would you hire someone to kill Haley?"

He lets out a bitter, hollow laugh. His eyes flash with fury. "Why? You don't know, Elliot? Any idea how angry that makes me? You destroyed my entire life, and it's not even on your mind. It's not keeping you up at night or gnawing at you day after day."

"Is this about the accident? About Becca? For seventeen years, you've blamed me for a senseless tragedy? Our friendship was all a lie?"

Lance glares. "Not a lie. A long game. Since then, I've wanted to take things from you, too. Misery loves company, Elliot."

"You also lied to Jules. Sabotaged my marriage. I know that now, too. I guess if you couldn't have your wife, you didn't want me to have one either. You convinced her that I cheated."

Lance laughs. "It wasn't hard to do. Tricking Jules was just a start. Ever since you took Becca from me, I've wanted you to suffer."

CHAPTER 68

Seventeen years ago.

I remember every excruciating moment.

The three of us were on our way to an engagement party for Becca's sister. I'd volunteered as the designated driver. I had a tennis match the next afternoon and wasn't planning on drinking. The weather was terrible. Rain pelted the windshield. My wipers barely kept up. I put my hazards on and leaned forward, squinting into the darkness. "We should pull over. Wait for the storm to let up."

"No, we can't," Becca pleaded from the backseat. "We're already going to be late. I'm the maid of honor. I should be there already."

Lance turned around to face his wife. "We can barely see through the windshield. Elliot's right. The weather will let up soon. We'll be ten minutes late at most."

I was already scanning for a safe spot to pull over. There were no shoulders on that stretch of the road.

"Please keep going," Becca said. "My sister has turned into Bridezilla, and she won't let me hear the end of it if I'm late. It's not much farther. We're almost there. I promise."

I sighed, caught between the desire to please everyone and the fear of driving off the road or someone crashing into us. I slowed down even more.

"Okay, but if it gets any worse, we're stopping, no matter what your sister might do to you."

"Thank you, Elliot. We'll be fine the way you're driving. You're the best," Becca said. "After Lance, of course."

The party was in a renovated barn in a remote area used for weddings and similar events. Darkness lined the road to the venue. No streetlights. I drove slowly around the unfamiliar curves, checking the nav system to make sure we didn't get lost. A few more miles and the storm eased up. The rain lessened to a steady smattering of large drops, but no longer obliterated visibility.

"Not much farther," Becca said as we approached a sharp bend.

A car appeared, coming toward us, headlights blazing straight into our lane. The driver made no attempt to swerve.

I yanked the wheel hard to avoid a collision.

What happened next unfolded with such quick violence, I'll never properly piece the sequence of events together. My head slammed sideways into the window, then forward. We came to a stop on the wrong side of the road. A stunned silence enveloped us, broken only by the heavy patter of rain and our ragged breathing.

"Holy crap," I whispered, shaking as the windshield quickly fogged. "Is everyone okay?"

"I think so." Lance touched his fingers to a dark gash on his forehead as he turned to the back. "Becca? Are you hurt?"

No answer.

"Becca!" he shouted, sounding more frantic than I've ever heard before.

"I'm fine," Becca finally answered. "Just rattled. That was absolutely terrifying. Are you guys okay?"

"Yeah. Yeah. I'm good." Still shaking, I turned to look at the road behind us and saw no other car.

"That jerk didn't even stop to see if we needed help," Lance said.

I pulled onto a long driveway to get off the road and calm down.

Blood flowed freely from Lance's cut. Becca handed him a package of tissues from her purse, and I grabbed the Kleenex box I kept in the console compartment.

He used a giant wad of tissues to sop up the blood dripping down the side of his face. "It doesn't even hurt. Head wounds just bleed a lot. It's a thing. But why didn't the airbags inflate?"

I let my gaze drop to the exclamation point lighting up my dashboard for a few months. I planned to have the airbags fixed when I took the car for its next service visit.

"Thank goodness no airbags," Becca said. "You can't push them back in, can you? We'd be stuck waiting for someone to tow the car or whatever they'd have to do, and my sister would kill me."

We vented about the drunk or distracted driver who could have gotten us all killed, morphing some of our terror into anger.

"We're all right," Becca said. "Let's get going. Drop me off, and then Lance should have that cut checked out."

Lance protested, but Becca insisted he needed stitches.

When we resumed our trip, I drove at a slower speed, afraid of what might be around every bend, shaken from our sudden stop and grateful none of us got seriously hurt.

We got Becca to her sister's party late, but not tragically late, or so I thought. After dropping her off, we drove back to the city and the hospital. We promised to return as soon as possible. An hour or two at most.

Lance's injuries weren't an emergency, and there were loads of other people waiting. Hours later, when a tired-looking physician's assistant stitched up Lance's temple and proclaimed him good as new, Lance's phone rang.

"Probably Becca wondering how much longer." He looked at the screen. "It's her sister."

Lance had his phone against his ear, but I heard the frightening sound of a woman sobbing as she tried to talk.

During the party, Becca had complained of a headache and went to lie down. Much later, a guest found her unresponsive and called an ambulance. She was on her way to the hospital now, the same hospital we were getting ready to leave.

Much later, a doctor came out to speak with Lance. "I'm so sorry. Your wife suffered a severe brain hemorrhage. She didn't make it."

I'll never forget the sound Lance made. His inhuman, anguished cry echoed through the hospital corridor. I can still hear it today. It has the same power to make me cringe, shudder, and feel as if I'm going to throw up.

Days later, the news only got worse. Becca had been six weeks pregnant with their first child.

In the days after Becca's passing, I replayed that night over and over in my mind. If only I'd insisted on stopping, we would have been off the road when that idiot driver passed us. If I'd gotten my car serviced and the airbags went off, Lance might not have cut his head, and he would have been with Becca at the party. He could have called an ambulance sooner.

Each of us played an unknowing role in the tragedy. Becca is the one who insisted we keep driving in the rain. She also insisted we take Lance to the hospital for stitches. She's the one who went to a separate room to lie down without telling anyone just how bad her headache must have been. Or perhaps the other driver's recklessness sealed our fate the moment they rounded the bend.

We never learned who caused our accident. I'm afraid of what I'd do to that person if given the chance. It was his fault.

Until now, I never knew Lance saw things differently.

CHAPTER 69

The sun coming through my office window creates a wide swath of light that reaches my bookshelves and settles on a small sailboat sculpture. It was a gift from Lance on my thirtieth birthday. I stride across the room, grab the object, and drop it into the trash.

He pretended to have my back for the past seventeen years while plotting my destruction.

A month has passed since I learned the truth about his betrayal. At first, with each flare of anger, I had the instinctive urge to call him for advice and to vent, before remembering he's not my friend anymore; he's the cause of my fury. Eventually, the urge to consult with him faded. Thank God I have Carol now and can turn to her for advice.

I spend more time working from my home office these days, not wanting to miss an opportunity to have lunch with Carol or do a quick errand with her. Her latest scan results were excellent. Her treatment is complete. She's talking about going back to work soon.

Moose likes to curl up in an armchair by my window. He stretches and yawns and occasionally chases the toys I've bought. He doesn't do much else, but there's something about his self-assured presence that relaxes me. I enjoy having him around.

I don't want any of my current "guests" to leave.

My phone beeps. It's Reeves. He wants to meet in person, so we arrange for him to come by the house this afternoon. The last news he delivered turned my world upside down. I'd almost rather not hear what else he's discovered.

I'm watching the monitor when he approaches the front door, empty-handed. No briefcase, no files.

Once we're in my office, he doesn't waste time. "I've completed the review of Frank James's death. It took a while to get the lab testing completed."

I check the door, making sure it's fully closed. "What did you find?"

"I had two independent forensic pathologists analyze the autopsy reports. They both flagged something. Traces of adulterants. I have the info if you want it. A standard toxicology test wouldn't pick it up. Might be contamination in the original lab. Or it could be used to hide another drug in his system, if a person knew what they were doing."

My stomach sinks as if I just experienced a quick drop on an amusement park ride. I'd hoped for clarity, for evidence that would absolve Haley. Instead... this. "The medical examiner ruled it natural causes."

Reeves shifts his weight. "That's still the official finding. But there are inconsistencies. Frank's overall health was excellent for his age. No history of cardiac issues. None of the typical patterns aligned with cardiac arrest are present."

"Is there any proof of foul play?"

"Nothing conclusive. But a good lawyer could build a solid case based on this information if they knew about it." Reeves uses his fingers to tick off the next items. "Two witnesses place your daughter, Haley James, as the last person to see him alive. Multiple neighbors reported hearing a heated argument that afternoon. There were traces of coconut oil on the victim's glass, and no sources of the oil in his home. Ms. James is a registered nurse with access to—"

"Stop," I cut him off, unable to listen to another word. "It all sounds circumstantial. Is there anything concrete?"

He rubs the side of his neck. "There's no smoking gun. But Mr. Rhodes, in my experience, when you have this many red flags—"

"Thank you, Jack. You can cease the investigation. Send me your final invoice. Don't breathe a word of this."

"You paid for my discretion. There's nothing to share."

After he leaves, I sit in the growing darkness, wrestling with what I've learned. The evidence isn't conclusive either way. It neither proves Haley's guilt nor confirms her innocence.

Questions swarm me. Is this how Adam felt, trapped in this limbo of uncertainty? Can I continue to form a healthy relationship with Haley when doubt has taken root? Or will a nagging suspicion gnaw at me as it must have done to her husband? I'm grinding my molars together as I contemplate the situation.

I have options. Tell Reeves to keep digging. Or confront Haley with what he already found. But the question I'm wrestling with now is whether I want to know the truth.

As I stare out at the newly empty space on my bookshelf, jaw clenched, I make my decision. I am strong enough to ignore my suspicions. It won't be easy, but I can do it. Like it or not, I'll watch her more closely now, always wondering, always uncertain. But that's what family does. They carry each other's burdens and keep each other's secrets. That's what unconditional love entails, and I'm ready for it.

Haley agreed to keep Carter's deception quiet. She never involved the police. Instead, unsettling as the experience was for her, she respected my wishes. We handled the situation as a family matter.

I grab my phone and call my daughter. "Hey." I keep my voice light. "Are you up for dinner tonight? Just you and I."

Haley agrees, and it's a date.

As I hang up, I wonder if she heard or sensed the slight change in my tone because of the secret I'm holding in. A secret I will keep buried.

CHAPTER 70

A terror-filled shout echoes through the large house, jolting me from sleep.

It's my mother.

I'm out of bed and in the dark hallway before I'm fully awake, my heart pounding. I burst into Mom's room and flip on the light switch. Her bed is empty. The sheets and blankets are neatly made. Undisturbed. It's almost two a.m. Where is she? Why isn't she in her bed?

A woman's moan pierces the silence, coming from the other end of the long hallway. Elliot's room.

Oh.

Is sleeping in Elliot's room a new thing, or have I been oblivious?

I hurry in that direction but hesitate outside his door, unsure of what I heard. Is she okay or not? As I'm hovering there, my mother cries out again.

"No, I didn't—" Her voice breaks off in a sob.

"Mom!" I pound against the wood, concern overwhelming my reservations. I'm about to barge in when Elliot opens the door wearing boxers and a T-shirt.

I look straight past him and into the room.

My mother is sitting up in bed, gathering sheets around her. "Oh, Haley. I'm so sorry I woke you. Everything is okay. I just had a nightmare."

"I heard, and I was worried." I try to sound casual, as if I'm not at all fazed by finding her in Elliot's bed.

"I'll get you some water," Elliot offers, leaving the room.

"Are you sure you're okay?" I ask from the doorway.

"Yes, yes. It was nothing. Only a bad dream. What time is it?" She glances at the bedside table. "Oh, dear. I hope you can fall back asleep."

This isn't her first episode with nightmares, but it's the first time I've found her in Elliot's bed. I've asked about her dreams before, but she won't talk about what haunts them. She says she doesn't remember when she wakes up, but I'm not sure I believe her. I forget my dreams, but I can always recall my nightmares. It could be the stress of everything we've gone through catching up with her. The investigation, my separation, Adam's arrest, then Lance's arrest. Possibly guilt on account of my father, the man she married. All of it.

Despite the strangeness, I'm glad my mother and Elliot found each other.

"It's okay, Mom. Everything's okay. We're all safe now, and where we need to be."

Lance is in custody, and the evidence against him is solid. Carter's deception was messed up, but as Elliot says—misguided, not malicious. And Adam, well, ever since he moved on with Jessica, I try not to think about him. This isn't the life I imagined for myself, but plans change. There's hope for the future. If my mother can find love again, surely I can, too.

Elliot returns with the water, and Mom accepts it. "Thank you, and again, I'm so sorry."

Something in her voice keeps me rooted to the spot, as if she's apologizing for more than just waking us up. Before I can question it, she forces a smile. "I'm fine now, Haley, really. Go back to bed. You have a long day at work tomorrow."

Elliot gently touches my shoulder and follows me into the hallway. "We were going to tell you together soon."

I manage a small smile. "I'm happy for you both."

"Are you sure?" he asks.

"I am. Promise. Don't worry about me slipping something into your drink when you're not looking." I laugh but also cringe at my morbid humor. Where did that come from? Too many of Adam's accusations must have lodged in my brain. It's the middle of the night. I'm still groggy from sleep. I hope he knows I'm joking.

He nods, but there's something troubled in his expression. "Go back to sleep," he says finally. "I'll take care of your mother."

CHAPTER 71

With my chemotherapy finished, I can finally enjoy an early, peaceful morning without feeling like an invalid. Haley is on her way to work, and Elliot is in his home office.

Wearing a winter coat, I ease into the cushions of what I now consider my seat on the patio and turn on the heat lamps. There are two now, and two is better than one.

Frost covers the dead vegetation in the backyard, turning the brown stalks a sparkling silver. It won't survive long past sunrise.

I cradle my coffee mug, running my thumb over and around the handle. I've left my mark on this house. My newest novel sits on the side table. My potted herbs are thriving in a kitchen planter. New Christmas wreaths hang from red velvet ribbons on every window, just as they always have in my home. Little pieces of myself mark the path to belonging. Pieces I'll have to leave behind if my past ever catches up with me and my secrets come out.

At least there's one thing I don't have to hide. Haley knows about my current relationship with Elliot now. We had to be sure of what we were doing before telling her. I never intended to have another fling. From the start, it was more than just the pleasure of being desired and our attraction, but I had to be certain Elliot felt the same.

As I sip my coffee, I look back on how we got here. Over thirty years ago, I had to do what was best for myself and my unborn child. Alone, I made a critical, terrifying decision. I chose not to tell Elliot about my pregnancy. Instead, I took a different risk and lied to my college boyfriend, the young man I knew and trusted. Together, we built a beautiful family and raised a wonderful daughter. We were all happy. It was the right choice, and I have no regrets.

I took another risk this year when I contacted Elliot to tell him we shared a daughter. So far, my decision has proved to be better than I ever imagined. Things are good with us. Very good. Our love for Haley is a tight bond.

My decisions also brought unexpected consequences. Who could have known that finally telling Elliot about his daughter would lead to his "best friend" trying to kill her? Lance came so close to taking Haley. The prospect makes me shudder.

As disturbing as his actions were, Lance's behavior isn't what haunts me most. It's my past that visits me in my nightmares, causing me to wake the house with my screams.

It comes down to two moments in my life. One intentional, and one a mistake. Two moments I would do anything to get back and do over. But I can't change what I've done, no matter my regret.

The memories intrude when I let my guard down, like when I'm sleeping. Uninvited, they poke and prod at my serenity. Try as I might to shove them down, they keep surfacing.

Just like Frank.

Adam's grandfather came to his door with a snarl on his face and a half-full tumbler in one hand. He stared at me as if I were a complete stranger and made me wonder if perhaps he didn't recognize me.

"Hello, Frank."

"I'm watching the game," he said, as if everyone in the world should know "the game" was on and which teams were playing. "What are you doing here?"

His rudeness wasn't born of ignorance but choice, and his disdain no longer surprised me.

I smiled at him anyway and used my most agreeable tone. "May I come in?"

With a grunt, he opened the door wider and turned around. "Right in the middle of the third quarter," he muttered as I followed him deeper into the house.

Frank plopped into a large leather recliner, facing the football game playing on his television.

"Why are you here?" he asked again, without looking at me.

"Haley told me what happened between you two earlier, when your remote wasn't working and you needed someone to fix it."

He scoffed. "Did she?"

"Listen, Frank. I have cancer."

"I heard. I'm sorry." He glanced at me, then turned back to the television.

"Thank you. I appreciate your concern. Because my time might be limited, I have to speak my mind on important matters."

He narrowed his eyes at me. "That so? Well, here's a piece of *my* mind for *you.* Your daughter is disrespectful."

The words stung, but I pushed my anger aside. This wasn't about me. I was there for Haley, for her happiness, hers and Adam's. Frank's constant demands and unrealistic expectations were tearing their marriage apart.

Frank took a generous gulp from his glass. A nearly empty bottle of expensive scotch sat on the table beside him. Maybe it wasn't the best time to reason with the man.

"How many of those have you had?"

"More than usual, thanks to your daughter."

Based on what Haley told me, Frank was the difficult one, not her. And I'd believe Haley over Frank any day. She'd never lied to me. But I held my tongue.

"I'm going to get myself a glass of water." I needed a moment to calm down.

When I returned, a commercial played on the television, and Frank stood by the window, facing away from me. His glass was empty on the table.

"I also want what's best for Adam," he said, his voice not as gruff.

In that instant, I saw a glimmer of the hope Haley had mentioned. Selfish Frank was occasionally thoughtful.

He turned to me, and his face hardened. "But Haley needs to learn family comes first."

A surge of protective anger made me tighten my grip on my water glass. "What are you talking about, Frank? Haley *is* Adam's family now. They're married."

Frank laughed, a harsh sound. "I'm talking about family by blood."

His choice of words bothered me. Haley didn't have a drop of my husband's blood, yet he treated her with all the love in the world. Although... he didn't know the truth.

"Haley better learn some respect. She better not speak to me that way again," Frank muttered.

I glared at him. "Or you'll what, Frank? What will you do?"

He didn't answer

I took a deep breath, still attempting to talk some sense into him. "Give them a chance by stepping back and letting them live their lives. They deserve our support. They're wonderful people. We've raised them well."

He waved me off and plopped back into his chair. Was he aware of the trouble he was causing and just didn't care? How many more years would my daughter's marriage suffer under his influence?

"Let me get you a glass of something nonalcoholic," I told him.

In the kitchen again, my heart raced. I dropped my hand into my purse, then gripped the small bottle inside. Just one liquid drop from the container was enough to lower blood pressure. Several full droppers mixed with alcohol could stop a heart.

Seconds later, I'd "enhanced" a tall glass of orange juice. I brought another drug with me, a masking agent, so no one would ever be the wiser, though I doubted it would matter. Frank was old and grumpy. He wouldn't be missed.

The football game had resumed when I rejoined him, carrying his juice with a paper towel between my hand and the glass. I set it on the table. "Drink this so you don't get dehydrated. And think about what I said."

Rather than turning to acknowledge me, Frank responded with a thunderous shout directed at something happening on the television.

I left him with the full glass, wondering what would happen next. Would my visit change nothing? Or everything?

Frank and I might have disagreed on the meaning of family, but I agree it's what matters most. And I'll do anything to protect my daughter.

When I poisoned Frank, I truly believed I was helping Haley. Instead, I ruined her marriage. The damage can't be undone. Which brings me to the second moment I'd give anything to undo.

Haley was thirteen. I worked night shifts so I could be there for her when she got home from school. It was raining hard on my way to the hospital, and I looked away for a split second too long. I crossed over the yellow line and caused an oncoming car to drive off the road. They didn't crash into anything, so I assumed everyone was okay. But I was wrong. Someone got hurt.

Later, I learned I knew the driver. Of all people, it was Elliot Rhodes. If not for my daughter and the secret I carried with me day and night, I might have forgotten his name the way he had probably forgotten mine.

I saw him and Lance together at the hospital that night. They were telling a doctor about the accident. The estimated time. An old dark-colored sedan. The street where it occurred. I knew the unknown driver they were cursing. It was me.

First, they prayed for Becca's recovery, and so did I. Hours later, they mourned her death. My heart broke for them, but I couldn't say anything. Aware that I was now hiding not one enormous secret from Elliot, but two, I wasn't about to approach him. That night was the last time I saw Elliot until after my husband passed away.

Footsteps approach behind me, pulling me back to the present. It's Elliot. He's coming to join me on the patio.

"You ready?" he asks, leaning in to kiss me.

"I'm ready."

What he doesn't know won't hurt him. It didn't before, and it won't now.

EPILOGUE

Three months later

I'm in my downtown Chicago office when Jenny comes in from the adjoining room with the news.

"Press release just went out. It's official," she says, eyes beaming and clasping her hands over her heart.

We're finally announcing the Granite Global merger to the world.

This deal will reshape the industry, setting the foundation for a new era of growth, and I'm pleased. My computer chimes with incoming emails, no doubt reactions from key stakeholders. The only message I respond to is from Carter.

Are we still on for dinner tonight?

I send a quick confirmation to say I'm looking forward to it. These Sunday dinners with Carter, Haley, and Carol have become a highlight of my week.

Despite the strange start with Carter's deceit, which I've labeled a misunderstanding, Carter and Haley have forged a friendship that continues to surprise me. They've found common ground, and they get along. I admire Haley's forgiving nature, though I don't intend to extend the same grace toward Lance. I can't. What he did is unforgiveable. His actions are now a matter for the law, and I hope justice gets served. It makes me sick to think of what he might have taken from me.

I'm not the only one amazed by how it all played out. Haley and Lauren's story has taken on a life of its own. A production company plans to make a movie about the commuter train incident, with Haley serving as a consultant. They're calling it "The Last Seat on the Train." It focuses on the split-second decision that changed everything. Haley gave up her seat, unknowingly saving her own life, and allowing her to save Lauren's in return. The bits involving Carter and Adam won't become public knowledge.

After all these years, who would have thought Carol and I would find our way back to each other? The woman I had a fling with one random college weekend is now the woman with whom I share a home and a life.

Stepping into the elevator, I focus on all the positives. Life is good. I have my daughter. I have Carol by my side. All things I never thought I'd have. It should be perfect. Yet despite the way we've all grown closer, I haven't been able to eliminate my unease when it comes to Haley. I can't forget the mysterious circumstances Reeves uncovered surrounding Frank's death. Adam had the same doubts based on less evidence, and that drove him away from Haley. He simply couldn't trust her. But with our children, it's different. We can love them unconditionally. A parent's love is strong.

When my wariness surfaces, I try to conjure up rational explanations. If she did it, if Haley actually killed Frank, there must be a justifiable reason.

If only I could talk to Carol about it. I'd love for her to convince me Haley could never have done such a thing, that it's crazy and impossible. But I won't. I'd never tell Carol. I refuse to burden her. I don't want her to even suspect her child could do something so terrible. I won't plant the seed of doubt in her mind. She's been through enough. I'll let her keep her image of our daughter untainted.

After all, family is about acceptance, isn't it? Even when we don't like what we see, we keep on loving. Haley might not be perfect, but her mother is, and that's enough for me.

NOTE FROM THE AUTHOR

With so many good books competing for your time, I'm honored you chose *The Last Seat.* I hope it kept you turning pages and guessing until the very last page.

If you enjoyed the story, leaving a review or recommending it to a friend is one of the best ways you can support an author like me. Word of mouth is what allows these stories to continue.

If you're looking for a next read, you'll find a list of my books on the following page. I recommend *When She Escaped*, a psychological thriller with a twist that flips everything, or *The Numbers Killer*, the first in my Agent Victoria mystery-thriller series.

Happy reading,
Jenifer Ruff

ALSO BY JENIFER RUFF

The Agent Victoria Heslin Thriller Series

The Numbers Killer

Pretty Little Girls

When They Find Us

Ripple of Doubt

The Groom Went Missing

Vanished on Vacation

The Atonement Murders

The Ones They Buried

The Bad Neighbor

Lies in the Snow

THE FBI & CDC Thriller Series

Only Wrong Once, Only One Cure, Only One Wave

The Brooke Walton Series

Everett, Rothaker, The Intern

Psychological Thrillers

The Last Seat

When She Escaped

Lauren's Secret

JENIFER RUFF

USA Today bestselling author Jenifer Ruff writes suspense novels, including the award-winning Agent Victoria Thriller Series. She adores peace and quiet, animals, and exercise, especially hiking. Jenifer lives in North Carolina and Virginia with her family and a pack of greyhounds. If she's not writing, she's probably devouring books or out exploring trails with her dogs. For more information you can visit her website at Jenruff.com

amazon.com/stores/author/B00NFZQOLQ

facebook.com/authorjruff

instagram.com/author.jenifer.ruff/

tiktok.com/@jeniferruff.author

http://bookbub.com/authors/jenifer-ruff

www.ingramcontent.com/pod-product-compliance
Ingram Content Group UK Ltd.
Pitfield, Milton Keynes, MK11 3LW, UK
UKHW041634190726
13854UKWH00006B/2492

9 781954 447530